This is a work of fiction. Names, characters, places, and incidents either are the product of the author's imagination or are used fictitiously. Any resemblance to actual persons, living or dead, events, or locales is entirely coincidental.

Cover design by Julia Gerbach

ISBN (paperback) 979-8-9861259-5-4

ISBN (ebook) 978-1-7343813-9-9

www.katherinegrantromance.com

ALSO BY KATHERINE GRANT

The Countess Chronicles:

The Ideal Countess
New Year's Masquerade
The Duchess Wager
The Husband Plot

The Prestons:

The Baron Without Blame
The Viscount Without Virtue
The Governess Without Guilt
The Charmer Without a Cause

Northfield Hall Novellas

(an unordered series for the mood reader)
The Hellion of Drury Lane
It's In Her Kiss
Three Nights With Her Husband

Plus, a free short story, The Spinster, available exclusively at www.katherinegrantromance.com

The Viscount Without Virtue

Katherine Grant

The Viscount Without Virtue

Katherine Grant

CHAPTER ONE

May 1811

Readers, I have arrived. At long last, yet after a short journey, I am here at Northfield Hall.

Northfield – that infamous hall whose name is whispered in the corner of every London drawing room – is unassuming upon first glance. No gilded windows shine in the glint of sunlight; no Roman folly gleams atop a cresting hill; no ornamented garden beckons to the curious adventurer. The house is built of brick whose reddish hue is muddied by sun, peeling Tudor plaster over dark rotting beams, and creeping green vines. Aside from its seven chimneys and three stories, it resembles a vicarage more than the house of a lord. Surrounding it are green fields no different than the fertile land found throughout England. A generous pond reflects the clouded sky; an assortment of brick outhouses serves as the kitchen, laundry, and storerooms; a stone stable shelters seven horses and assorted conveyances; farmers of varying degrees of industriousness till the soil. Even the sheep look no different, their coats no whiter nor fluffier for all the Honorable Lord Preston, Second Baron Ashforth, claims a superiority of wool.

No, there is no difference between Lord Preston's holding and yours, my honorable readers, except one: his dangerous ideas slice his loyal English subjects from the healthy blood of their mother Empire.

M AX STILLED HIS PEN at the sound of approaching footsteps. He was tucked away in the shadows between the storerooms and the laundry, his writing desk balanced across his knees. If anyone were to see him – Mr. Maulvi, the Ashforth private secretary, or a gardener, or even a laundrywoman – then the game would be over before it even started.

His heart beat madly as the footsteps grew closer. Max could see the passerby now: a young woman in a simple gray dress and sturdy boots. A clasped wicker basket swung from her arm, while her head was carefully covered by a straw bonnet over a white cap. She was the type of woman Max wouldn't even notice, except for the risk that she might at any second glance up from her study of the ground and discover him.

She didn't. In a matter of short, silent breaths, the woman passed, and Max was once again alone with the shadows.

Victory surged through his body. As it always did when he got away with something. He couldn't help but grin to himself, even as he packed away his portable writing desk. He had only stopped to capture the lines racing through his head, anyway; he would finish the rest of the report in the safety of the night. Swinging his pack over his shoulder, Max sauntered back into the yard. His lips pursed around a whistle, one of the drinking shanties he'd sung at the roadside inn the night before.

Yes, this adventure was exactly what he needed. In one tidy scheme, he would escape from the tedium of London and prove to his father once and for all that he was ready to take up the family legacy.

Max followed the instructions given by the innkeeper to find the Northfield carpentry. He had already made it past the main Hall without incident, and now he followed the path through the woods until he hit a clearing with a circle of simple brick buildings. This was the trade village, where Northfield Hall journeymen toiled away to supply the estate with everything it might need: a blacksmith, a stone mason, and a tanner or tallow maker that diffused the air with unpleasant scents.

Max's destination, the carpentry, was easy to identify. It occupied the western half of the clearing. One half was an enclosed building; then the roof extended the same length to cover a sawpit, upon which a great piece of timber sat on three rollers. As Max approached, he smelled the peculiar mix of sawdust and turpentine.

He peered through the window before knocking on the door of the enclosed workshop. A thick worktable spanned one side of the room, tools hung along the wall like well-trained regiments. None of this startled Max, since it was what one would expect from a carpenter's shop. No, what gave him the jolt were the people in the room: one man and two teenage boys, all Chinese.

He shouldn't have been surprised. Everyone in London knew Northfield Hall was home to outcasts. And yet, the sight of them slipped across his skin like a gasp.

Shaking himself, Max knocked on the door – and remembered just in time to sweep his hat from his head in deference. He stretched his words into a lower-class brogue. "Good afternoon. I heard in town you have need of a carpenter, and I have come to offer my services. My name is Maxwell Sims, lately of London."

The man stared at him in silence for a long moment. He was, like most people, shorter than Max, but otherwise one could sense the muscles brimming beneath his work clothes. The breadth of his shoulders narrowed at his waist before disappearing into stocky legs.

His hair was almost completely gray. All in all, the kind of man easily underestimated.

"Assistant," the older man said at last. "Carpenter's *assistant.*"

Max nodded gamely, as if he were accustomed to being corrected by men with strange accents. "Of course. That is what I meant." Nervous – and cursing himself for it – Max spewed out the cover story he had concocted on his journey from London. "I am down on my luck, sir. Recently returned from transportation, on account of theft. I am only looking to save enough quid to return to my sweetheart in Norwich."

It was a story designed to guarantee him a spot at Northfield Hall. Rumor had it that was the primary requirement for employment here: Lord Preston did not hire people unless they were unwanted elsewhere. Already, Max had seen four Black servants, a handful of Hindustanis, and a man with a scar across his face and only one leg.

When *The Perceptive's* Jewish editor had demurred this assignment, the Earl of Meretta had challenged Max to do it. Despite the fact that he walked and talked exactly like a viscount.

This was an opportunity to prove, in the Earl of Meretta's words, that Max could sacrifice his personal comforts in the name of the greater good. And so Max had planned this story, spent an extra week on the road to appear that much more bedraggled, and dressed in clothes nearly too large for him. Now he forced himself to look embarrassed.

The man offered no sympathy. "Where are your tools?"

Tools. Max hadn't considered he would need show up with anything other than the pack at his back. "Ah, I am a man of all work, sir. I'm handy with a saw and hammer, but I don't have my own tools."

"Have you ever worked in a carpentry before?"

At least the man was emoting now. Even if the emotion leaking from his glare was cold skepticism. "Yes, sir. With John Holloway, back in Van Diemen's Land. We built the houses for our settlement." Max delivered this last lie as innocently as possible, knowing as he did that the carpentry needed hands to erect new laborer cottages.

That stole the man's interest. Max read it in how he leaned ever so slightly forward and his expression relaxed. Infinitesimal changes, but evidence enough: if Max could say the right next thing, he would have the job.

That very instant came from behind him: "Oh, I beg your pardon!"

A soft, female voice. Distracting enough to knock Max's next words from his head. He nearly growled with annoyance – and impatience.

He needed to secure this position.

Pasting on as polite an expression as he could muster, Max turned to find the intruder was the same woman who had almost discovered him at his writing.

Her eyes widened as she saw him, her pink lips parting into a little "o" of surprise. Up close, he could see the freckles dancing across her nose.

"I didn't..." For a moment, the woman gaped without further words. Then she looked away from Max to the Chinese carpenters. "I'm back with provisions. Mrs. Chow told me specifically to make sure you each eat two cakes."

A serving girl, then. Max imagined her in the kitchen, an apron over her drab gray dress and patches of flour dusting her cheeks like the powdered makeup of old.

The elder youth took the offered basket and set it on the worktable. He and his brother stuffed their faces indecorously with the honey cakes inside.

In the exchange, the woman ended up standing beside the head carpenter. She looked politely at Max's shoulder. "You must be the man come from Thatcham about work."

"This is Maxwell Sims, lately of London," the Chinese carpenter replied. "Man of all work."

"Wonderful. We certainly need whatever help we can get." The woman's eyes drifted over Max again.

He wondered what she saw. As the Viscount Berwick, presented in a parlor wearing a tailored suit, Max had never failed to snag a female admirer, even if her appreciation was limited to a knowing blush. Today he was not Berwick. What message, exactly, would a serving woman such as herself read of his oversized coat and scuffed boots?

His skin heated under her clear gray eyes. Max retaliated with his own scrutiny. So much of her was covered that Max couldn't say what color hair she had or whether her figure curved around the waist or even how full her bosom was. He could see only the delicate face, pale neck, and bare hands at the ends of her long sleeves.

And those freckles.

Catching himself, Max brushed the observations away. As she herself had said, he was there for work, nothing else.

He angled himself obsequiously to the carpenter. "May I consider myself hired, then? I can get to work straight away."

The man drew the moment out in silence for longer than Max thought humanly possible. Then, with a grimace, he said, "We work from dawn to dusk. I do not tolerate slothfulness or deceitfulness. Wages paid at the end of each quarter by Mr. Maulvi."

Triumph. Max bit down on his tongue to hide any reaction; his friends loved to point out when he gloated, because he was apparently very obvious about it.

"Thank you, sir. You won't regret it." Lies, of course. Victory turned Max to the woman, who still stood there. As if he were Berwick, he caught up her hand in his. "And you are, miss?"

All eyes in the room, it seemed, swung to where his bare hand wrapped around her palm. It took only that instant for Max to realize where he had gone wrong: the straw bonnet, the lace trim around her sleeves, the clean fingers. This was no serving girl.

"May I present the Honorable Miss Ellen Preston," the carpenter replied, his tone harsh and clear. "The eldest daughter of Lord Preston, Baron Ashforth."

Fuck.

THE MAN'S HAND WAS warm as it clenched more tightly about hers. Ellen watched as alarm replaced the curiosity with which he had just been regarding her. She *should* be offended that he had so confidently grabbed at her, as if she were a tavern wench or worse.

Instead, she wished he would hold onto her forever.

"I apologize," he said, dropping his hands, his gaze, his chin.

"A pleasure to meet you, Mr. Sims," Ellen said, since Mr. Chow was watching. If she launched into a monologue on how she did hate the way the laborers avoided her gaze, Mr. Chow would only tell her father, and then her father would summon some sort of lecture, and Papa's lectures only ever reminded Ellen of how much she missed Mama.

Mr. Sims did not look in her direction.

Ellen angled her attention back to Mr. Chow. The sooner this awkward moment ended, the better. "I'll get to work on the shutters, then." There were eight sets to make, and she had only finished one so far.

But Mr. Chow said, "I'm afraid not, Miss Ellen." His eyes slid to the new man, as if that explained everything.

Surely, Mr. Chow wasn't being maidenish about her reputation. Mr. Sims had assumed a posture of humility: chin down, shoulders back, eyes averted. Rather like a dog whose ears had pulled backwards to show respect. Except the man was so tall – and muscled, everywhere a man could have muscles. He had stepped three feet away from her, yet Ellen could feel him as if he were beside her.

He was, perhaps, the most handsome man she had ever seen.

Still, he was a mere man. She would not expire simply by working beside him. "I'm sure Mr. Sims would not object, Mr. Chow."

The man's gaze flicked upwards. There was amusement there. Ellen couldn't tell if it was at her expense.

"Mr. Sims does not have tools," Mr. Chow said. "He must use yours."

Her tools. In the hands of this man. His fingers caressing the handle of her hammer. His palms guiding her plane across timber planks. His thumbpads testing the sharpness of each blade.

Envy heated her gut. Envy of Mr. Sims, for stealing her tools. Of her tools, for stealing Mr. Sims.

Ellen swallowed back the temptation to argue. It was unkind to be selfish when a man had so little in life that he had to seek work without tools. The only concern was whether the shutters would get done. "Do you have joinery experience, Mr. Sims?"

"He built houses in Australia," Mr. Chow answered. "We will get by."

The man in question nodded, as if to agree. Ellen would have liked to ask whether those houses even had shutters. She would have liked to question why Mr. Chow should prefer a man with brute strength over a woman with skilled labor.

She did not. After all, Mr. Sims had walked the five miles from town, and perhaps further, in search of work. He would have difficulty finding wages elsewhere, being a former convict. This was not about whose labor would complete the cottages better. It was about being gracious and generous.

Ellen could rise above her dismay, if it was the right thing to do.

"Allow me to show you the shutter design, then."

Her following actions were ones she did almost every afternoon, as familiar as the smell of fresh wood. Tie on her leather apron. Slip on the heavy work gloves. Open her toolchest and assemble her old friends, the chisel and bevel and plane. Yet that afternoon, with the weight of everyone's eyes on her, Ellen nearly fumbled her tools to the floor.

Heat flooded her cheeks. She cursed that feeling, cursed her complexion for blushing so casily, cursed herself for being so awkward. Mr. Sims would think her embarrassed, when in truth she was only uncomfortable. Perhaps a little nervous.

He was very handsome.

"Right then," she said with as much confidence as she could muster. "Come have a look."

The Chows, finishing their cakes, took the cue to return to work. Spencer and Oliver set to sanding down the planks to be carted to the build site, while Mr. Chow settled at the drafting table with pen in hand.

Ellen's attention remained on Mr. Sims. Setting his pack in a corner of the workshop, he approached her bench. He was a large man, both tall and broad-shouldered, and there was something about the way he walked that took up even more space in the room than he should have. From beneath his cap, blond hair flowed in a loose, old-fashioned queue.

She caught herself biting on her lower lip in interest.

He paused about two feet away from her, as if to come closer would cause mortal offense.

"You won't be able to do much joinery from there." Beckoning him nearer, Ellen took a step to the side to make more room. Mr. Sims looked to Mr. Chow before taking up a spot at the very edge corner of the table.

Ellen ignored that, as well as she ignored noticing that his eyes were a deep, rich hazel. She flipped open the reference book with the shutter design. "Now, here you see the scheme for what I'm trying to do." She pointed with the end of her chisel to the relevant drawings, explaining where the angles got tricky and the modifications she had made. Not wanting to assume he could read, she stuck to the illustrations.

Nearing the end of her explanation, Ellen peeked up, to make sure Mr. Sims was following. He had leaned in so close that she could practically see the gold stubble sprouting along his strong, sharp jaw.

She forgot the rest of her sentence.

Mr. Sims didn't seem to notice. Bracing one elbow on the scarred tabletop, he focused on the book. Ellen saw his eyes dart across the page. He could read, then. She watched him – couldn't tear her gaze away, really – until, after too long, Mr. Sims turned from the book and opened his mouth to ask a question. He caught her looking straight at him.

A guilty blush rushed her neck and cheeks. She felt it as much as he could probably see it. Clearing her throat, she reached for the shutter base she had been working on that morning. "You may begin by finishing the planing on this piece."

Mr. Sims smirked at her. It was a twist of his lips, one that felt neither cruel nor kind. One that said, *I can tell you find me attractive* yet did not assure, *I find you attractive, too.*

He wiped it away soon enough, taking up the plane and shutter base, but Ellen caught it.

If only she had more experience at this sort of thing to know whether she should smirk back or not. Since Percy Thistleman had left three years ago, there weren't many men at Northfield Hall who would flirt with her. She was Miss Preston, the daughter of their benefactor, a prim and proper miss whom they would greet but not a person with whom they would become familiar. Besides, Ellen was too shy to offer up sly smiles casually. Her sister Sophia flirted as naturally as she breathed, whether the other person wanted to receive suggestive comments or not. Sophia would know exactly how to respond to Mr. Sims's smirk to regain the upper hand without pushing the exchange beyond a friendly conversation.

In any case, the moment had passed. Mr. Sims's attention was on the oak base, which he now held in his palm at the same time as attempting to bring the plane down across its surface.

Like some kind of maniac.

"Not like that!" Her screech echoed across the workshop. From their positions, Spencer and Oliver ducked their heads to hide snickers.

Mr. Sims only stared at her, as if she were the one about to plane her own skin.

"Perhaps that is how you did it in Australia without proper tools," she pretended, to save him embarrassment. Relieving him of the wood, Ellen locked it in the vise and positioned the swing-arm plane on its edge. "Here, if you would be so good as to exercise caution."

She stepped back to allow him to take up the plane. The tool offered two grips: one each at the front and back so that the joiner could exercise equal pressure across the surface of the wood at all times. Mr. Sims put his right hand in front and left in back, which meant he wasn't in position to hold the frog just ahead of the back grip.

No matter what he said, the man had clearly never done any kind of joinery work before.

"Your grip, Mr. Sims."

"My grip?"

Oh, his voice was so pleasantly deep. Ellen could feel it vibrating in her bones. Her mouth went dry from the sensation; she swallowed as she replaced him at the plane to demonstrate.

"Like this." Curling her right-hand fingers around the back grip, she showed him how her index finger extended to kiss the frog, then palmed the front tow with her left hand. "Don't forget to use the power of your legs, either."

Why had she said that? Immediately, she wanted to bite back the words. There was nothing unusual in them being said from one carpenter to another. But while saying them, her eyes dropped to his legs. Her thoughts blanked to everything except his body.

And she knew he could tell, too.

Ellen slid the plane across the wood to move the moment along. It was a motion she had done a hundred times before. The oak yielded, shaving ribbons up onto the table, a reaction Ellen usually relished.

For the moment, she could think only of Mr. Sims beside her. Watching her. Perhaps – though she couldn't tell – admiring her.

Ellen pushed away the thought. She had never been the type to lose her head over a man, and she had no interest in beginning now. There was no reason to get in a dither every time he looked at her. He couldn't help being handsome any more than she could help being attracted to him.

She did hope he reciprocated the feeling, even if just a little. It would be so lowering to spend all this energy losing her breath over his proximity only to discover that he was indifferent to her.

Stepping back, Ellen gestured Mr. Sims to the plane. "Let's see what you can do, then."

He imitated her grip carefully. Pressing down into the front tow, he pushed the plane forward and back along the wood. Again. Ellen kept her gaze on the wood, rather than admire his arms or the slope of his nose or anything else about him.

Mr. Sims paused. His chin rose, and his hazel gaze collided with hers. For a moment, Ellen panicked, thinking he had caught her staring again.

She was making a fool of herself.

Then he smirked. "How is my stance, Miss Preston?"

Oh, he knew she had been staring at him. But this time, Ellen knew what his smirk intimated, too.

He would stare back, if she wanted him to.

Ellen wasn't sure that she did. She hadn't contemplated a flirtation in a long time, not one within the realms of reality, anyway. It was one thing to wish for someone to keep company with and another entirely to be offered an actual human being with his own personality and hopes and dreams. Ellen wasn't sure she truly wanted to fan the flames of attraction between herself and Mr. Sims.

For the moment, however, it couldn't hurt to be friendly. So she smiled back and said, "You have good form, Mr. Sims."

Chapter Two

M ISS PRESTON WAS EITHER going to be an opportunity or a problem. Max couldn't yet tell which. On the one hand, as the daughter of Lord Preston, she would be a treasure trove of information, if Max could coax it out of her.

On the other hand, Max wasn't sure he could withstand her steady gray gaze for another afternoon and *not* flirt the skirts off her. She had him spend most of those first hours planing grooves into the shutter bases. It was tedious work that should have made conversation easy. Yet every time Max glanced up at her, she was watching him, and he couldn't stop himself from trying to earn a blush, a smile, a laugh. She flirted back, too.

If he were the Viscount Berwick, that would be one kind of problem. As Maxwell Sims, carpenter, it was sheer stupidity to be forward with the baron's daughter.

Max was glad when, at twilight, Miss Preston finally retreated from the workshop. His day was far from over, however. Mr. Chow set him to finishing two-by-fours with linseed oil until well after the lanterns had been lit and his nose dull to all smell. Only when the entire pile of planks were completed did Mr. Chow lead him to a one-room building closer to the Hall, where a table stretched from one door to the other. Laborers shoved in shoulder-to-shoulder along the table, helping themselves from great cauldrons of stew and baskets of rye bread. The room fairly boomed with chatter.

Max felt the usual quiver of apprehension at joining a group so large. It was an instinct he had long since mastered after being forced by his mother to attend so many London squeezes, and after a gulp of country air, he plastered on his invincible smile and found a seat towards the end of the table.

The man to his right held out a palm. "You're the new carpenter's assistant. I'm Killian, the blacksmith."

Max shook his hand. Killian looked about the same age as him, though his black hair had retreated near to the back of his scalp. True to his profession, he boasted massive shoulders and forearms, and he nearly crushed Max's hand.

"You don't have to look so worried," Killian said. "You found yourself a good position here. Mr. Chow is exacting, but other than that, count your blessings. Good food every day. Roofs that don't leak, and wood for fire all winter long."

Max had not been worried; he had been contemplating how a carpenter would respond to an Irishman shaking his hand, since it was surely not the direct cut a viscount would deliver. Now he smiled along to Killian's description. "Have you been at Northfield long?"

"Since I ran away from my master at the age of thirteen." Killian raised an eyebrow, as if Max was supposed to know what this meant.

He assumed the master was a blacksmith and that Killian had been the apprentice. Perhaps the smith had been cruel to Killian or refused to feed him. That type of abuse was not unheard of, particularly if the apprentice was lazy or full of backtalk. It was unfortunate, but not necessarily undeserved. Certainly nothing to run away from, not when the master had the legal right to the apprentice's labor.

In any case, Max didn't need to know. His assignment was about Northfield Hall itself. He helped himself to a bowl of meat stew as he asked, "Did you come directly here, then?"

"I hadn't heard of this place. No, I ran away to Dublin, and then I stowed myself on a ship. I thought I was going to America. Spent two days in Liverpool thinking I had arrived to Boston. Can you imagine that?"

Max could not. "How did you discover the truth?" He tried a spoonful of the slop and was pleasantly surprised to discover it resembled the ox rumps Monsieur D'Eon served at Montchampion Manor.

"A moll corrected me while kicking me off her corner of the street."

That sounded about right. "How did you come to Northfield Hall, then?"

"I asked that moll if she had need of a blacksmith. After she about died of laughing, she told me of this place and said they might take me in. She didn't know how to get here any more than I did, but she knew it was in Berkshire. So I started walking, and eventually, I made it here."

Max couldn't help frowning in incredulity. The walk from Liverpool to the middle of Berkshire would take weeks, and that was assuming one didn't get killed by highwaymen.

In the interest of rapport, Max let the blarney slide. "And as soon as you arrived, they took you in here?"

"Well, same as you, I expect." Shrugging, Killian stuffed a crumpet into his mouth. "One of the gardeners found me wandering about the fields. He gave me a hot meal and a bath, and then Mr. Maulvi interviewed me. I'd never seen a Hindustani in so fine a suit, I can tell you that much. I stared at him more than I answered him. Guess he's used to that, though, because he didn't hold it against me. Anyhow, they let me stay and work for wages learning from the last blacksmith. When she got married a few years ago, I got the top job."

Too many questions swamped Max's mind. He took a big swig of ale to wash it all down: the food, the story, the responses.

"Didn't your old master ever come looking for you?"

"He wouldn't have, not when it required coming to England. Doesn't matter, anyhow. Lord Preston paid him out for the remainder of my service. Not that the bastard deserved it." Killian shoved at the man to his other side. "They never do, eh, Hamlyn?"

The man – a scrawny, dark Black man – clanged his mug to Killian's in agreement. His gaze fell to Max, but he looked away before Max could say anything.

"Don't mind Hamlyn," Killian said, his voice lowered. "He doesn't trust any White man further than he can throw us. Not any more than I can trust an Englishman, I suppose. Nor you trust a copper, eh?"

Max nodded in agreement, though his stomach twisted. He didn't mind lying. It was the sentiments he didn't understand. He knew of these prejudices, in an academic sense. But he had never felt the steel-edged words pressed so closely against his own neck.

It stirred an ugly defensiveness in him. The kind that might start a brawl in a taproom over the honor of his kind.

He pushed the instinct away as the youngest Chow plopped into the seat across from them. His plate boasted a fruit tart, which had clearly not come from the communal table, and Max remembered that Mrs. Chow had sent special snacks that afternoon. Lucky Young Chow.

"How is Sims doing, then, Oliver?" Killian asked. "Has he made any unforgivable cuts yet?"

Max filed the name away; he would try harder to remember it this time.

The youth grinned. "Not unless you count pawing at Miss Preston."

Max choked on his stew. Killian had to thump his back before Max could speak, and even then, his eyes smarted. "I didn't paw at her. I introduced myself. I didn't know she was the lady of the house."

"And after that, it would have been rude if you hadn't flirted with her, I'm sure." Oliver smirked. "What would your sweetheart think?"

The boy had spent all afternoon at his own tasks in silence. Max could hardly believe that now he teased him with a toothy grin, as if they were best friends.

"Oh, a sweetheart, have you?" Killian leaned back, as if setting up for a tale. "Come on then. Let's hear all about her."

Tangy fear rushed Max's blood deliciously at the prospect of a lie. He flexed his fingers around his mug and conjured his most recent paramour to mind. "Her name is Delia. Most beautiful creature you've ever seen. Perfect features, perfect body. And her hair. Red as fire. There's nothing I love more than a redhead. Flame in the hair, flame everywhere, I always say. Especially in bed."

Oliver and Killian exchanged a look. "Not all redheads have the same personality, surely," Oliver said. "That's like saying all convicts are drunkards."

Perhaps he was laying it on a bit thick. Max grinned, as if he weren't hiding anything. "All the redheads I've met. Fierce, fiery, anxious to argue. The best kind of woman, if you ask me."

"Funny how so much of that is said of us Irish folk, too." Killian's expression was halfway between a grimace and a smile. "And this Delia is waiting patiently for you after all these years? What was it, seven years transportation?"

"Three." Max shrugged. "I can only hope she has not forgotten me. I certainly could never forget her."

The conversation shifted into a more general discussion of the nature of love from there, pulling in their other seatmates and even Hamlyn. Max tried to take note of everyone, looking for who would be most likely to tell him the truth about Northfield Hall.

Twenty years or so ago, Lord and Lady Preston had declared they would divest from any economic system that profited from slave labor or – taking it farther than any other Whig clattering for reform – even labor from colonies. In his writings, Lord Preston threw out accusations of exploitation and subjugation; Max thought the man simply did not have a firm grasp on reality. In either case, Preston transformed Northfield Hall into a self-contained estate that grew or crafted everything its inhabitants could need. Anything imported – such as coal for the winter – came strictly from English shores, and even then, Max had heard the family preferred to burn wood or grass instead.

Even more striking, Lord Preston sold very little of the estate's products. Most of it was consumed by the family and laborers. Whatever surplus they did sell went to markets within fifty miles of the Hall, and the profits were split evenly among every worker – or so rumor had it. Because of that, the public liked to paint Northfield Hall as a bastion of pure English nobility, where the ruling class shared its wealth and resources with everyone on its land.

A bunch of rubbish, Max supposed, and a thorn in the side of his father, the Earl of Meretta, who Lord Preston loved to paint as the devil in his public writing. Which was why Max was there in disguise. Max was on the search for the cracks in Northfield's veneer.

The hypocrisy where greed won out after all. The failures where the Prestons did worse than a free market would. The unnatural bonds that held these strange people in the baron's thrall.

Anything that would disprove Northfield Hall's nobility, once and for all.

He decided he would start with Hamlyn, whenever he could get a chance to pull the stone mason to the side.

By the end of supper, deep night had settled in, leaving the fields lit by a weak moon from behind clouds. Killian procured a lantern from a shed beside the dining hall, then clapped a hand to Max's shoulder. "Come on, then. I'll show you to the lodgings."

As they picked their way down a dirt path, Killian explained that all the single male laborers lodged in the same outbuilding, while the women stayed on a house on the opposite side of the fields. Married couples and families got their own cottages along the eastern border of the property. "There is no strict rule about comingling with the fairer sex," Killian said, "but if Lord Preston catches two single people in the act, he expects them to marry. So you'd best be careful, or ready to shackle yourself."

A little belatedly, Max remembered to say, "My heart already belongs to Delia."

"Aye, but what of the rest of you?" This with a chuckle. Then Killian stopped walking and grabbed Max's shoulder again. "Watch out for Miss Preston. She means well. But I don't trust a woman born into her station who wants to spend her days working with her hands. If you ask me, it is only a matter of time until she gets the rest of us into trouble. Besides which, Lord Preston may believe in the equality of man, but not when it comes to who will marry his daughters. No, the Misses Preston are destined for gentry, and you might be thrown off the property if you look at them too long."

Max flashed back to Miss Preston gripping the hand plane, her gaze flickering to him with unmistakable heat. Under different circumstances – if he weren't pretending to be someone else – he would enjoy the challenge of unearthing the personality beneath her layers of bonnet and cap and gown.

Killian was right, though. Miss Preston might as well be marked on a pirate's map: there be danger there.

"My heart belongs to Delia," he repeated.

"That's right," Killian said, as if he had coached Max on the line himself. Then he led Max into the lodging house. A fog was rolling in, chilling the air even inside the building. Killian climbed with him four stories to the top floor, then showed Max a room about the size of a fireplace. "There you are. Breakfast is served at dawn, and Mr. Chow will be expecting you just after."

At last, Max was left alone. Except Killian took the lantern with him, plunging the little room into darkness.

No writing could be done, then. Stretching his arms to either side of him, Max palmed his way to the straw pallet on the floor. It was even lower than he expected, and he fell backwards a little bit as he sat on it, his head knocking against the brick wall. Eyes adjusting to the blackened room, Max unlaced his boots. He set his pack beside the mattress and folded his coat and waistcoat on top of it.

That was it. The sum of actions to make himself comfortable for the night. No calling for a glass of claret, no warming pans to be removed from between his sheets, not even a clean nightshirt to change into.

Max ignored the dismay whispering deep in his gut. This had been a successful day. He had gotten himself hired. He had begun building trust with the laborers. He already had the first draft of his report under way. He would not admit discomfort or doubt or fear into his psyche.

There was too much at stake to do anything but believe he could do this. And he could. Max knew it: he could connect with anyone, so long as he didn't let the specter of Viscount Berwick get in the way. From there, it was only a matter of finding something worth writing about and turning it into a report.

Before he knew it, Max would be in his father's London study again, only instead of lecturing him on taking life seriously, the earl would be appraising Max of when he could expect to be named the nominee for the House of Commons seat in Great Yarmouth.

Max closed his eyes and ignored the lumps in the mattress. He could do this. He would do this.

Miss Ellen Preston and her freckled nose would just have to be ignored.

PAPA WAS LATE FOR supper. Ellen made everyone wait, even though ten-year-old Caroline put up a fierce wail that she was hungry. Nate, who even at fifteen was always good for cheering anyone up, folded her napkin into the shape of a goose and made it start to honk.

"Perhaps he is eating in his room," Sophia suggested. She looked longingly towards where the footmen guarded the food. She may as well have been hungering for the male attention as she was for the meal. She had a particular fondness for their footmen, Jacques and Uriah, always making them blush with her smiles.

"He would have let us know." Ellen refolded her own napkin for the third time. Papa never used to be this way, but in the three years since Mama had passed, he was scatter-minded, swept up in whatever held his attention for that moment. He loved supper with the family, though. He always said so. "Uncle Maulvi, how were his spirits today?"

Uncle Maulvi took his meals with them on nights when Aunt Croft – his common-law wife – hosted card games. He was not their uncle by blood but by choice. His own parents had come as servants to Ellen's great-grandmother from the Bengal, and he had lived his whole life at Northfield Hall. When they were children, he always dug up a sweet from the secret pockets of his embroidered jackets. In more recent years, he was their sounding board whenever they were too overcome with emotion to be rational.

"It is not your burden to worry over his spirits, my dear."

Ellen disagreed. She was his daughter. She had every right to wish her father into better humors. Although in this particular moment, she had asked out of habit, not concern.

Her heart still raced a little from the afternoon in the workshop. A natural reaction, she was sure, to prolonged proximity to a man who looked as if he had stepped out of an artist's imagination of perfect form.

Surely, she would grow immune to his aesthetic in a matter of days.

"How long do we have to wait?" Caroline moaned, the napkin-goose having finished its honking.

"Indeed," Benny chimed in, using that voice he thought made him sound old and wise, despite him only being eighteen. In truth, it was so ridiculously fake that Ellen couldn't even look at Sophia or else they would both burst into laughter. "It has been a quarter hour already. He won't mind if we start without him."

"*I'll* mind," Ellen said. It was the principle of the thing: a family did not begin supping until they were all present. Only her voice was too soft, as usual, to break through her siblings' own opinions.

"We could at least have the soup course before it gets cold," Nate suggested.

Ellen raised her voice. "We are waiting for Papa."

"Jacques!" Benny raised his hand towards the footmen, not hearing her. "The soup, please."

"No!" But Jacques was following Benny's instructions, not hers.

Sophia slammed her palms onto the table, rattling the pewter plates. "Ellen says we wait for Papa. Therefore, we wait for Papa. You ingrates will just have to take this opportunity to contemplate the reality of hunger that our lesser-fortunate countrymen experience every day."

They heeded Sophia. Everyone always did, in a more instinctive way than they did Ellen. It was the confidence that oozed out of Sophia's every pore. She wasn't afraid to glare at anyone, either, or cut one's esteem in half with a well-timed barb.

Ellen counted herself lucky that Sophia almost always sided with her.

Of course, as soon as the matter was settled, Papa strode into the dining room. He vibrated with energy and, taking his customary seat opposite Ellen at the head of the table, said, "You didn't need to wait for me."

The footmen served the asparagus soup. Caroline exclaimed, "I've never been so happy to eat asparagus!"

Papa smiled at her. "I can't imagine why not. Asparagus is one of my favorite foods. And did you know, they say the great Duchess of Surrey eats asparagus every day when it is in season."

Caroline's eyes widened. She loved any mention of London society and was particularly captivated by the legendary Duchess of Surrey who had gallivanted across Europe with her husband before his recent death.

Papa widened his attention to the whole table. "Now then, what entertainment shall we have tonight? A debate on economic regulations?"

There was something playful in the way he said it, and so their chorus of groans was also teasing. Even though it was fully within the realm of possibility that he would force such a debate on them. Ellen relaxed into the familial pattern.

"Ah, a history lesson, then? We can turn our attention to the great Moghul kingdom at last."

This, too, was a real possibility, except Papa usually saved such lectures for after dinner, when they all gathered in the garden conservatory and he could reference his various history books.

"Couldn't we just the once have a regular conversation?" Nate asked.

"I see. If none of those appeal..." Papa's eyes twinkled. "...then perhaps a letter from Aunt Charlotte will pique your attention."

Sophia squealed, as if she were Caro's age and not all of twenty years old. "Did Aunt Charlotte truly write?"

Their Aunt Charlotte was the only member of Mama's family that had stayed in touch with them after Mama and Papa married against their grandfather's wishes. She usually wrote once a year, around Christmastime, and had only visited the one time to say goodbye to Mama.

In spite of that, she was Sophia's hero.

"I have the letter right here," Papa said, withdrawing it from his breast pocket. It was a thick packet of pages, as Aunt Charlotte's letters always were. She never worried about the weight of the letter, either, and wrote in wide, looped cursive that took as much space as she wanted it to, without any frugality. "Shall I read it aloud?"

Papa read the letter in his dramatic storybook voice, pausing every now and then for dramatic effect that made Caroline giggle and the rest of them squirm in their seats. The first half of the letter seemed entirely devoted to *ton* gossip – including none other than the Duchess of Surrey's remarriage to the Earl of Gresham. Benny, catching Ellen's gaze, rolled his eyes.

Ellen wasn't quite following the narrative. Her mind had wandered to the question of Mr. Sims. Specifically, whether it was wise for her to return to the carpentry, knowing he was such a distraction to her. At Benny's cue, she signaled to the footmen to replace the soup with the roast.

Finally, Papa arrived at the more salient portion of the letter. "Certain friends of mine can speak of one topic and one topic only: the possibility that Lord Perceval will push through an abolition bill at last. I am a silly old bird, but I understand the bill is currently being drafted by the House of Commons and, like a woman at the birthing bed, will need even more *accrouchement* to make it to the House of Lords from someone more knowledgeable and practiced than the dandies flitting about Hyde Park. If you know of anyone, do send them my way. Partridge House boasts five more bedrooms than I can possibly fill, and I would be so very happy to usher dear Ellen and Sophia through their first Season, if my lord permits it."

Papa dropped the letter dramatically to the tabletop. He was the very picture of triumph, as if this invitation from Aunt Charlotte were the fruit of twenty years of work and not simply a kindness from family. It was the abolition bill that excited him, of course, not the lure of the center of Britain's evil empire. Ellen cut uneasily into her roasted venison.

"So?" Papa prodded. "Would dear Ellen and Sophia enjoy a Season in London?"

"Oh yes!" Sophia had been begging to leave Northfield Hall for years, since even before Mama died. "Oh, finally!"

For Sophia, it would be a lark, probably. She was the younger sister, only twenty, and would never let herself be bullied into a marriage, anyhow.

But Ellen was twenty-two. Approaching that dreaded *shelf* that marked one ineligible. And she knew very well what happened in London. One found oneself on a balcony with a man one had never met, and the next day, the two of you were betrothed.

"I should like to go, too," Benny said. "I should start meeting my peers and learning the ins and outs of Parliament."

"Naturally. There are five guest apartments available, after all," Papa agreed.

There was no flirting over a block of wood in London. Probably the only conversation topics were fashion and gossip, two topics Ellen knew nothing about.

"May I come?" Caroline asked. "And may I get new dresses and gloves and do my hair up like a lady?"

"Those dresses are made of fabrics imported from the slave territories and oppressed colonies, Caro," Ellen said, noting that the gravy had too much salt. "I'm sure you do not mean to say you wish to give our money to such evil enterprise."

She didn't need ears to know that Sophia harrumphed at this. Sophia had never cared for the free produce movement, no matter how many times Mama and Papa explained its virtues in thwarting the slave economy by supporting only goods produced by paid labor.

Little Caroline frowned. "No, but I want to go to London."

"You and Edward are in charge of the theatric to inaugurate the new cottages, remember?" Ellen prodded her sister. "How could you rehearse properly if you are in London?"

"We don't need to rehearse that much."

Papa ran his hand through her hair. "You've a few more years of life to live before you'll be ready for London, poppet."

"I'll stay home with you, Caro," Nate said. "Until I run off to the Navy, anyhow."

Nate threatened this about once every day. Ellen still wasn't sure if he really meant it. Nate was known to say things just to get a reaction. But he also kept saying it.

Uncle Maulvi looked to Papa, who then looked to Ellen. She felt their looks as surely as if they had shared words about her.

She pushed her plate away. "I couldn't possibly go, Papa. The new man in the carpentry hasn't his own tools, so he is using mine, but he doesn't know the first thing about joinery. I must train him, else the cottages will have no shutters."

Ellen was rather sure she successfully said this without belying any interest in Mr. Sims himself, until Benny teased, "Is that the man the maids are all chattering about being so handsome? Oh yes, you *must* stay and train him."

"We could hire a joiner from the Reading guild to fill in," Uncle Maulvi suggested before Ellen could defend herself. "If you should prefer to go to London.

Typical Uncle Maulvi – completely helpful until one had a point to make, and then he had to ruin it by being the voice of reason. Ellen shook her head. "I haven't the proper outfits, and I can hardly count on readymade gowns from a *modiste*'s. If I were to go to London, I would need months in advance to plan, Papa."

Benny snickered. Sophia did not quite join him, but she did skewer Ellen with a look that said she would require more details about Mr. Sims later.

None of this was about Mr. Sims, though. Ellen didn't know the man well enough to want anything to do with him, except admire him from afar. She didn't want to go to London because she hated the idea of leaving Northfield Hall. Of being away from her woodwork for more than a day at a time. Of chatting and smiling with people who happily consumed sugar from slave labor.

There was no use convincing her siblings of that, not when she had likely already blushed up to her ears at the mention of Mr. Sims.

Papa offered her a sad, understanding smile. "As you wish, Little Light."

Ellen struggled not to feel selfish in her triumph.

Chapter Three

CARPENTRY WAS HARDER THAN it looked.

Max spent two days performing this task and then that for Mr. Chow to demonstrate his skill. Staining wood. Sanding rough planks into even surfaces. Heaving the frame of a cottage wall to standing. Hammering boards into place.

He had watched his carpenters at Montchampion Manor do this sort of thing for years. When he was a boy, they had let him swing the hammer and cut practice boards with a handsaw.

Max realized now they had been humoring him. Left to his own devices, he could barely even aim the hammer properly; three times, he hit the board instead of the nail, and when he did successfully make contact, the nail bent sideways instead of lodging into the wood.

"How did you build houses in Van Diemen's Land?" Mr. Chow asked. "Out of mud?"

This, when Max had managed to saw a joint piece to the wrong angle. He pushed away the plummeting feeling of despair. He would not fail at this. "You've heard of sea legs. I only need a few more days for my hands to remember what to do."

Mr. Chow relegated him to the shutters for the rest of that second afternoon. "I have no time to train you, but perhaps Miss Preston can."

The lady in question did not look particularly eager to cede her tools to him. From her little corner of the workshop, she had been watching him make one mistake after another. Max wondered if she even found him remotely attractive anymore, given that he was so clearly incompetent at carpentry.

He got his answer when a blush crept up her neck at his approach. She looked away, busying her hands with brushing wood shavings from the table, but Max saw the telltale pink rising all the way to her cheeks. If the tips of her ears had been visible instead of tucked within her starched cap, he wagered he would see them burn bright red, too.

Max kept a smile from his lips. At least he could still charm a woman, even as a supposed criminal.

Perhaps he could use that to discover her family's dark secrets.

"May I be of service to you, Miss Preston?"

Her eyes flashed upwards. The irises were a clear gray, a hue that didn't quite consist of any color. The freckles speckled beneath her lashes stood out like a smile.

Max wished he had time to count them.

"Let's see if you remember how to use the swing-arm plane," Miss Preston was saying in response to his question. She stepped aside, leaving him to select the right tool and a proper piece of wood.

Lucky for Max, that first day remained etched in his memory. He recognized the swing-arm plane immediately because of the grip that Miss Preston had so elegantly demonstrated for him. He took up a block of wood from the available pile, clamped it in the vise, and set to planing.

As he drew the tool across the grain, Max lifted his attention back to Miss Preston. "Is this how you wanted me to do it?"

The corners of her lips lifted in a smile. "Keep at it, just like that, for a while longer, and I should be satisfied."

Mr. Chow organized Spencer and Oliver to join him to the build site to work on the framing. He paused at the door. "Will you be alright, Miss Preston?"

"Oh yes." She lifted a knife from her work dress's pocket. "Mr. Sims can do me no harm."

The country was always more informal than town about rules like leaving young women alone with men. Still, Max wondered what Lord Preston would think if he discovered his daughter left without a chaperone.

He shook the thought away. Miss Preston's reputation was not his concern. In fact, the closer a relationship he could forge with her, the more likely she would tell him things about her family that he could use in his report.

Still operating the plane, Max decided to begin with vulnerability. "I have been hoping to find a moment to apologize to you, Miss Preston. For grabbing at you the other day. I made a cake of myself, I'm afraid."

"Oh, no need to apologize. I only thought you were being friendly." Settling onto a stool to watch him work, Miss Preston picked up a discarded piece of wood and started whittling at it with her carving knife. "I wish more of our people would be familiar with me. They used to be, when I was young, but now everyone seems concerned with being polite."

"You are the lady of the house, after all. It is only proper to keep a distance."

She turned the wood skillfully, shaping it into something soft and round. "Proper by whose rules?"

"Well..." Max couldn't figure out how a carpenter would respond to that.

"I'm sorry, I don't mean to fluster you. You are quite right that everyone is only being polite. It's just that I was raised to believe rules deserve to be questioned. Replaced, if necessary." Her eyes flew upwards, meeting his gaze in a flurry of gray iris. "I should like to replace the rule that requires me to be lonely even though I am surrounded by people."

And then she bit her lip. To stop herself from saying more, perhaps.

Max couldn't help thinking of other reasons a lip might be bitten. A kiss. A throe of passion.

He forced his attention back to the plane. Slowly, the wood was beginning to show evidence of the groove. "Let me break that rule with you, then. Even ladies of the house should have friends, I suppose."

They both glanced up in the same instant, their gazes colliding. Miss Preston looked away first. "Now I am the one who has made a cake of myself."

"Then we are even."

Her carving was beginning to take shape. A sheep, Max guessed, and he marveled that she could draw that out of wood in such quick cuts.

"How have your first few days been here?" Miss Preston asked.

Max lied, "The best few days since I was arrested, and that is the truth."

"It must have been very hard to be transported. Everything I have read about it sounds horrible." She frowned down at her sheep, her lips twisting in concentration.

Max didn't much want to invent a whole miserable experience of Australia. To steer the conversation in a more productive direction, he said, "My father expected better of me. It is especially hard to have disappointed him. I'm sure you do not know that feeling."

Miss Preston tilted her head. "Many of the people here have expressed similar sentiments. Our parents shape so much of our lives, don't they? Either one is trying to make them proud, or to prove them wrong, or simply to earn their love."

In Max's case, he realized, he was trying to do all three. When he published his report, he would prove to his father that he was not a frivolous spendthrift, and with that would come the pride – perhaps love, too, if the Earl of Meretta was capable of such emotion.

A lowering thought, that Max's private turmoil was no different than a common laborer's.

"Which is your goal?" he prodded her.

"Oh." Liberating the sheep from its wooden frame, she started adding in more details to the face and wool. "I want to make Papa proud, I suppose. I'm at the age that I need to decide for myself what my life will be from here on out. I hope he – and Mama, if she were alive – will be proud of what I do." More quietly, she added, "When I leave Northfield Hall."

"Leave?"

"When I marry. Or, if not marry, dedicate my life to a noble pursuit. Run a school for the poor or join the abolition speaking circuit."

Max couldn't imagine anything drearier. "Wherever you go, will you continue Northfield Hall's practice of avoiding imports?"

"Of course. I should hate to support the slave economy in any way. I'm sure you feel the same."

Max spotted this for the opportunity that it was. No one had quizzed him on his political or economic practices before hiring him, but would he lose his position if he admitted to being an avid tobacco smoker? "I think slavery is as evil as the next man does, but I don't see how my smoking a pipe or not makes a difference."

Miss Preston turned her entire attention to him. "Oh, but how could it not? The only reason they grow tobacco is to sell it to us. If we stop purchasing, they will stop growing it, and then they won't need slave labor anymore."

"You'd need to convince a lot more people than me for that to be effective." Max nearly forgot, in this response, to use his accent.

Luckily, she didn't seem to notice. Instead, she offered him a slow smile. "What makes you think I would stop with you?"

She was very pretty when she smiled. The captivating kind of pretty that made Max forget what his hands were doing. He lost himself in admiring her – and then found himself planing pure air instead of solid wood.

It stole his balance so much that Max nearly fell face-first onto the ground. He caught himself just as Miss Preston burst into laughter. "Oh, I'm sorry, I don't mean to laugh at you!" she cried between peals.

"If we are keeping score of who has made a cake of themselves most, I believe I am winning."

It was too bad, though, that he had done so, because their conversation had been veering towards something useful. Now Miss Preston rose from her stool and relieved him of the plane. "Perhaps you had better watch me for a while and see if you can learn that way."

"Quite," Max agreed. He sank onto the stool only to kick something that had fallen to the ground; her little wooden sheep.

He held it out to her. "Where would you like me to put this?"

"Oh." Busy at the plane, she looked from the sheep to him. Then she smiled – almost shyly. "Keep it. A gift. In the name of friendship."

She might have fooled him, if a blush hadn't crept into her cheeks again.

This wasn't friendship, and they both knew it. Max should exercise more caution. He took the report seriously, and he didn't want to risk it by doing anything too untoward with Miss Preston. But so far, their flirtation was proving entirely harmless. Helpful, even.

He tucked the sheep into his pocket.

REFUSING A TRIP TO London was not so simple as saying no, of course. It took four days for the household to prepare for the journey, which meant Ellen also suffered through four days of Sophia placing hints in conversation and Benny teasing her for being afraid of London and Caroline asking over and over again why Ellen wouldn't want to go. Nate was the only sibling to leave her in peace, largely because his tutor had finally set him to reading *Odysseus* and Nate had no interest in returning to the real world.

Her only respite was in the workshop, which was not nearly as relaxing as it had been before the arrival of Mr. Sims. Now, instead of losing herself in the puzzle of shaping wood, Ellen spent all her energy testing whether Mr. Sims was the kind of man she might want to kiss.

Well, she knew she *wanted* to kiss him. What she needed to determine was whether she admired his character enough to not regret it.

Papa saved his cajoling for the final evening. The rest of the household was racing around to finish packing, so Ellen took her needlework into her dressing room – where she could catch some evening light – and tried to put her mind to something else, so as not to dread the farewells tomorrow. Papa interrupted with a gentle knock at the door.

"May I have a word?"

He wore his old dressing gown, which Mama had made him a dozen years ago when he was larger and happier. Now, having lost nearly two stone in grief, the wool swam about him, giving him the look of a little boy in his father's clothes.

Ellen made room for him on her bench. "Do you regret inviting Sophia and Benny along yet?"

"I expect the regret will come tomorrow after about an hour in the carriage when they realize there are still five hours left, and when I realize I still have five hours of listening to them bicker." Papa smiled. "In truth, I am looking forward to having two of my favorite people in the world as my travel companions. I only wish you were going with us."

Ellen held her needle up to the light to thread it with green.

"I know you feel the weight of many responsibilities here," Papa continued. "I am glad for it because Mama and I above all wanted to raise you children with a sense of duty. However, I worry that you do not feel any duty to yourself. Northfield Hall can spare you."

Evidently, since Mr. Chow kept trying to foist unskilled Mr. Sims upon the shutters instead of trusting her to finish them. "I am not so altruistic as that, Papa. I choose to stay at Northfield Hall because I do not want to go to London, not because I feel that I am indispensable here."

"Ellen." Papa stood and grimaced out the window. "We all still grieve Mama, but it has been three years. At your age, most young women are anxious to marry. Do you not want to turn your thoughts to the future?"

She decided not to point out that it was about *him* they all worried because of his grief. "When I marry, it shall be to a man who does not look to worldly considerations for happiness. That type of man is unlikely to be found in London."

Her father asked uncomfortably, "Is it young Thistleman? Are you still waiting for him?"

A blush burned hot on Ellen's cheeks. She turned away. Those letters were supposed to have been clandestine. The idea that Papa knew about them – knew, too, that she had imagined a future with Percy – mortified her.

She had been nineteen the summer that Percy visited his father, the rector. Ellen supposed she had fancied herself in love. She had certainly drunk up every second of his attention when he walked her home from the glebe. And her body had craved his in new, exciting sensations. Between kisses, they had whispered to each other about marriage, enough so that Ellen had decided to consummate their relationship – a few times.

Then he had left for his own curacy, promising to save enough money for a family. And then Mama had died. Percy's letters arrived further and further apart, and Ellen had taken even longer to write her replies. By now, it had been over two years since she had heard from him.

She couldn't even quite remember who had written the last letter.

"I am not waiting for any one person in particular. I am waiting for…" Ellen searched for the right words. When she thought of the future, she could only do it a few months at a time, following the rhythm of Northfield Hall. Building the cottages. Harvesting the flax and barley. Pickling vegetables and brewing ale. Shoring up the estate against the cold rains of winter.

She could not picture a life away from Northfield Hall. Certainly not if it meant marrying a man who drank tea and smoked tobacco. If she had to part from Northfield, then Ellen wanted it to be for a reason greater than marriage. Mama had given up her whole family because she had believed in Papa's vision of a life free of goods stolen from the rest of the world. Ellen needed a reason at least as good as that to leave Northfield Hall.

And so she waited, hoping she would be strong enough to make the necessary sacrifices when she discovered her greater purpose.

It wouldn't hurt if that future included a man handsome and winsome, such as Mr. Sims.

Papa sank into the seat beside her. "When your mother died, I...well, there was a part of me that felt there was no reason to go on. I wanted to refuse my meals and waste away to join her in whatever comes next. It felt as if my heart had died."

Ellen didn't know why he said this aloud. She had been there. She had seen the heartbreak written in white pain across his face.

"I worry that you are afraid to live with your heart because you saw how terribly I handled my own grief. I still miss Mama, of course. I am so glad to have remained, though. The days I have with you children, and the work I have been able to do. Sometimes even just waking up and watching dawn embrace Northfield Hall is enough for me to feel close to her. Close to myself, too."

Ellen bent over her needlework so she didn't have to see whatever expression was on Papa's face as he muddled through this speech.

"Marriage is worth it, Ellen, that's all I am trying to say. Even though it brings its own pain, it is worth it. I don't want you to shy away from it because of fear."

Ellen couldn't think what he wanted her to say. She reverted to the advice he most often gave: "If you cannot be proud of an action, then don't do it."

"Conversely, if you *can* be proud of an action, then do it." Papa sighed. "There is much I wish for you, Little Light, not least of which is the peace of expressing your true thoughts instead of always choosing your words to please me or whomever you are speaking with."

I don't do that. "Thank you, Papa."

He cupped the back of her head over her house cap, as if she were still a girl and not nearly as tall as him. "You are intelligent, kind, and beautiful. There is so much of you to be proud of. And yet, you hide yourself in this cap and in politeness, so that no one may truly find you. I worry about that."

Ellen had spent so much of the past three years worrying about Papa. It was disorienting to have his gaze turned back on her, as if she were the fragile one. "I am not in need of finding, Papa. I am happy."

"I hope that is true." Dropping his hand, Papa slapped his palms to his knees. His whole manner cooled into something brisker. "One last thing, then. This new man..."

"Mr. Sims?" Her voice hiked up nearly an octave. Surely Papa wasn't listening to Benny and Sophia. Ellen couldn't stand it if he asked her whether she found the man attractive. It was one thing to admit it to herself, and entirely another to say it aloud to one's own father.

Luckily, Papa only said, "Mr. Chow thinks he may have lied about his carpentry experience. Apparently, the man can hardly even tell the difference between a hammer and a nail."

Ducking her head over her embroidery hoop, Ellen exhaled a sigh of relief. "Indeed, Mr. Sims is rather hopeless at carpentry."

"Mr. Chow worries that he lied maliciously."

The image that popped to mind was of Mr. Sims at the swing-arm plane, admitting to the shame of disappointing his father. Before he said the words – when they had just been thoughts rattling in his head – Ellen had almost seen his body shrink in upon itself, as if beneath the hulking frame of his shoulders he was still only a little boy. And then, he had offered up the truth so easily. Almost with a smile.

A man like him couldn't be malicious.

"For what purpose? I'm sure he only exaggerated in hopes of the job. It must be difficult to find work once the employer hears you've just returned from the penal colonies."

"I'm not sure," Papa said in that distant, circumspective way of his that meant he wouldn't say more on the matter. "Mr. Chow will be keeping an eye on him. I know you have been helping Mr. Sims, too. Let Mr. Chow or Uncle Maulvi know if you notice anything out of place."

"I will." Ellen wasn't sure she meant it. Just because Mr. Sims couldn't properly hold a plane didn't mean he deserved suspicion. "Don't worry about Northfield Hall while you are away, Papa. We will make sure everything runs smoothly. All you have to do is abolish slavery at last."

"Oh, is that all?" Rising, Papa pressed a kiss to her forehead. "Your optimism gives me hope. I shall write as often as I can."

Ellen didn't know why he needed her optimism. He was the one who had taught her to believe that the good of humanity could conquer over greed. She squeezed his hand before letting him drift back out of the dressing room. Then, looking out the window, she allowed her thoughts to return to Mr. Sims.

One lie did not make a man a liar. Being a liar did not make a man evil. No matter that he had overrepresented his carpentry skills; Ellen couldn't believe Mr. Sims harbored bad intentions. If Mr. Chow would not give Mr. Sims the benefit of the doubt, Ellen would.

It was what she had been raised to do.

CHAPTER FOUR

My dear readers, there is one thing I can tell you for certain:

Lord Preston has not rescued the common man from overwork. They may count themselves fortunate for being fed and housed and tended at times of illness, but they are required to work for such privileges, much harder than myself or other lordships reading this would ever expect from our tenants.

I offer to you my own experience as Mr. Maxwell Sims, carpenter, as example. Before dawn, I wake to the crowing of a dozen roosters. I fetch breakfast – a meat pasty

– from the communal dining room and report to the workshop just as the first pinks of sunlight illuminate my path. My master, Mr. Chow, already awaits me, a scowl on his face at my tardiness. He sets me to various woodworking tasks to build four cottages, all of which are expected to be completed by the end of July. This I labor at for hours, until the sun is high in the sky, at which point young children of the estate come by with bread, cheese, cold meats, and ale for dinner. Mr. Chow watches me eat, as if every bite steals from him a plank of wood. Then it is back to my work, although my muscles are screaming and my eyelids are drooping and my stomach still growls. This ends only once darkness has fallen. A dull bell rings, calling us all from each corner of the estate to crowd in for supper. Afterwards, we are all too tired in mind, body, and spirit to do anything other than limp to our straw pallets and collapse into sleep.

That I am able to write this to you proves only that I love you, my dear readers, more than I love the comfort and rest of my own body.

I T HAD BEEN ONE week. One terrible, long, import-free week. Breakfasts without tea or coffee. Meals without sugar. Days without even one whiff of tobacco. Max tried to enjoy each detail, so that he could spin it into his report.

But he wasn't sure how much more of it he could take.

The trouble was that no one around him seemed to think it was a hellhole at all. When he complained of overwork to Oliver, the youth only laughed. "You should hear what my eldest brother Martin had to put up with from his master in London."

When Max exclaimed about sleeping on a straw pallet to Killian, he earned only a quizzical look. "What did you sleep on in Australia, then? Feather beds?"

And Max didn't even try to complain about the food, since each night, every single person crowed over how great it was to count on Cook's fare at the end of a long day.

The only thing Max could find agreement upon was that Miss Preston's presence in the workshop was unnerving.

She didn't keep the same hours as the rest of the laborers. Whereas Max was expected to awaken with the first crow of the roosters in the barnyard, Miss Preston strolled in most days long after the sun had already come up.

She always wore the same work dress, too, that dull gray serge that completely disguised her figure. If Max had wanted to describe her for the paper – which he didn't, as it felt ungentlemanly to comment on a lady's appearance even in an objective report – he wouldn't even be able to guess at her hair color, since she kept it carefully wrapped in that bleached white cap like a spinster.

When Max flirted too obviously with Miss Preston, he earned dark looks from Mr. Chow, and so he tried his best to ignore her. The last thing he needed was to be tossed out on account of being impertinent with the lord's daughter. Every day upon her entrance, he resolved not to inhale the pleasant soapy smell that floated like a cloud around her and instead fixed his attention on the timber at hand. He listened to Oliver wax on about the heroism of his older brother Martin. He distracted himself with strategies for how to question his fellow laborers without giving away his purpose.

He absolutely did not allow himself to sand an entire length of wood while picturing the breasts hidden beneath Miss Preston's apron.

In his second week, Mr. Chow and Spencer worked at the cottage build site and assigned Max and Oliver to the sawpit to split fresh timber into planks. It was a task that required more brute strength than skill. As sawyer, Oliver perched atop the log and positioned the whipsaw into place, following a line drawn in ash that would ensure an even, two-inch-thick plank. Max took the role of pitman, standing in the five-foot-deep pit and yanking the saw downwards to make the cut. Over and over and over again.

His arms ached after the first five pulls. By the end of the first quarter hour, his hands were blistering even beneath the work gloves. He tried to lose himself in the motion of the work, but all he could think about was how uncomfortable he was, especially as the morning grew hotter into an unseasonable summer day.

When Max's hand slipped, Oliver let out a great string of curses, first in Chinese and then in English, ending with, "Why do I have to work with a child?"

The viscount in Max wanted to snarl back. He tempered that and huffed out as politely as he could, "I apologize."

The youth glared at him. "Why are you even here? You don't know the first thing about carpentry."

If he had to respond to that, Max just might quit the report altogether. He climbed from the pit instead, ignoring Oliver's question. "I need water."

Miss Preston, he noticed, was watching the exchange from her worktable inside the shop, where she patiently chiseled a shutter pull into its proper shape. She looked down quickly, as if she did not want to be caught.

Max rattled the water pitcher noisily against the cup as he poured himself a drink. If he had to suffer through pure manual labor, he at least wanted to keep Miss Preston's attention.

"My father thinks you are a thief," Oliver said from his seat on the timber.

"Oh, does he?" Max considered this. On the one hand, he wasn't fool enough to think Mr. Chow believed he had any experience in carpentry. On the other, he didn't want anyone wondering about where he had come from or why he was at Northfield Hall. "Why haven't I stolen anything yet, then?"

Oliver clearly hadn't considered this and pulled an answer out of thin air. "Perhaps you are waiting for the new moon so you can sneak into the house in the dark and slit everyone's throats."

"Really, Oliver." Miss Preston shook her head, readjusting the clamp of her vise. Max expected her to chastise the boy's manners, but instead, she said, "Then he would be a thief *and* a murderer."

Max grinned. He couldn't help it. She was funny. Gulping down the water, he refilled the cup and sauntered over to her table. "It is true that I am a thief." Setting the cup beside her, he winked. "However, I am only here to steal Miss Preston's heart."

She rolled her eyes. Her cheeks were already flush from the heat, so Max couldn't quite tell if she blushed, too. But he liked to think she did.

Before Oliver could respond, Spencer ran up to the workshop. "Oliver, Father wants to show you how to frame the floor." With less enthusiasm, he said to Max, "You're to stay here and help Miss Preston with the shutters."

An order Max could accept with no qualms. He waited for Oliver and Spencer to disappear onto the path to the cottage site, then turned to his instructress. "I am at your service, Miss Preston."

Her eyes, he noticed, had roamed downwards. Examining the sweat soaking through his coat, perhaps. Admiring the ripple of his muscles, he hoped.

"You may remove your jacket, if you like." Now her cheeks definitely blazed. "It is too hot to stand on ceremony."

Max could have taken that opening and turned it into something naughty and delicious. Invite her to strip to her smock or offer to remove as many clothes as she liked.

He restrained himself to a mere eyebrow raise and shrugged out of his coat. He hung it on a peg beside one of the saws. He removed his necktie, too, so that he wore only his waistcoat and shirt above his torso. Still too many clothes, but his skin breathed a little easier with fewer layers.

Miss Preston pretended not to watch him. She stripped off her leather work gloves to take up the cup of water. Max noticed the strength in her fingers as they flashed through the air. In a ballroom, they would look mannish; in the workshop, they were competent.

She drank the water in long, slow sips. Her eyes closed with pleasure. Her throat moved in greedy gulps. When she finished, her tongue darted out to lick a stray bead of water from her lips.

Never had Max found a simple act so arousing.

This time, when their eyes met, Miss Preston didn't blush. She held his gaze, an eyebrow tilted in a challenge. One Max recognized.

He could kiss her, if he wanted to.

Max retreated to the stool beside the worktable. "You did not join your father in London."

"No." Miss Preston returned her attention to the chisel. Lightly – as if there was no chemistry fizzling between them – she added, "I am not interested in the marriage mart at the moment, and of course, there is no other reason for a woman such as myself to go to London."

"Of course." Max did wonder about her marriage prospects. Lord Preston carried enough of a reputation himself; his daughters would be limited to the Whigs who didn't mind a radical in the family. Max couldn't imagine any of his peers offering for Miss Preston if they discovered her interest in carpentry. They would take one look at the wood shavings clinging to her cuffs and leave the room.

Their loss, of course. Max wasn't sure he could imagine Miss Preston in an evening gown, much less recognize her in one. She wouldn't be herself without a block of wood in her hand.

"There are the shutters to complete, anyway," he continued. "I have been meaning to ask, by the way, how you became such an expert joiner. Surely Lord and Lady Preston did not encourage such a hobby."

"I am useful to Northfield Hall. Papa has no objection to that." Miss Preston adjusted her position to better angle her chisel against the wood. "Martin Chow began his apprenticeship here – a decade ago, now – and since he is like an older brother to me, I followed him. Curiosity at first, I suppose, and then very quickly I found it much more interesting than anything in the schoolroom."

Max had been curious about carpentry, too. Only when his father had discovered him following the workers about, the earl had set Max to twice as many hours with his tutors and lectured the grounds men on letting the heir do common tasks.

"I have heard quite a few theories about you," Miss Preston said, chipping away at her chisel. "Mrs. Chow thinks you are a common criminal who is too afraid to admit what felony you committed.

Others speculate you are a spy here to uncover how Northfield is so profitable. My brother Nate is convinced you are a pirate who has followed a treasure map to our property." Pausing, she lifted an eyebrow at Max. "Nate is taken with all things to do with the sea, I'm afraid."

He tried to project confidence. Nonchalance, even. Mr. Sims would not be alarmed by such accusations because he knew he had done nothing wrong. He was only an ex-criminal trying to earn enough money to return to Norwich. "To which theory do you subscribe?"

Max heard how his tone didn't quite sound calm. There was a defensiveness in it. Miss Preston paused, chisel hovering over her wood, to reply, "I should like to believe you tell the truth, Mr. Sims. That is the magic of Northfield, after all. We believe in each other and forgive each other our sins. Of course, that is easier to do if we know what each other's sins are."

As if Max would confess his black heart to her, simply because she asked.

He scoffed. "Is that it? I thought the magic of Northfield Hall was money in everyone's greedy little palms."

Now Miss Preston set down her tool altogether. "I have agitated you."

"No." But she had. And since she had noticed, Max had to do something about it. Find some excuse for why her line of questioning upset him, without getting anywhere near the truth.

"I do believe you, Mr. Sims. There is nothing sinister in claiming to have some carpentry experience in order to get a job. I daresay I would lie, too, if I needed wages in a scrape. I was only teasing when I mentioned what everyone else is thinking."

She was too good-hearted for him. Max hated to have her believe the best in him. One day, she would discover the truth – that he had been lying to her this whole time – and he hated to think she was willingly blindfolding herself to the hints everyone else saw.

At the very least, he didn't want her to feel a fool for flirting with him.

"You have not agitated me, Miss Preston," he reiterated. "It is only that I do have something to confess to you. A transgression for which I hope you might forgive me."

"Oh." One word rippled between them. She swallowed. Her hands stilled in the midst of brushing shavings from the table onto the floor. And she looked at him. In such a way that changed the temperature in the air.

Again, Max knew: he could kiss her. He could take her in his arms, lay her across the shutters, and relish in the sweet heat of her lips. If he wanted to.

Which was why he had to confess this lie. Tell her he was promised to another. Because one day – soon, he hoped – Miss Preston would find out who Max really was. It would be easier for both of them if there was no kiss.

He opened his mouth to confess to his fictional sweetheart. Except before he could speak, Miss Preston slid from the worktable and stepped before him. With him still on the stool, she was almost exactly the same height as him.

"It's only—before you do—I just—"

She grabbed him by the waistcoat. And, instead of finishing her sentence, she kissed him.

E LLEN CAME TO HER senses sooner rather than later. Or maybe it was later rather than sooner. Because she was already kissing him. A deep, messy kiss. Her fingers curled under the edges of his waistcoat. Her nose scraped against the stubble on his cheek. Her tongue tangled desperately with his.

Precisely the kind of kiss she had been fantasizing about for the last week and a half.

In the end, deciding to kiss him had been simple. He was about to tell her something she wouldn't like. Something that would be hard to forgive.

Before he did that, Ellen wanted to know what it would be like to sear her skin against his.

It was better than she imagined. She had to remember to heave him away, rather than let his hands creep up the back of her dress.

"There. We have gotten that out of the way."

Mr. Sims blinked at her. His eyelids drooped from desire, and he brushed his thumb across his lower lip – an almost innocent gesture, like a virgin second-guessing his first kiss. "Out of the way?"

"Yes." Ellen checked the tie of her apron. "You were about to confess a transgression. I'm afraid it will complicate things, and I wanted to kiss you at least once. So, now we have. You may confess."

She sounded like an idiot. She was well aware. She felt like one, too. At least she was a blissful idiot who had just now claimed the best kiss of the decade.

He stared at her a moment longer. Ellen wondered what exactly prevented him from understanding her meaning. Was he shocked that she might kiss him?

It was a depressing thought. Too many people wanted her to fit the image of a pure angel that they vaulted her onto an unreachable pedestal to keep her there. It was, she suspected, one of the reasons the laborers had grown so distant from her. They were afraid to wobble the statue of Ellen.

Before she had tied her hair up beneath its cap, the Northfield Hall gossip had veered in the other direction, claiming her to be bold and independent, all because her hair was red as a flame. No matter what she did, it seemed, those around her would see what they wanted of her.

She returned to her stool at the worktable. "What was it you wanted to tell me?"

"Oh." He cleared his throat. Perhaps for the first time in their acquaintance, he blushed. "Only that...I am not sure that you know this because I did tell Mr. Chow, but…I have a sweetheart in Norwich. Delia. I am here to earn enough money so I may return and marry her."

Almost immediately, mortification overwhelmed her. Here she had been flirting with the man for the better part of two weeks – had forced her lips directly onto his – and he was in love with a girl in Norwich!

"Oh, I do apologize. I didn't mean to…oh, how awful of me!"

Had he kissed her back? Ellen suddenly wasn't sure.

"Don't." Rising, he leaned into the worktable. "You are not at fault here. I have been having too much fun with you, Miss Preston. That's why I thought I had better mention it."

She thought he was being rather generous, considering she was the one who had thrown herself at him. Still, she accepted the grace he offered. "Perhaps we had better get back to work and forget it ever happened."

"Back to work." Mr. Sims smirked. "I'm not sure I'll forget that kiss anytime soon, though."

He said it to be kind. To make her feel better. Still, Ellen didn't think his Delia would appreciate it.

She had expected him to confess to something terrible. He would disclose that he had once killed a man; that he was plotting to blow up Parliament in a radical protest; that he was a French spy. Whatever he had to say, she had feared it would make her stop liking him, and so she had wanted to seize the kiss first.

It hadn't occurred to her that he might be spoken for.

"I hope I haven't made you uncomfortable." Ellen noticed her hands trembling as she reached for the chisel. "You needn't humor me simply because my father is Lord Preston."

Mr. Sims reached out and closed a hand around hers. "You haven't. I haven't. I promise."

It was strange how even now, knowing he was promised to another, Ellen felt the undertow of connection. Looking into his eyes was as comfortable as tying on her work apron at the beginning of the day. Holding his hand was as natural as a chisel in her palm.

Kissing him had been like a winter evening's fire. Intense. Necessary. Comforting.

She pulled away. She knew now; there were no excuses for either of them. Mr. Sims was her colleague and nothing more, from here on out.

Ellen handed him the chisel. "Show me what you can do with a shutter pull."

Chapter Five

Miss Preston ignored Max for the rest of the week.

Max knew it was for the best. Their flirtation had passed the point of a friendly game. If he had allowed it to grow, he would be inviting trouble in. And the whole purpose of this report was to prove to his father that he knew how to turn his back to trouble.

Only he wanted desperately to steal another moment with her. Just the one. Blush. Kiss. Then Max might be satisfied.

Except, of course, he wouldn't be. That kiss had not yet left Max's lips. Perhaps because *she* had seized *him*. In hands so competent they could transform raw wood into elegant shutter pulls. She had been no novice. She had known exactly how to kiss him senseless. Exactly when to pull away, too, and smile like a cat who stole the cream, leaving Max haggard and breathless.

He shouldn't want it to happen again. He shouldn't even look Miss Preston's way again, not when she had only mention it to any person on the estate to ban him from Northfield Hall. Even as Maxwell Sims, he should be dreading the memory of it, since he was supposed to be saving his wages to return to marry Delia in Norwich.

Max spent the week stealing glimpses of Miss Preston anyway. Brow furrowed, body shapeless beneath leather apron and wool dress, hair hidden away in that dratted cap. Max had never imagined the mere flash of gray serge would quicken his blood, and now here he was.

His only respite arrived on Sunday morning, when everyone at Northfield Hall had a weekly holiday. Unless he attended the sermon – which Max wouldn't stoop to, even for a woman – Max had little hope of catching a glance of Miss Preston, and therefore, he could use the day to clear his head.

Get his focus back on the mission at hand. Find out the truth behind some of his compatriots at Northfield Hall.

So far, Max had only the obvious to write in his report. The description of the estate, the catalog of imports banished from its grounds, and an analysis of human nature. If nothing else, Max had a draft upon how not even precious Lord Preston could abolish social hierarchy. At Northfield Hall, it lurked just below the surface: the farmers who worked the common fields kept apart from the rest of the Northfield society, the tradesmen held themselves above the servants, the servants who worked inside the Hall considered themselves yards above those who worked outside, and the grounds workers had precious little nice to say about anyone from beyond the estate.

But Max knew that alone was not enough for *The Perceptive*'s purposes. The report was supposed to make Lord Preston the laughingstock of England, not provide an opinion upon why the nature of man was impervious to intervention.

He woke Sunday morning with the memory of that last meeting with his father ringing in his ears, like the screech of a wrong note from the organ. He had answered a summons from the earl. They arrived occasionally, usually spurred by the earl hearing something unsavory about Max, and as usual, the idea of the meeting alone had set Max to drinking too much. A few whiskeys. A pint or two of ale at one of the rougher pubs, deep in the early hours of the morning. From there, he couldn't quite recall what he had done or what he had drunk.

Some perversion inside him had driven him to show up hungover, when he knew that alone would set his father off. This pattern had been set ages ago. Max could do nothing but follow it.

He was shown to the dining room, where the Earl of Meretta sat at the very end of the gleaming mahogany table. It was midafternoon, not a usual meal time, but the earl ate what he wanted, when he wanted it, regardless of what the rest of society might do. As Max took the seat to his father's right, the earl cut into a steaming meat pie.

"If your mother saw you, she would think you ill," the earl said by way of greeting.

Not true: Max's mother would smile indulgently and defend a young man's right to his youth while he had it.

"I have a headache." Speaking of which, Max reached across the table to seize the silver coffee urn and filled his porcelain cup. "You indulged in too much drink."

And here the pattern continued. Max had expected it. Therefore, it shouldn't have stung him. Yet his stomach soured; he had to set down his coffee before tasting it. "I was with Lord Peters last night. We discussed the army appropriations bill."

The earl spoke around a great mouthful of pie. "For exactly two minutes, I would wager. The rest of the night you were...what? Drinking, gambling, and whoring?"

Max sifted through the responses available to him. *And what did you do before taking a seat in Parliament?* Or *Not all three, in fact* or *If only you would give me something to do...*

"You are the heir to one of the oldest families in England," his father intoned, as he always did. "You must not give into the common ways of the fops who can't believe their good luck they wormed their way into titles."

Most of Max's friends were the third or fourth generation of their titles. For all that his father harped about the quality of a family, distinguishing between recent dukedoms and ancient baronies, Max cared more about whether a man would stand by him while he puked into the gutters than whether he had been knighted by George III or Edward IV.

"If you would stand me for election in Great Yarmouth, my lord, then I might be of more use to you."

"Ah, so you can drag our name through the scandal sheets as an MP? I think not."

"That was only..." Max aborted the argument before he could even begin it. He *had* landed in the gossip rags, years ago when he had first come to London, fresh from Eton, and somehow ended up bedding the Prime Minister's mistress without knowing it. "If I could only be of some use to you, then I would not find myself struggling to fill my days."

"You will not be of use to me until you can go three days without putting your own carnal needs ahead of good sense."

The pattern continued, then. Max had been summoned, he had been lectured, and now he would be dismissed, sent back into the abyss of London with nothing but the heavy expectation of fucking up.

As he always did.

Nausea rose, from the alcohol still roiling his stomach. From frustration, too. Was this his destiny, then? Not to rise to the top of his generation, not to earn the distinction as a statesman or politician, but to disappoint his father day after day until by the time the earl died, Max didn't recognize himself anymore?

Max wasn't even the man his father saw him as. Yes, he went out for evenings with friends. He drank at the theater, flirted with actresses, bought jewels for the paramour of the moment. But that was what everyone did as the sun set on London. During the days, Max tried to find ways to be useful. He took coffee at his club to read the newspapers and keep a finger on the pulse of national politics.

He went to soirees hosted by various ladies and diplomats to build friendships with players who might be crucial to one bill or another. He was even trying to get appointed to the board of the foundling hospital so he could learn more about how such institutions functioned.

None of this was enough.

"How can I prove myself to you, then, my lord?" Max cried out in frustration. "Would you have me take rooms with the Quakers, disavow all my worldly goods, and preach for the salvation of mankind?"

For the first time, the earl looked up from his meat pie. His eyes were surprisingly small in his face, and Max caught sight of new lines around them. "Don't be ridiculous."

"I am not being ridiculous. I am desperate. How many times must you lecture me on my behavior? How many days must I contemplate which of the useless activities will make me less of an embarrassment to you? Give me something, Father, anything, to prove that I am ready for the Great Yarmouth seat."

"You haven't even been to Montchampion Manor for two years, much less Great Yarmouth."

"I'll go. I will travel to Great Yarmouth and knock on every door, introduce myself to every resident – voter or no – if that is what you want me to do."

"You are being tiresome, Berwick." There was a glimmer, however, of interest about the earl's eyes.

Max leaned forward. "I would prove myself to you, my lord."

His father looked at the newspaper in his hand, the week's edition of *The Perceptive*. Hope sparked in Max's heart. When his father had first funded the paper, Max had asked to be made editor – or at least to be given space in each edition to write opinion pieces – only to be reminded that his tutors had consistently decried him for missing assignments entirely.

The earl tossed the paper to Max. "Lord Preston has been railing against us in *The Progress Gazette* again. He is an annoyance, and I am ready for the public to be as tired of him as I am."

"I am surprised they are not, since all he does is lecture us on how evil we are. Surely we get enough of that from our Sunday sermons."

The earl did not twitch his lips in amusement. Why would he – he had never found anything Max said humorous.

"I want someone to go to Northfield Hall. Pretend to be one of them. Find out all of Lord Preston's little secrets. Then expose it to the world in *The Perceptive*."

"In other words, you want to prove to the public that Lord Preston is a kook or a fraud. The way all of us know him to be."

Max's father returned his attention to his meat pie. "Cabot refused to do it, since it means living as a laborer, perhaps for weeks. You would have to be clever with your hands, do a lot of lying, and not get in your cups or let your cock tell you what to do."

Here is where the earl would poison the well: *In other words, I do not think you can do it.*

But instead he said, "If you write a report that Cabot will publish, then I'll consider the seat at Great Yarmouth."

Max swallowed. "Yes, my lord. I will."

He was halfway out of the room when his father intoned, "Oh, Berwick, above all: don't get caught."

The words hung in the air, unexplained. Max didn't need his father to say anything else. The consequences were clear. If he were found doing manual labor, it would be the scandal of the century. His father would disavow any knowledge of the plot. Max would be sent into the country, no doubt, and not let out until someone had eloped with someone else's wife.

He would never take a seat in Parliament, not until his father died and he inherited the earldom.

Well, he wouldn't get caught. It was that simple.

That had seemed the biggest risk when he set off on this little adventure. It hadn't occurred to him that he would struggle to find so much as a complaint about Lord Preston for the report.

Max used the memory as fuel. He had a point to prove to his father, and he wouldn't let a good kiss get in the way of that. Rising from his straw pallet, Max dressed in his only change of clothes and followed the throng of laborers into the nearby village of Thatcham. Most were dressed in their Sunday finest for the church service, but a handful veered farther to the inn at the edge of the main road. Max noted the non-conformists: the Hindustani gardeners, the Black stone mason Hamlyn, and Irishmen like Killian.

Max decided to claim to be a Quaker, if anyone asked why he was not at the regular service. That seemed the type of religion that a Preston would admire.

No one did ask; they simply invited him to join them among the inn's half-full dining room. Settling in beside Killian, Max was delighted to discover the Sunday roast included pepper and nutmeg – ingredients denied him at Northfield Hall – and ordered a wine to accompany his food, even though he knew full well it was beyond a carpenter assistant's budget and likely tasted of piss.

This was one of Max's favorite ways to pass an afternoon. Relaxed in one place with nothing to do but connect with the men around him. In his years traveling from Rome to Zagreb to Constantinople and back, Max had luxuriated in spending whole days with strangers, learning how they took their meals and why they dressed the way they did and hearing the trials and tribulations of their lives. If he was good at anything, it was inviting people to unlock their stories for him – usually without even trying.

When the lads had spent nearly a half hour on the subject of who could lift an anvil above their head for more than ten seconds, Max decided he might as well guide the conversation in the direction of his curiosity.

"So lads," he said, leaning in to grab their attention, "what do you think are the odds that Lord Preston is mad?"

At his club in London, this question would have landed with a laugh. The Whigs would have put up some pretense of offense, but even they admitted Lord Preston went to extremes.

Here, Max was met with a bank of faces contracted in horror.

Killian recovered enough to slap Max's back with a manufactured scoff. "You haven't met his lordship yet, that's all."

"Why?" These were common men, after all. Everyone knew there was nothing they liked more than to bitch about lordships when no one of import was listening. "Is he so precious about his reputation that he can't handle some friendly speculation about whether he has joined the king in insanity?"

One of the gardeners said, "Which is madder: a baron who takes care of his people, or a carpenter's assistant who needs a woman to show him how to use a hammer?"

The other men liked that one. Max, resisting the urge to react, said only, "He has a funny way of defining 'his' people. How many of you are even from Berkshire?"

"It is true that he doesn't use geography to define his relations." Hamlyn set a cold stare on Max. "To what do you object? That it is different from the way your masters always told you the world should be?"

Max forced out a smooth smile. He wasn't sure where he had gone wrong, but it was clear he had. He needed to get on some other footing, and fast. "So defensive. I am only wondering what kind of man we are following. The way you carry on, one might think you worship Lord Preston more than you do the king himself."

"Lord Preston is a good man," Hamlyn growled.

The air crackled with the energy of twelve angry men. Max had fucked this up. That much was clear. The only question was how he could redeem himself so they would let him stay at the table, much less tell him about their experiences at Northfield Hall.

Luckily, the innkeeper interrupted. "Post for you lot."

From the corner of his eye, Max caught a flash of movement out the window. A familiar figure marching down the street. For an instant, his mind told him it was Miss Preston. But when he turned his head, he saw no one.

His heart raced, anyway.

The innkeeper started handing out the envelopes, one man at a time, pausing with each delivery to collect the price of the postage. Hamlyn, receiving a letter, glared at Max. "Only reason I can read is because of Lady Preston, may she rest in peace."

The innkeeper handed Max an envelope. Instantly, Max recognized the handwriting: Daniel Cabot, editor of *The Perceptive*.

His first draft of notes had made it to London already, then. Max wondered what Daniel had thought of it. Whether Cabot had shown it to the earl. Whether that was enough to convince the earl to stand Max up for election in Great Yarmouth.

He pushed the hope away. Max had no time to indulge in fantasies. First, he had to fix this interview. He had to regain his rapport with these men so that he could uncover the information *The Perceptive* needed.

Summoning as much charm as he thought the room could handle, Max pressed a handful of coins into the innkeeper's hand, far more than would cover the cost of his letter. "Another round of ale for the table, at my expense."

The innkeeper served up the drinks. The men thanked him — warily. Max raised his tankard in toast. "To Lord Preston's health!"

"To Northfield Hall!" Killian added.

"To the slaves toiling without freedom!" cried Hamlyn.

"To the Tiger of Mysore!" from one of the Hindustanis.

Each man piled on his own toast, until at last they were all satisfied and Max dared take a drink. He swallowed vigorously; the ale splattered out the corners of his mouth. The men were too busy devolving into arguments of whose families had been worse betrayed by the empire to notice.

Max tried to listen. He knew that was key. He had to be curious about the men in order for them to believe they could trust him with their stories.

But the envelope sat heavy in his pocket. To hear from someone in London – to be reminded that he was, in fact, Viscount Berwick – to hold a physical memento promising he would one day be free of the sawpit – Max's hands almost itched with desperation to open it.

He was jolted back to the table by a direct question from Hamlyn. "What about you, Sims? Who fucked you over?"

"Oh." He tried to remember what the others had just said. Heartless landlords turning out tenants. Brutal soldiers burning villages. Rich owners selling off children.

Max couldn't lie about something like that.

"No one. I stole two yards of calico, just as they said. For my sister. I shouldn't have done it, but I did, and now I've paid the price."

Killian prodded, "Aye, but why did you need to steal the calico? Who set the price of calico so high and your wages so low that you couldn't afford to buy a nice fabric for your sister?"

"Fucking Parliament, that's who," one of the men towards the end of the table said.

Max opened his mouth, then closed it. He couldn't argue the principles of economics to these men. Maxwell Sims wouldn't know anything about the invisible hand of the market any more than these laborers wanted to learn about it. He decided to say, "It doesn't matter why. I knew it was against the law, and I did it anyway."

Hamlyn asked, "Do you think it was fair that for two yards of calico, you were sent to Australia for three years?"

"Aye." Killian was a little drunk and red in the face now. "Do you think that mercer lost three years' worth of profits because of your little thieving?"

The ale was turning sour in Max's stomach. He adjusted his seat, and the envelope crinkled in his pocket. A reminder: this was all a lie. "Without just punishments, why would anyone pay for goods? What would stop every man from stealing?"

"It wasn't just. What they did to you." Hamlyn set Max with a long, sad stare. "They upended your life. Your family's life. Tried to break your soul, too, if I know them. For two yards of fabric."

We forgive each other our sins here, Miss Preston had said. Max wondered if they would forgive him if they ever found out who he really was. The lies he was spinning. The sins he could truly own.

Someone broke the mood. Max didn't know who. He didn't have it in him to switch back to Sunday joviality and jape about who could let loose the biggest fart on the walk home.

He needed a reprieve from all this. From being someone he was not. From failing to crack open the puzzle of Northfield Hall. His thoughts drifted again to Miss Preston, yearning this time not for a kiss so much as for a simple conversation. About anything. About nothing. Somehow, Max felt that just being close to her would lend him the encouragement he craved.

Sentimental drivel, that's all that was. Disgusted at his own thoughts, Max excused himself from the inn. He was better off taking a nap than brooding among the men.

The morning sunshine had dissolved into a drizzle. Max kept his hand on the letter in his pocket to protect it from the rain. He tried to think positively about what the editor might say. It would be good news. Praise. Perhaps – miraculously – even an invitation home.

Max liked that idea. Perhaps he needn't muddle through being a carpenter and liar much longer. Perhaps he had done enough to prove himself to his father.

Perhaps he could return to London, and, one day, meet Miss Preston there in someone's drawing room and pay her a compliment as himself, Lord Berwick.

The instant he was out of view of the village, he opened the letter.

> *This is drivel about what it is like to live outside a palace. We do not need to explain to readers what hard work is (though it brings me pleasure that your lordship is finally learning the meaning of that phrase).*

What about disappearing profits? What have you found about Berskhire linen? Send more when you have actual findings to share. Until then, spare me your complaints.

Max tucked it into his pocket. Ignored the way his stomach plummeted. He should have known better. He never had done anything well enough. Never had he satisfied even a school tutor, much less his father.

In an hour or so, he would reread the letter. He would use it as a reason to keep trying. It would motivate him to work harder and cleverer. By the end of the week, he would have the facts he needed to expose Lord Preston's great experiment as flawed and hopeless.

To humiliate Miss Preston's family once and for all.

For the moment, however, Max only focused on putting one foot in front of the other.

Ellen fled the inn on her tiptoes. She didn't think anyone from Northfield had spotted her, except perhaps Mr. Hamlyn. Mr. Sims hadn't seen her, that was for sure.

What are the odds that Lord Preston is mad?

At least Killian and the like had stood up for Papa. Mr. Sims hadn't wanted to let the subject drop. Like their neighbor Lady Traymer when someone dared wear the wrong type of gown to an assembly. It was almost as if Mr. Sims believed Papa was the devil himself.

The innkeeper had seen her fingers trembling as she retrieved the three letters waiting for Northfield Hall. He must have heard what Mr. Sims was saying, too, because he set aside his work to interrupt the conversation with their post.

Ellen removed herself to the street before any of the laborers might greet her. Letters tucked in her reticule, she started for home. She was too disturbed to carry through with any of her intended Sunday socializing.

She had kissed that man! It wasn't that Ellen believed Mr. Sims to be an angel. The few basic truths about him were the picture of a scoundrel: he admitted to being a committed criminal; he lied about having any carpentry experience at all; and he had kissed her back, even though some woman waited in Norwich to marry him.

None of that had mattered much to her. Ellen had even indulged the fantasy all week that he would be trying to kiss her again, if only he weren't promised to Delia.

Apparently, all he had been fantasizing about was whether her father was a lunatic.

This was precisely why Ellen had waited to kiss Mr. Sims. If only she had deliberated one week more. So that she could discover him for the toad he was.

Mr. Chow hadn't trusted him from the start. Ellen wondered why the rest of them hadn't listened to Mr. Chow. Perhaps everyone else had. Perhaps it was only she who was so beguiled by the way he could settle his eyes on her and *listen* that she had concocted an entirely different personality for Mr. Sims. She thought him kind. Compassionate. A man trying his best to get back on his feet.

But a compassionate man would not disparage her family like that.

She should have told Papa to turn Mr. Sims out rather than give him the benefit of the doubt. If this was how they were repaid for kindness – Ellen shook herself, as if that could rid her of the shame seizing her body.

Her frenzy had carried her all the way down the village road to the turn-off to Northfield. Now she tried to collect herself. The question was not how she felt about Mr. Sims, but what she planned to do about it. She could tell Uncle Maulvi what she had overheard and ask him to send Mr. Sims away.

Only that wouldn't answer the question she most wanted answered: *why.* Why lie about his carpentry experience, when it was so obvious how incompetent he was? Why apply to be employed at Northfield Hall only to disparage it so?

Ellen didn't need to wonder why he might kiss her when promised to another. That was a story as old as time.

As the Hall rose on the horizon, Ellen decided her course of action. She would tell Uncle Maulvi – after discovering Mr. Sims's motivations.

Mrs. Chow kept records of each laborer's lodgings in her little office beside the still room. Slipping in, Ellen discovered which room belonged to Mr. Sims and tucked the skeleton key into her pocket.

It was quite the climb up the men's lodging house steps, especially with the afternoon heat trapped in the stairwell, and Ellen was huffing by the time she reached the top. She paused to catch her breath. The corridor was dark, as the only window was in the stairwell behind her. It was narrow, too, and the ceiling hung low. She couldn't imagine all of Mr. Sims squeezing into this space. He barely seemed able to fit in the sawpit.

His room was at the end of the corridor. Looking over both shoulders – just in case – Ellen unlocked the door.

It smelled like Mr. Sims. She hadn't realized he had a particular smell, but as soon as Ellen inhaled within his room, she felt as if he were there. Her skin tingled.

Shaking herself, she focused on discovering everything she could about him. For one thing, the bed was not neatly made at all. A sheet and blanket lay crumpled at its foot, as if he had thrown off his covers and expected someone else to come fold them into place. Near the window, a chipped basin sat on the bedstand with an inch or two of dirty water still inside it.

The wooden sheep she had made him sat forgotten on the windowsill.

Then Ellen spotted the satchel beneath the bedstand. It was an inelegant canvas sack with two sturdy ropes as handles. Glancing over her shoulder – as if she would find someone watching her, when she was the only soul in the building – Ellen pulled it from its hiding place and started rummaging through.

The top layer produced only clothes: an argyle sweater, a knitted cap, and a fine wool scarf. Ellen threw these onto his dirty mattress, then reached deeper into the sack.

Now her hands landed on a wooden, portable desk. A curious belonging for a man-of-all-work who didn't even own tools. Ellen drew it out carefully, then tilted open the lid to discover a whole sheath of papers.

Sinking onto the floor, Ellen started reading. The first paper looked like notes he jotted to himself. *Carpentry workshop. No coffee or tea. Some men don't eat pork. Men and women live separately.*

Fear coiled in her stomach. There was no reason to make such observations about Northfield – unless one planned to *do* something with them.

She flipped to the next page. This was in the same handwriting – his, she assumed – which was perfectly formed, except for where letters should curve elegantly, they slanted in hurried dashes. As if he couldn't be bothered with the courtesy of properly forming letters.

Ellen shook off this observation to read what he had written. It was a description of the Hall itself, addressed to anonymous "readers," and its tone was hardly friendly. In three swift paragraphs, it skewered the community at Northfield as fractious and small-minded.

She couldn't name the emotion seizing her. It sank her stomach. Stung her eyes. Quickened her breath.

She knew what kind of man he was. But apparently, the stupid part of her that had kissed him had been holding out hope that she would discover reasons to trust Mr. Sims.

Yet here it was in plain writing. A newspaperman, Ellen guessed, though it didn't really matter. All that signified was that they had let a lion in amongst their lambs.

Somewhere down the hallway, a door slammed. Footsteps – heavy and booted – marched along, growing louder and louder.

Ellen's skin turned to cold sweat. In a panic, she threw the desk onto the straw pallet and shoved the papers under her bodice. Just in time, too – as she straightened her dress, Mr. Sims opened the door.

He stared at her. At first, his hands curled into fists in surprise; then he simply looked puzzled. "Miss Preston?"

As the mistress of the household, Ellen had every right to inspect her servants' quarters. Only her family had never made a practice of it. She couldn't think of any explanation for her presence except the truth.

Ellen wasn't ready yet to confront him. And so she said the first thing that popped into her mouth. "There you are at last, Mr. Sims."

He swallowed. Visibly. "Have you need of me?"

Heart hammering, Ellen suddenly realized what it looked like. If she wasn't inspecting his room, then she had to have a different purpose. A seductive purpose.

She sidled against the wall, trying to get closer to the door. The sheep, looking mournfully out his tiny window, caught her eye. "I am collecting my figurines. To donate to the summer fair at the village. May I have my sheep back?"

Sims – or whatever his name was – blinked. He looked to the windowsill, then back at her. "I thought she was a gift."

"She?"

He blushed. "I named her Elin-o-o-or." The last syllable he drew out into a sheep's bleating. "She is my good luck talisman."

Ellen ordered her heart not to thud in desire at the way he so earnestly ducked his head. She had been taken in by his soft gaze before. Now she knew better.

Crossing the room in two steps, he retrieved the sheep. Ellen rotated so that her back was to the door. She held out her hand. All she needed to do was take the blasted Elinor and retreat. Then she could turn her discovery and the papers and the whole problem over to Uncle Maulvi to sort out.

It was a small room. He stepped close to offer the sheep, close enough that Ellen could smell the dust of the road on his skin. He was too handsome by half. The way he looked at her with those deep, hazel eyes made him seem so earnest. She wished he would smirk, to remind her that he was an arrogant liar.

Instead, he placed the sheep in her hand. It was surprisingly smooth. Ellen glanced down to confirm what she felt: at some point, he had taken the time to sand and seal little Elinor.

His fingers closed over her palm. "May she bring as much peace to the next fellow as she did me."

Ellen was supposed to be fleeing. Wresting this traitor from the heart of her family. Doing the right thing, or at least something she could be proud of.

Her skin was not supposed to tingle at his touch. And she absolutely was not supposed to want to kiss him again.

Yet that was precisely what she did.

A goodbye kiss, she told herself. The price he paid for teasing her with his lies. She pressed her lips into his greedily, drinking in the taste of ale in his breath, nipping her tongue against his, imprinting every last of her desires onto his skin. Let him wonder about what he could have had, if only he hadn't lied. Let him agonize over betraying his precious Delia. Let him lay awake at night, remembering the best kiss of his life.

Ellen swore to herself that she would remember him as nothing more than a handsome, lying piece of flesh.

His hand landed at her ribcage, just beneath her left breast. It hesitated, as if asking for permission to drift higher, and at first Ellen thought only of that. Of how her body yearned for his touch on her bare skin.

It took another half-second for her to hear the crinkle of paper. Her eyes flew open as he pressed – gently – again into her bodice.

There was a new, cold steel in his voice when he asked, "What do you have in there?"

Ellen did the only thing she could think to do. Pressing the sheep back into his palm, she turned and ran.

CHAPTER SIX

M AX DIDN'T KNOW WHY Miss Preston fled. Why there were papers crackling in her bodice. Or why she had left Elinor in his hand. But even through the fog of desire, Max reckoned he could guess.

Glancing over his shoulder, Max took in the state of his room. His pack gaped open, the writing desk with his inkwell and pens resting on the straw pallet. If he investigated further, he suspected he would discover his papers were gone.

Miss Preston's footsteps clattered on the stairwell. Panic at last seized Max. If she had his papers, then she knew – or was about to discover – not only his true purpose but also his identity. In which case, Max could kiss the report and his seat at Great Yarmouth goodbye.

He vaulted out of the room.

Max raced down the stairs, taking them two at a time. Miss Preston had a good head start on him, so he had to make a guess that she had chosen the path that led toward the Hall. He forced himself not to run – in case anyone happened to look his way – but he moved fast enough that soon, he spotted her. She had just reached the grove of lilac trees that bordered the Hall's garden.

"Miss Preston!" he shouted, manners be damned.

She turned, her pink dress flapping against her legs. "You have gall, sir."

Max stopped a few yards from her. "Please, let me explain."

"I do not need an explanation. Your intentions are plain enough." Pulling at her bodice, she retrieved the haphazard sheaf of papers and began to read from the top one. "*The naivete of some inhabitants of Northfield Hall beggars belief. Either they believe whole-heartedly in the goodness of one man – Lord Preston – or they use it as a frontispiece to distract one from a darker truth. I, dear reader, am determined to discover that darker truth for you.*"

There was not much of a defense to that.

And yet, just a few minutes ago, Max had been kissing this woman. Perhaps she would still respond to his charm. "It is a good paragraph, is it not?"

She was not amused. "What, precisely, is your goal at North-field Hall, Mr. Sims?"

Max weighed his options. On the one hand, he was tempted to lie. On the other, she had already read his draft. Max decided his best bet was honesty. "To uncover the hypocrisy at Northfield Hall. The reasons it is not all your father claims it to be. To prove, once and for all, that this little experiment in utopia is a failure."

"Utopia?" Miss Preston raised an incredulous eyebrow. "No one has ever claimed Northfield as some kind of utopia."

He almost laughed at her naivete. Then he realized, having grown up here, Miss Preston likely had no idea what the rest of the world thought of it. "The papers have. Popular imagination has. A place where any man or woman down on their luck can find honest work? Where money stained by slavery is not welcome? Where everyone shares the estate's yields?" Max found himself prowling just a little bit closer to her. "Everyone in England has heard of Northfield Hall, Miss Preston. Everyone in England has an opinion. And that makes this the most dangerous landholding in the empire."

He was close enough now to see her eyes widen at his words. Her lips parted in surprise.

He pushed away all thoughts of kisses.

"So you are here to describe the reality of a fable." Miss Preston clutched the letter tighter to her person as she met his gaze. "You hope to share enough stories of how you are forced to work all day and live without tea that my family becomes a laughingstock instead of a legend."

Max didn't like the way she phrased it. "It is not about your family. It is about what Northfield stands for. The idea of so idyllic a place thriving gives people ideas. It makes people want to throw off slavery altogether. To stop importing from the East Indies. To fundamentally change the British economy so that all of our island can live in such a principled way as Northfield Hall."

"And that would be so bad?" she asked, her voice little more than a whisper.

Max didn't know how, but they were within reach of each other now. He could see each freckle dotting her nose. "We would lose all our wealth. All our political power outside the channel. Napoleon would likely sail to our shores and have his way with us, and we would be so weakened by lack of gold that we would let him. Your children, Miss Preston, would grow up speaking French and pledging sovereignty to a foreign emperor."

She raised that slender eyebrow again. "Alternately said, others would do to us as we have done unto them."

"Would you rather be the wolf or the lamb?"

They both looked down at his hand, where he still clutched little elm Elinor.

"I am sorry to have lied to you," Max said. "I didn't like doing it."

Miss Preston worried her fingers across his writing. "Have you found these dark secrets yet?"

Max hesitated. The card player in him said he should bluff. Except, if he claimed to know everything he needed to about Northfield Hall, she would turn him out in the next breath.

Max didn't have any of the proof he had been hoping for. When he arrived, he had expected to find Northfield Hall overrun with confidence men, whores, and thieves. The types of characters one recoiled from on the streets of London. He had thought to find storerooms of imported goods in the woods, or at least discover that all of Northfield was dilapidated and inoperable.

Whatever sins Northfield Hall hid, they were deeper than Max had expected. He needed more time.

Which meant he had to somehow convince Miss Preston to let him stay.

"No, I haven't. I would appreciate if you would permit me to remain."

She flushed. "You presume I would do so because I have kissed you?"

Recently enough that Max could still taste her on his lips. That did not seem to be a winning thing to say. "I have more respect for you than that, Miss Preston. I hope you would allow me to stay out of mutual interest. The more information I have, the more thorough my report can be. So that I may write the truth about Northfield Hall. Good and bad."

Her eyes flicked up from the paper. Her irises were so gray and clear. Beneath the lilac blossoms, they almost reflected purple at him.

"How long do you hope to stay?"

"A week more, perhaps two." Max couldn't afford to take much longer than that. "*The Perceptive* is eager to publish it as soon as I can finish."

Miss Preston chewed on her lower lip as she stared at him. He wished he could read her thoughts. All he could tell was that she was considering her options.

"I don't even know your name."

Victory dropped Max into his best courtesan's bow. "Maximilian George Christian Sutton Hainsworth, Viscount Berwick, at your service."

It was a strange relief to claim his identity again. Although he didn't particularly like the way it drained all color from Miss Preston's face. Her mouth rounded out, "Viscount Berwick?"

"I am afraid so."

"Heir to the Earl of Meretta."

He was not surprised she knew his lineage. Their fathers, after all, dragged each other through the mud in the London papers just about every other month. "I aim to do nothing but report the truth, Miss Preston."

She shook her head. "You will ruin my family. You'll get my father arrested like Sir Francis Burdett."

"Only if he has done something illegal." Burdett, after all, had published his Parliamentary speech in the papers, which was blatantly against the law. So far, Preston had proved to be more cautious than that.

Though Max did hope to discover that Lord Preston had crossed a line or two.

He took up Miss Preston's hands to calm her down. "Let me stay for a week or two longer, Miss Preston. Help me learn about Northfield Hall. I give you my word that I will only write truthfully. If there is nothing to be found, then you have nothing to fear."

She dug her fingers into his palm, as if he were her last grip before falling from a cliff. "Are you going to write about how I kissed you?"

"Never. I would never disparage a lady, and particularly not you." Max pulled her close but stopped himself from holding her in his arms. "Even though I know I shouldn't be, I am very fond of you."

Saying this – not lying – felt dangerous. Max's stomach somersaulted, and he couldn't decide if it was pleasant or not.

Miss Preston pulled her hands away. "Do you have a sweetheart in Norwich?"

"No. My heart belongs to no one but me."

For some reason, this earned him a glare. "I don't trust you."

Like an idiot, Max said, "I will prove myself to you."

Miss Preston stared at him for a long time. Max felt himself evaluated, not for the strength of his shoulders but the merit of his character.

He wasn't at all sure he passed muster.

Miss Preston tucked the papers back into her bodice. "You may stay. To earn my trust. I will help answer your questions about Northfield Hall. If you publish your report and it is untruthful, I..."

Max waited patiently, wondering what consequence she could possibly conjure up. Blackmail – she could earn money from him annually if she decided to accuse him of misusing her. Embarrassment, if she preferred to simply publish that as an account in the gossip rags.

In the end, eyes wide and gray, Miss Preston threatened him with: "I will never forgive you."

He didn't deserve to be within ten feet of a woman as pure as she. "You have my word," Max promised.

To himself, he promised that he would actually live up to her expectations.

CHAPTER SEVEN

E VEN AFTER SUPPER – hours after the *episode* – Ellen's stomach roiled with anxiety about what to do with Mr. Sims. Except he wasn't Mr. Sims.

He was Maximilian Hainsworth, Viscount Berwick. Heir to one of the most powerful families in Britain. Just last year, the Earl of Meretta – Lord Berwick's *father* – had tried to get Papa arrested alongside the radical Sir Francis Burdett. With no proof whatsoever, other than that Papa and Sir Francis had supped at the same club the night before Sir Francis published his infamous speech questioning the power of the House of Commons in the *Weekly Register*.

Thankfully, no one else in Parliament had agreed to lump Papa into the arrest warrant.

Now that earl's own son was here, spying on Northfield Hall. Ellen didn't know what he could hope to find, but she was sure his goal was to disgrace Papa, if not send him to the Tower of London.

She was not naïve enough to believe that she held any sway over him at all. The viscount had promised whatever he needed to in order to keep her quiet, all because of his precious report. He would not alter his course for her sake.

Still. They had kissed. Twice.

Even though I shouldn't be, I am very fond of you.

It complicated things.

Ellen sank into the settee in the garden drawing room, where the summer evening light still streamed through the windows. Her pocket crinkled with the papers of the day: the three letters from the inn and the ones she had stolen from the viscount. Two of the envelopes were addressed to Uncle Maulvi. Ellen supposed she could tell him the truth about Lord Berwick.

Except Uncle Maulvi would most likely do the obvious thing and turn the viscount out on his ear. Ellen could only imagine what his newspaper would make of that. *LORD PRESTON CUTS LORD BERWICK* or *EARL OF MERETTA MORTALLY OFFENDED BY TREATMENT OF HEIR.*

They could embarrass the earl right back and publish an account of all the manual labor Lord Berwick had undertaken at Northfield Hall. The two families could drag each other down with endless stories in the scandal sheets.

That would accomplish nothing, other than to drown all of Papa's work on the abolition bill with pointless gossip.

Whereas if Ellen kept the viscount's secret, she could steer him towards a more informed report than rehashing the rivalry between the inside and outside staffs. At the very least, she could forestall his publication, stringing him along with promise of this discovery or that, until Papa had a chance to lay the foundation for the bill.

Caroline and Edward Chow came tearing into the room before Ellen could turn the matter over again. "You said you would read the post after supper!" Caro accused. "Won't you read it aloud now?"

"This very minute? Perhaps it would be better to save for morning," Ellen teased. In truth, the last letter – news from Sophia – was precisely what she needed after such a day. She couldn't guess how her sister would find London, but she desperately wanted to hear how Papa was faring and whether Benny was behaving and how many young gentlemen Sophia had wrapped around her finger so far.

"Oh, please read it, Miss Ellen," Eddie pleaded. "Caroline has been waiting for eons to hear from Sophia."

Edward was the sweetheart of the Chow family. Only six months older than Caroline, he had always guarded her closely, as if she were his responsibility alone, and in her hours free from the schoolroom, Caroline was almost constantly at his side. Ellen only worried what would happen over the next few years, as they reached the age when such a friendship would no longer be appropriate.

But that was a problem for another day. Breaking the seal on Sophia's letter, Ellen began to read:

My dear Ellen,

I apologize for not writing sooner. I would claim a headache, an overly scheduled visit, or a bad journey, but in truth, I am simply a slothful person. I know that were our positions switched, you would have written me twice per day. Alas, God made us different for reasons we cannot know, so I must simply embrace my own personality rather than castigate myself for not being you.

A classically Sophia opening. Ellen resisted the urge to roll her eyes as Caroline giggled.

Thus far, London is very tiresome. Papa is suspicious of every shop that does not stock free labor products, which is to say all of them, and therefore I may not partake in the joys of Bond Street. Aunt Charlotte sneaks me contraband – namely, chocolate! – but I will not tell you much about it for fear you will drop dead of shock and envy. In any case, everyone sleeps here until noon or after, which suits me well. Then we must receive visitors or return calls ourselves, which suits me not at all. Everyone in London prattles without saying anything of substance, and the gentlemen think themselves more worthy of devotion than they are. Then there are dinner

parties, dances, or the theater, which are marginally
more interesting but still packed with too many people
for my taste.

Caroline's eyes had grown wide. "It sounds wonderful. Oh, Ellen, why mayn't I go to London?"

"When you are older, you may." Ellen didn't miss the way Edward's brow furrowed at the idea of Caroline going away.

"But you never have."

"I don't choose to." Ellen flipped the page to continue reading.

"How will you find a husband without going to London?" Caroline asked.

A memory of telling Mr. Sims – *no*, Lord Berwick – that she had no interest in the marriage mart flashed across Ellen's skin. What a fool he must think her. Throwing herself at a carpenter's assistant while poo-pooing a respectable marriage!

She shook the thoughts away. "I am not concerned with finding a husband. If I'm meant to have one, he will find me. Now, shall I finish the letter, or no?"

Caroline bit her lip to signify she would behave herself for the remainder of the letter.

As for Papa, I don't see very much of him, so concerned
is he in the passage of this bill. When he is not at
Parliament, he is at various clubs or dinners, work-

ing to get the necessary support. He has read Benny and me a draft or two of his speeches, which start off dreadfully but get marginally better after our feedback. Aunt Charlotte's friends don't have much faith this bill will pass, but Papa is quite enthusiastic that change is around the corner. This is more than I care to write on the topic, but I know you worry for him. Benny, by the way, intersects with me only at evening engagements, and even then, he is so busy flirting that we hardly speak. If I don't find better amusement soon, I am afraid I shall have to invent some myself! All in all, I miss you sorely. My love to you, Nate, Caroline, etc.

"What about Eddie?" Caroline asked. "Does she send her love to him?"

The boy in question blushed scarlet.

Biting back a laugh, Ellen invented, "Ah yes, here it is. *An extra heaping of love for young Mr. Edward Chow.*"

Caroline beamed with satisfaction.

"Now, I believe Mrs. Chow will be looking for you at this hour, Eddie. And Caroline, you have to finish your sampler this evening or else Miss Lockyear will be sore with you tomorrow."

Taking all the papers with her, she herded the children out of the drawing room.

Sophia's letter, playful as it may have been, gave Ellen the insight she needed into Papa's state of mind. He was consumed with abolishing slavery once and for all, and he believed it within his grasp. Which only reinforced: he did not need the Viscount Berwick publishing a hateful account of Northfield just now.

She couldn't stop the viscount from writing a report, no matter whether he made up lies about Northfield Hall or told the truth. But she could delay him. The longer he took to write his report, the more time Papa would have to secure the abolition bill.

Ellen couldn't turn the viscount over to Uncle Maulvi after all. He needed to be distracted and delayed, not turned away from the property.

There was no choice about it, really. Ellen would have to handle the Viscount Berwick herself.

I T HAD BEEN THREE days since Miss Preston showed up in his bedroom.

Three days since he had confessed to every secret he had tried so hard to keep. His mission. His identity. His feelings for her.

Three days since Max had even *seen* the blasted female.

He had braced himself on Monday to be escorted by Messrs Chow and Maulvi to Thatcham with a one-way ticket back to London. Yet the day had proceeded as if no one knew the truth. Oliver and Max worked the sawpit. Mr. Chow and Spencer framed the cottages.

The only difference was that Miss Preston didn't show up. Nor did she appear on Tuesday, even though two shutters sat incomplete on the worktable. Now, on Wednesday, Max concluded she must have decided the best way to protect her family was to remove herself from his presence entirely.

Her physical absence meant she only consumed his thoughts that much more. He fantasized about her lips. Her freckles. Her breasts and legs and arse hidden beneath her gowns. Worse, he collected up things he wanted to say to her. Assurances that his report was not malicious. Observations about Northfield Hall he thought she would appreciate.

He even fantasized about apologizing to her again for lying.

Max didn't want to speculate about whether he had ever before been in such a frenzy about a woman.

He knew the answer was no.

Gripping the whipsaw, Max tried to return his thoughts to reality. Timber above, shavings below. Blade in his hand. Only, he caught a whiff of something that might have been Miss Preston's soap and –

Oliver glared at him just as Max pulled the saw down sideways, cutting the timber into a hopeless slant.

"Sorry."

"We will only have to saw more if you keep messing up," Oliver grumbled.

"I said I was sorry."

A light female voice interjected, "Oh, well, if you *said* you were sorry..."

Max swore in surprise. His heart hammered as he whipped around. Sure enough, it was Miss Preston in her terrible gray dress, gloating from the threshold.

At least he hadn't begun fantasizing scents.

"I didn't mean to startle you. Only, I have just come from a chat with Mrs. Shayler. Their mule kicked through the barn door. I thought, Mr. Sims, that you might help me hold the heavy timber while I do the repairs."

Max would not have predicted her to be such a good liar, yet she didn't even flush as she called him by his false name.

"I could help," Oliver volunteered.

"Very competently," Miss Preston agreed. "Only I assumed whoever doesn't go would best help at the cottages and..."

They all knew what she left unsaid. Max would only do harm at the cottage build.

She concluded cheerfully, "I should like the practice myself. So, can you spare Mr. Sims?"

Oliver finally recognized this as an opportunity for slacking. "Oh, go on, then."

Max tried not to look too eager as he hopped up from the sawpit.

They took the path that led from the trade village across the orchard, past the pond, and up the northern fields to where the textiles sat in the northwestern corner of the estate. Miss Preston carried a wicker basket of food while Max ferried a thick wooden box of tools.

He drank in her presence. After three days of thinking about her, Max was surprised to remember that she rose only to the top of his shoulder. He had forgotten, too, that her nose curved upwards at its tip.

"I hope you don't mind my little subterfuge," Miss Preston said when they were well clear of the trade village. "The door is not actually damaged. I only needed an excuse to take you to see the textile works."

Before parting on Sunday, Max had listed for her what he wanted to learn about Northfield Hall, and the textiles were at the top of his list. It was one of *The Perceptive*'s pet theories: that the popular Berkshire linen sold in London was actually the product of Northfield Hall.

He hadn't mentioned that to Miss Preston, of course. Max tried not to feel guilty.

"You have not told your Mr. Maulvi or Mr. Chow about who I am."

"I did not want Mr. Chow to be intimidated should he need to discipline you." Miss Preston slid her eyes sideways to steal a glance at him. Max was careful to arrange his features into disinterest. "Although he has a particular hatred of viscounts, so perhaps really I am protecting you."

"A hatred singularly of viscounts?"

Miss Preston smiled at his incredulity, that pretty grin that Max could admire for hours. He looked away, lest he trip on the path staring at her. "Yes. You see, Mr. and Mrs. Chow were brought here from KwongChow – you may know it as Canton – to serve in a viscount's household, but when Mrs. Chow found herself in the family way, the viscount turned them out. They were homeless and without work for months until they found Northfield."

An employer had the right to sack a maid who became pregnant after she started service, since after all, it limited the work she had promised to do in exchange for wages. Still, it was better done when she had family to go to. Max would have at least given the Chows money to tide them over until she was fit for work again.

"One would think he would hate all of the aristocracy, then, or perhaps even all Englishmen."

Miss Preston tilted her head. "It should be very sad if viscounts were representative of all Englishmen."

Max deserved this. Still, it made his stomach swim uncomfortably.

He poked at her basket. "Is there anything in there for me? I haven't eaten all day."

"All day?" Miss Preston raised a wary eyebrow. "Surely you exaggerate."

He slapped his palm across his heart. "Upon my family's honor, Miss Preston. I slept through breakfast, and I have not had even a moment to drink water since. It is punishment, though I do not yet know my crime."

She pressed her lips together in thought. "Perhaps Mr. Chow is simply grown tired of uneven planks and half-bent nails."

Max couldn't argue with that.

"However, I should hate for you to swoon. I don't carry any vinaigrettes, and I fear I couldn't catch you before you hit your head on the ground." Reaching into the basket, Miss Preston retrieved an oatcake. "Have this."

Never had a dull, unsweetened mash of grain ever tasted so good. Max ate it in two bites, and he couldn't keep a grin off his face at the sensation of food on his tongue. "You are an angel, Miss Preston."

"Hardly." Yet she handed him a flask. "You may have one sip."

It was ale, and Max made that single sip last so long that Miss Preston had to reach out and tear the flask away from him.

"Poor Mrs. Shayler won't have anything to drink if you carry on like that."

"That would be a shame," Max agreed. "Those oatcakes are inedible if one doesn't have some ale to swill them down."

Miss Preston scoffed. "May I remind you that you are a carpenter's assistant, sir? You are hardly in a position to criticize what food comes your way."

And yet, he couldn't help himself. "A whole section of my report, Miss Preston, will be dedicated to criticizing the food that comes my way at Northfield Hall. No tea, no coffee, no sugared sweets."

"Nothing whose taste has been fouled by human evil, you mean?" Miss Preston retorted.

"If I never taste honey again, my dear, it will be too soon."

Their exchange might have continued if he hadn't thrown in too familiar a term. Instead, Miss Preston straightened. Her gaze locked on the path ahead of them. "Yes, well, you are welcome to return to the comforts of the slave trade at the moment of your choosing, my lord."

Max took two conscious steps to his left to put more space between them. "I will suffer through a few more weeks if it means I may complete my report."

They walked in silence for a moment. And then a moment more. Miss Preston had turned her head so that even when Max looked at her, he could only see the brim of her straw bonnet.

"It is good you don't let me say whatever I want," Max found himself injecting to revive the conversation. "I like to tease. Sometimes, no one stops me. I appreciate that you don't let me fill the air indefinitely with nonsense."

"If you are not teasing, then you are complaining." She lifted her chin enough that Max could see the curve of a smile on her lips. "Or lying. Do you ever say what you truly mean?"

"Occasionally. For example, when I said I am fond of you. That was the truth."

She didn't respond. Max supposed he couldn't blame her. He wouldn't believe a cad like himself, either.

"And you, Miss Preston? Do you ever jest, or is every word from your lips completely honest?"

"My father accused me recently of not being honest. Not like you – I don't lie to people on purpose. But I suppose I try to say the right thing for the moment, rather than the honest one. I never want to offend." Miss Preston smiled again, turning up her whole face so that she could beam directly at Max. "Except with you. I am a more honest version of myself with you."

His breath caught in the power of the moment. Without even thinking, he skipped over it with a tease, "You are not afraid to offend me, you mean. A dangerous way to live, considering I am heir to an earldom." Then, regretting his glibness, Max said, "Shall we practice being honest with each other, then?"

"Only if you go first."

It had been his idea, and yet for the life of him, Max couldn't think of a single honest thing to say. He looked about for inspiration. "I think Northfield Hall is a beautiful prospect, even if it is entirely designed for use and not at all for decoration."

"There is some decoration. My mother planted these lilacs. She said they made everything look more cheerful when the world is just beginning to wake up from winter." Miss Preston gestured to the trees lining the path. They nodded lazily with purple flowers.

Max was more interested in the expression on Miss Preston's face, which was somehow a mix of happiness and sorrow. "My condolences. I know you lost her only a few years ago."

"She was ill for a while before that. A wasting disease. We had time to say goodbye." The lilacs came to a head at the pond, where they spread along the southern bank across from three ancient oak trees. It gave the pond the illusion of a fairytale oasis, where anything might happen.

Miss Preston paused. It was only a moment, and Max didn't see her lips move, but he had the impression she stopped to make a wish upon the pond. Then she resumed their northward walk. "My mother never spoke to her family after she married Papa. My grandfather did not approve of Northfield Hall. Did you know that?"

Max did. All of London did. It was part of the legend of Northfield.

"She chose this life because she knew it was the right thing to do. She and Papa both. We define *fellow man* differently than the rest of Britain. For you, for a man to receive your sympathy or aid, he must be of a similar class, of good Anglican character, born into a legitimate marriage, and look like you. At Northfield, he must simply be a person in want of a helping hand."

Miss Preston's earnestness embarrassed Max. He wanted to throw a shawl over her neck and instruct her to cover herself. Instead, he said, "Your claim is that Northfield Hall is a more Christian institution than any other in all of the British Empire."

"Well." She thought about it for a few paces. "Christianity doesn't have much to do with it. It is that any person in trouble – man or woman – may rely on living an honest life here without worry of exploiting another human being to steal more coin for themselves."

Max's arms shouted in protest that *they* felt exploited. "As for the laborers, do they share your family's unusual philosophy, or do they go along with it to take their cut of the estate's profits?"

"Everyone here believes in everyone else's right to be here. We are not a fractured community the way you wrote in your report." This she said hotly, and her skin burned pink, too.

"No more so than anywhere else." Max hated to admit it, since it was, for the moment, the only truth he had been able to uncover about Northfield Hall. Yet she was right: there was nothing particularly remarkable about one set of servants considering themselves better than another. "That section doesn't say much of anything, does it? I keep overwriting, as if adding another adjective will make my sentence more meaningful."

They walked a few more paces. Max brooded on the report – and how easily Cabot had condemned it. Before that letter, he had rather thought he was muddling along quite nicely. Now he wasn't sure he had the capacity to write the report, even should he find anything worth writing about.

Miss Preston shifted her grip on the hamper. "Why are you writing the report in any case? I should think the newspaper could find someone of less consequence to disguise himself as a carpenter's apprentice for weeks on end."

Max swallowed. She would not like the truth. *He* did not like the truth. Opening his mouth, he cast about for a lie. But in the end, he had promised her honesty. "I am proving to my father that I take our family legacy seriously."

The words sounded ridiculous out loud. Like he was a boy serving punishment for some transgression. Miss Preston evidently agreed, for skepticism dripped from her words as she asked, "By disguising yourself as a common laborer?"

"There is a rotten borough under my father's purview. My late cousin occupied its seat in the House of Commons until he passed last month. I asked my father to consider me for the replacement, since he only has to buy off the voters. He declined. I asked him what I had to do to earn it, and this is what he set me to. To prove, once and for all, that I care more about a political career than good drink and company."

Miss Preston's steps slowed. "Why should you need to prove yourself? You will inherit his seat in the House of Lords one day. Shouldn't he want you to gain as much experience now as you can?"

"That is my feeling precisely." Max sighed, as if that could shake off the familiar weight settling around his shoulders. It was enough to forget the twenty-pound toolchest hanging from his hands. "I have been Viscount Berwick all my life. I always thought one day, it would not feel like some giant specter into which I had to grow. But even now, all of twenty-five, I cannot make myself live up to what my father expects of me. At school, I didn't get high enough marks. Abroad, I did not wine and dine with enough ambassadors. In London, I get mentioned too often in the scandal sheets. I am Berwick, but not the way he wants me to be. Not the way he was, I suppose."

"And so you contort yourself into a carpenter in hopes that might at last be the answer." Miss Preston peered at him, her face soft with thought and compassion and confusion all at once.

Max fixed his gaze on the textile works, which they were fast approaching. Gratitude washed over him; he had said far too much, more than he had ever admitted to everyone, and he needed a reason to stop.

Taking his cue, Miss Preston brightened, almost like an actress on stage, and barreled forward to hand off her basket to Mrs. Shayler.

"I do hope you don't mind the disturbance. Uncle Maulvi asked me to show Mr. Sims around the other workshops at Northfield, since Mr. Sims is still quite new here. Have you been introduced?"

They had not. Max nodded respectfully in the woman's direction. She was a large-set Black woman with hair done up in intricate braids. She smiled at Max, the friendliest welcome he had yet received at Northfield Hall. When she spoke, she surprised him with an accent as native to Berkshire as the innkeeper's in Thatcham. "Let me show you the place, then."

The textiles occupied as much space as a stable and paddock. It included a barn, a brick outbuilding, and a traditional cottage with a thatched roof. They entered the barn first, where wooden contraptions sat at the ready. "Of course, the flax is still growing at this time of year," Mrs. Shayler said, gesturing to the fields they had just crossed where the plant grew green and about knee-high. "In the next month or so, we'll be asking anyone with time to spare to help harvest it and set it out to dry." She pointed to a series of half-barrels lining the far wall, face up. "It soaks for two weeks, dries again, and then Mr. Shayler comes in with his strong arms to do the scutching and brushing through the hackles. We welcome help from other strong arms for that part, too." This as an aside to Max, accompanied by an appreciative glance at his biceps.

He erred on the side of looking embarrassed and bestowed his attention upon the scutching stand. Mrs. Shayler said to Miss Preston, "The children are that excited for the performance. Little Henny stays up at night practicing her lines instead of saying her prayers and falling to sleep."

Miss Preston beamed. "I am looking forward to the theatric almost as much as I am to seeing the cottages completed."

"You're not as excited as the new inhabitants are, I'm sure." Mrs. Shayler turned back to Max. "We keep the seeds, of course, for planting and linseed oil. The tow we keep for burlap and twine and the like, so we are quite efficient in what we can get out of our little fields, you see." She led them out of the barn into the whitewashed building. Max could tell from its racket even before they entered that it held a loom. In fact, when he stepped through, he saw ten looms – each one as wide as a horse – and all of them at work.

Mrs. Shayler had to raise her voice. "We split the spinning up in our homes, but the thread all comes back here to be woven. We do both the linen and wool here."

"Our little textile mill," Miss Preston added, a smile wreathing her lips.

For her sake, Max tried to be impressed. He noted the industriousness of the weavers – a mix of men and women – who looked up to greet them yet didn't miss a breath in their patterns. Mrs. Shayler led him around the perimeter to a storeroom, which was nearly as wide as the main room but held nothing except finished bolts of fabric. Max counted nearly two rows of twenty bolts of fabric per shelf.

It was certainly enough bolts to supply to London as Berkshire linen.

But it was nothing compared to the actual textile mills Max had toured in his lifetime. That was something of a tradition among his set: whenever they visited each other's country homes, they toured the local industries, and more and more, that included steam-powered mills. The looms there could produce more fabric in a week than the Northfield enterprise could produce in a year.

He felt a little sad for Miss Preston that she could be proud of so provincial an establishment.

"And how long is the fabric stored here?" Max asked Mrs. Shayler.

The woman blinked in surprise at the question. "Why, until it is used."

"Every family at Northfield Hall is entitled to five bolts of fabric per year," Miss Preston supplied. "To be claimed upon need. For an individual such as yourself, you are permitted one bolt. If you liked, you could take a bolt with you now."

Excitement pricked at Max's skin. Perhaps this was the secret then: Lord Preston made his money up by charging the very laborers he paid. "At what price could I purchase the fabric?"

Mrs. Shayler grinned. "No price. It is part of your yearly wages."

"Same as the food and ale served for lodgers." Miss Preston had to tip her head back to frown at him from beneath the brim of her straw hat. "Surely Mr. Chow explained this to you when you applied for the position."

Max didn't know why *she* was the one frowning. He was the one thwarted at every hunch. "I am sometimes guilty of not listening very well."

Miss Preston arched an eyebrow. For her part, Mrs. Shayler said, "No harm as long as one can admit it, I always say. Of course, Mr. Shayler doesn't listen to me say *that*, so it is all a moot point."

Max had met this Mr. Shayler briefly at the inn on Sunday. He had been a quiet, cheerful man of similar complexion to his wife; there was something charming in seeing that his helpmeet was as convivial as he.

"Where do you dye the fabric?" Max asked.

"That's done by Mr. Griswick in Thatcham. We keep trying to find a dyer to come live here, but Mr. Griswick is a good master, and the rest of the guild is suspicious of Northfield Hall on account of how happy we all are. Think we're putting up some kind of front."

Miss Preston was quick to comment, "A ridiculous notion."

That excitement quickened his heart again. For the first time, a whiff of discontent. If he could speak to Mr. Griswick or perhaps even go to a dyer's guild meeting, Max might be able to finally grab onto something tangible that he could use against Northfield Hall.

Against Miss Preston's family.

Max reined in his reaction. His friends always said his emotions flew across his face. And he could feel Miss Preston watching him with those same gray eyes that just three days ago had threatened to never forgive him.

He offered her a smile. Pretended it meant, *I believe you.*

And felt his gut sink into self-reproach when she smiled back.

This was the last time he allowed a good woman to think him a good man.

Chapter Eight

E LLEN CAME TO THINK of him as Max. It was simpler than
Mr. Sims or Lord Berwick or *the viscount*. And she had to
call him something in her mind. He was almost always a mere
thought away.

It wasn't that she sought out reasons to think of him. Ellen
was perfectly happy to spend the evening correcting Caroline's
embroidery or debating with Nate the merits of etiquette in a
civilized society.

Her mind kept returning to Max, though. Snagging on little
honesties to share with him. Things that were previously stray
thoughts – how she absolutely *hated* it when the porridge was
served burned, how she loved when the rain fell so hard that
it spilled in sheets from the gutters, how she worried that she
couldn't quite remember what Mama's smile looked like – felt
like secrets she could offer Max. Secrets that would replace his
smirk with that wide-eyed, earnest smile that she was growing
to like so much.

It did not mean she *liked* Max. She never forgot he was a liar, or that he had arrived with the purpose of – at best – humiliating her family. It was just that he was a good listener.

At least he didn't truly have a sweetheart waiting to marry him in Norwich.

Still, Ellen had seen the way Max's eyes gleamed at the mention of Mr. Griswick and the dyers' guild.

She would have to introduce him to the dyers. If she didn't, Max would only find a way to speak to them on his own. The whole guild had been opposed to Papa ever since they tried to fleece him for an exorbitant annual payment. Mr. Griswick took the work, but everyone knew the worst rumors about Northfield Hall that circulated Thatcham began with him. At least if she was present, Griswick might hold his tongue.

Telling Mr. Chow that she was trying to find Max work to which he was better suited, Ellen arranged to introduce him to Mr. Griswick – at the end of the week, to stall the report that much longer. With her maid Layla in tow for propriety's sake, Ellen arrived Friday morning at the workshop to collect Max.

He was alone, back to the door, and he had removed both jacket and waistcoat so that the only thing between her and his bare skin was a sweaty, once-white linen shirt.

Ellen found herself frozen, just to watch the power of his back muscles as he moved the plane across a plank of wood. She knew that motion, a mesmerizing pull back and forth. She always felt it unlocked the flavor of the lumber as it smoothed the surface, like a lover coaxing a quim into wetness.

What a thought to have. That was one she wouldn't even share with Max. Shaking herself, Ellen announced her presence. "May I interrupt you?"

Max jumped, startled, then looked at her over his shoulder.

He really did look like a viscount, staring at her in that annoyed, put-upon manner. She wondered that she hadn't spotted it right away. His nose was quite patrician.

In the next instant, he smirked. "You may always interrupt me, Miss Preston."

"If you don't mind leaving off your work here for the afternoon, I thought I might introduce you to Mr. Griswick in Thatcham."

Max's eyebrows flew upwards in surprise. It was an unusual expression on him. "The dyer?"

"Yes. You seemed interested the other day. I arranged it with Mr. Chow, so he will not mind you stepping out."

Max opened his mouth as if to say something, but his eyes flitted from Ellen to Layla standing behind her. Swallowing his words, he stood and untied the leather apron that had been protecting his front. His shirt gaped almost all the way down to his navel.

Ellen gulped against the instant desire that lit between her legs.

Max did not comment on her gaping, though he did smirk again. Buttoning his shirt – slow as can be – he added to it the waistcoat and jacket, and finally he donned his hat. "I am at your service, Miss."

The walk to Thatcham was about five miles. Layla, who had been with Ellen nearly two years and could be perfectly flirtatious herself, was good enough to hang back, so that Ellen and Max might walk side by side in relative privacy. Ellen wore her good bonnet, rather than her usual straw hat, and a dress she didn't mind catching up too much dust. Max teased, "Mr. Griswick must be a handsome man. You are wearing an actual gown for this visit."

"What do you accuse me of wearing elsewise?"

He leaned a little closer. "A gunny sack."

Ellen pretended to be offended. "I beg your pardon. We use *tow* sacks here, rather than importing gunny like barbarians."

"Ah, is that how you see the rest of us? Do you imagine London is full of men gnashing their teeth and thumping their chests?"

She bit back a laugh. "Yes, that is how I imagine the average Englishman. Especially the viscounts."

"I suppose I cannot be offended. That is rather what I expected from Northfield Hall."

Sticking her hand to brush through the barley growing beside the road, Ellen wished he did not need to remind her why he was there. Why he was even walking beside her. All of it boiled down to that one purpose.

A month from now, Max would be back in London. Gnashing his teeth at reformists like her father, or whatever it was he did.

"What does your life look like when you are actually a viscount?"

"I spend every morning in the sawpit, same as here," he replied without pause.

Another joke. Ellen tensed. What if he had only been humoring her the other day when he said he could be true with her? "I meant that honestly."

Max sobered. "There is very little you would approve of. I am usually in London. I wake late in the morning, take coffee at breakfast, eat decadent food, go to my club where I am served imported spirits, flirt with ladies wearing Indian jewels, and get into arguments with Whigs over them being too soft-hearted."

It was easy to imagine. Max was a man of such energy. He must be a force in town. Everyone else must hang upon each of his words.

If only he saw life the way she did, Ellen imagined she could find Max to be the most fascinating man in the world.

"And if you were to take that seat in the House of Commons, would your life change very much?"

From the corner of her eye, she watched him think. His teeth claimed his bottom lip – only for a moment, as if he caught himself – and his gaze darted off into the fields. "Of course. I would be busy researching bills, negotiating compromises with my peers, answering to the two dozen men unlucky enough to be my constituents. Perhaps the matrons at the foundling hospital would at last deem me worthy of joining their board. They think my current application is a lark, you see, and they keep finding excuses to bar me from their meetings."

Ellen understood the ache for a life with a greater purpose than waking, eating, and sleeping. One that would be marked with accomplishments, or at least sacrifices, which others would remember far longer than one lived. Without that kind of purpose, the years felt rather like a spilled ball of yarn, unspooling endlessly to no rhyme or reason.

A stray, cold raindrop splattered on her nose.

"All this hard work you would do in the name of the Tories, I suppose. Protect the current interests, condemn the poor man for not having been born into wealth, that sort of thing."

Now he smiled, amused. "I believe in human nature, if that is what you are asking. Even your father who is determined to make every man, woman, and child welcome at Northfield Hall cannot stop the inhabitants here from organizing themselves into a hierarchy – and that is because it is useful. My goal in Parliament would be to focus on winning the war, expanding our resources, and otherwise strengthening the empire, so that our generation may march Britain towards a wealthier future. As to the poor man, our natural systems will sort him out."

"Our natural systems shuffle him into the poor house – if he is lucky – and work him to death."

Max clasped his hands behind his back, a gesture that immediately made him look like a dandy, no matter that he wore loose work clothes. "Perhaps there is some room for improvement. If only they would let me join the board of the foundling hospital, I would have first-hand experience to refer to."

"I am sure your fellow lodgers here would be more than happy to educate you as to their first-hand experiences." Ellen shook off another raindrop.

"Perhaps we had better call for a carriage," Max said. "I should hate to get caught in the rain."

That would add another half hour at best to their journey, since they would have to backtrack to the stables and then wait for the horses to be hooked into the gig. Ellen examined the clouds, which had descended to crowd the sky with dark gray but otherwise looked benign. They were as likely to drift away without so much as a drizzle as they were to let out a good rain.

"We would do better to walk faster so as not to keep Mr. Griswick waiting. He is rather cantankerous."

Max's lips fell into a grim, acquiescent line.

Ellen asked – though she wasn't sure she wanted to hear the answer – "Why are you so interested in our textiles? I never thought it would go as far as to include the dyeing process."

He hesitated. Ellen could see in the way he re-hooked his hands behind his back that he was considering not answering. She prodded, "I already know you are looking to humiliate my family publicly. It can't be worse than that."

She expected him to smirk. He grimaced instead. But he did, at least, answer her: "There is a textile gaining popularity in London these last few years known as Berkshire linen. It is very fine, hand-woven, and hard to come by. Therefore, its price is exorbitantly high. I suspect it is made here at Northfield Hall."

"We don't sell goods for profit like that." It was one of the creeds of Northfield Hall. Whatever surplus of their crops and goods that they did sell, Papa always made sure it was a fair price, something that the average yeoman could purchase at a town market. They only did it to cover their taxes and wages, not to turn a profit the way most aristocrats ran their estates.

Max tilted his head, as if to indicate he did not quite believe her. Then he said, "I should prefer not to humiliate you, Miss Preston. I only want to offer the public more truth than fiction about Northfield Hall."

The rain increased to a slight, off-kilter spatter. Not enough to muddy the road or drench their clothes, but more than a drop here or there.

Ellen decided they needed to lighten the conversation again, otherwise end up wet and angry at Mr. Griswick's. "When you take your seat in Parliament, will you stop flirting with those ladies in jewels, too? Or will you still find time for that?"

"I imagine I shall have to limit myself to only flirting with one or two at a time." Max leaned in again, smirking. "I don't think either you or I can credibly claim celibacy among our virtues."

"I was not aware that you could claim *any* virtues."

"That depends on how you define virtue. You do not seem to object to the virtues of my body."

Ellen blushed even as her skin burned with that familiar desire. "I should object. You are as good as a sworn enemy to my family."

"And I should be avoiding you like the plague so that I can write this report without any distractions." A raindrop fell on Max this time, flat on his forehead. He scrunched his face, which only encouraged it to drip all the faster.

She almost reached up to brush it away. "It is not as if I am falling in love with you."

"Nor I you." Max gave her one of those earnest, boyish smiles. "We feel an affinity towards each other. That is all."

"Precisely." Ellen felt affinities towards many people, all the time. She needn't waste her energy worrying what it meant in regard to Max.

"No matter what happens next, we may consider ourselves friends. In private, at the very least."

His words were casual, but an intensity ran under them that stirred against Ellen's skin.

Layla interrupted, darting forward with the umbrella. "Miss Preston, this weather is about to turn. Perhaps you would prefer to head back."

They were halfway to the village road, at least. Ellen hated to think of turning around. "I'm sure the drizzle will pass over in a few minutes. Mr. Griswick is expecting us. Come, stand under the umbrella with me."

A few minutes later, the rain had only grown worse. The clouds crowded the sky so that it was nearly dark as night. Poor Max, who walked outside the umbrella, was nearly soaked through already.

They were almost to the village road. Even turning back would be another quarter hour at least in the rain.

Ellen handed the umbrella to Layla. "You had better go back to the house and start up a hot bath for me. Mr. Sims will escort me to the tool shed, where we will wait out the storm."

Layla looked from Ellen to Max and back. "But Miss Preston...alone?"

"Mr. Sims will remain outside the shed," Ellen lied. "I am far more comfortable having him there than waiting on my own. I can send him back for the gig if it looks like the storm will last longer than I expect."

"If you insist," Layla said. She looked over her shoulder only once before hustling back towards the Hall.

Without the protection of the umbrella, the rain pelted Ellen in great cold bursts. Her woolen pelisse wouldn't keep her dry for long. She turned to Max. "There is a shed in the common fields. I'll show you the way."

The footpath was in worse condition than the road, uneven enough that parts of it were completely swamped. "I had thought to find shelter, not a swimming hole," Max complained.

The rain had darkened his hair to a dull brown, and thick tendrils were plastered about his forehead.

A storm *would* make him more handsome. Whereas Ellen likely looked like a poodle whose coat had gone limp, revealing skin and bones and ugly long limbs.

"Must you whine about everything, Lord Berwick, or do you only do it to needle me?"

"Why not both?" Max teased.

The puddles so far had been perfectly reasonable, nothing that Ellen couldn't step over herself. But now the path flooded for at least three feet, far too long for her to even leap across. On either side, they were walled in by rising barley.

Without so much as a word, Max scooped her into his arms. Ellen's elbow crooked around his neck instinctively. His skin was almost hot to the touch. Their eyes met for an instant, and he looked neither flirtatious nor annoyed nor teasing. This was Max at his core, glancing to ensure she was safe.

Then the brim of her hat collided with his. Max looked ahead again and, setting his lips in a grim line, splashed through the puddle. "It's a good thing I don't have a valet here, for he would not put up with the way I treat these boots."

He didn't put her down on the other side. Ellen considered asking him to. They were still a good way from the shed. But there would be more puddles, and she was much warmer pressed against his chest.

There was a part of her, too, that wanted to see if he could carry her the rest of the way without tiring his arms. To test whether the muscles he so loved to show off lived up to their boast.

"Next time you want to take me to Mr. Griswick's, we *will* take a vehicle," Max intoned. "A coach. A brougham. Even a pony cart would do, so long as it includes a roof."

"It is five miles to Thatcham. It is only because of your delicate city sensibilities that you find that worthy of horses."

"Your father has invested in horses for a reason. Instead, you use me as your horse." Ellen was close enough to spot the quirk in his lip that betrayed this as teasing.

"When I decide to ride you, my lord," she said in retaliation, "you will know."

The heat between them changed. If he had dropped her unceremoniously into the mud and plunged his tongue between her lips, Ellen would have welcomed it.

As it was, he kept walking.

The shed appeared at last. A simple wooden structure, it sat between the barley fields and the southern clover pastures and housed supplies for the farmers, mostly replacement wheels and emergency tools in case their ploughs broke at this end of the fields. It was not often visited, except for a few years when Sophia had turned it into her private clubhouse, nor did it offer any warmth for lack of a hearth, but it would do to wait out the rain.

Balancing her weight between his left arm and right knee, Max opened the shed door, then swung her inside. When he closed the door again, they were plunged into darkness, since the shed had no windows.

Ellen was glad she had sent Layla away. "There should be a lantern somewhere. If you put me down, I can find it."

His hands slid along her waist to do so. Ellen's palms landed on his chest. The rain brought out the smell of sawdust in his clothes, but there was something else to his scent today. Something sweet and natural that made her want to lean forward and drink him in.

"Would you like me to return for a vehicle?" Max asked, his voice gruff, his accent overly formal.

"No, I don't expect the rain will last much longer." She didn't know if this was true or not. Turning away, Ellen groped along the wall until she found the lamp. She cracked the door open to let in enough light for her to strike the lantern's match and ignite the stubbed candle inside it. Then, shutting out the rain again, she hung the lamp on the wall.

"That's better," she forced herself to say. In some ways, it was much worse, for now she could see Max properly. How he stood only an arm's length away. How his whole body glistened from the rain.

How his eyes traced her every move.

He cleared his throat. "Miss Preston, I am afraid I am a terrible flirt. You have been most generous with me, and I do not mean to take advantage of that kindness."

Ellen wondered if Max began most of his seductions with such a speech. Or if he offered it to her only because of her station in life.

She wondered if he actually thought she could turn away from him when he stood so near and looked so delicious. He was a handsome man – he *knew* that – and, despite everything she knew about him, she intended to enjoy it for herself while she could.

There was no point in pretending they had arrived at this shed for any other purpose.

"Let me continue our game of honesty." She unpinned her bonnet and set it on top of a tool chest. "In most cases, I try to guide my actions by what is best for all parties involved. That is not my guide today. Right now, I should like you to kiss me senseless."

A MAN HAD NO choice after a speech like that. Max spanned the distance – no more than a foot or two – between them and took Miss Preston in his arms. Despite her clammy clothes, she did not tremble. She turned her lips towards him helpfully – hopefully.

Max almost didn't seal the kiss, just to tease her.

Except he had already carried her through the pissing rain, and he had memorized the curve of her hip against his chest and knew precisely where her corset laces tied above her shift. And he had been thinking of this kiss since the last one.

He reached down, braced his hands beneath her arse, and hoisted her up against his waist. Their lips met mid-air. The impact clashed teeth against teeth. Miss Preston – breath hitching – caught his neck between her arms and repositioned her mouth from above. Her thighs clamped around his waist.

Max willed himself not to notice. There was one vestige of a gentleman left inside him, and that was who had heard her say *kiss*, not *fuck*. He would not press his advantage. He would merely take what she would give.

The kiss was enough to steal his attention, anyhow. Desperate. Needy. Tongue battling tongue. Hot breaths, and he couldn't tell whose they were. Her fingers tugged through his hair. His were still at her back, bracing her against him, until Max could take that no longer. He pinned Miss Preston against the door – remembering with a thrill that anyone could arrive at the shed at any moment – so that his hands could grasp her body in palmfuls. Arse. Breast. Neck – sinewy and vulnerable. Breasts again, in both hands, relishing how she whimpered around his tongue with each squeeze.

Damn, but it had been too long since he had been with a woman. He was hard as a fencepost, and he wanted to bite every inch of her skin. Yet Max couldn't tear his lips away from Miss Preston's. She was quicksand, and helplessly he could only sink further into her.

She was the one who commenced pulling off clothes. His, specifically, beginning with pushing his coat off each arm. It landed on the floor, which was probably dirt, and Max had been at Northfield Hall long enough to know that meant *he* would be cleaning it later. He didn't care. Miss Preston unbuttoned his worsted waistcoat. She hadn't stopped kissing him. Her teeth nicked against his lip in her hurry.

They did separate when it came to the shirt. Miss Preston tugged it free of his trousers – her fingers scraping deliciously against his bare hips and stomach – but then their lips had to part for her to lift it over his head. The air should have been cold on his skin. Max didn't notice anything except the heat in Miss Preston's eyes.

He retaliated. Setting her feet on the ground, Max charted his course. Her dress was a simple matter of unbuttoning the back. He hung it from the tip of a shovel that leaned against the wall. Miss Preston now stood breathless by the door in nothing but her petticoat, simple corset, a wet linen shift, and her stockings and boots. And that infernal cap enclosing her hair.

Max would let her keep the footwear.

Lifting the petticoat over her head, Max ordered, "Turn around." She did so, leaning against the door, hands above her head. Max grabbed at her breasts from behind before unlacing her corset. While he worked, Miss Preston pressed her arse backwards to nestle against his cock. He kissed the back of her neck. She tasted so good. Every inch of his body yearned to be against hers.

When he got the corset free, he released Miss Preston to hang it with her dress. He looked away for just that instant, only to find her lifting off the shift herself. She handed it to him to drape, as if he were a lady's maid and not a man two strokes away from explosion.

Hers was the first naked woman's body Max had seen in over a month. His cock ached at that fact. And at the shape of her. The softness of her. The tempting mass of curls at the joining of her legs.

That hair looked brown. Max wondered whether it would match the tresses she hid beneath her cap.

It took him a few moments to remember about the gentleman in him. She had only said *kiss*.

"We have gotten carried away," he forced himself to say. He didn't recognize his own voice.

Annoyance crossed Miss Preston's face. "Precisely what I asked for."

His cock throbbed in agreement. Max ignored it. "We had best stop before we do something we regret."

She thrust her chin upwards. "Do you *want* to stop? I rather thought you were enjoying yourself."

"I was. I am." His voice – horrifyingly – broke, jumping upwards an octave on his last word. Max cleared his throat. "I am mindful of your position in society and the dangers of what comes next."

Miss Preston took two steps forward. Surreal steps, for she still wore her boots and stockings, yet Max could see the skin of her thighs and the swing of her breasts. She smiled. "Lord Berwick, perhaps I have not made myself clear. You are not to concern yourself with the consequences of this morning. I should like to ride you like a horse. Swive you like the swine you are. Fuck you like a whore. May I, please?"

Max could hardly say no.

He did wonder, as she pushed down his trousers, where an idealist like her had gotten such a filthy mouth. She knelt square-ly in front of him, and Max's mind leapt – how could she know this and who had dared defile her? – before she took his cock inside her mouth. He moaned. He couldn't help it. She didn't do it with the expertise of a woman well-practiced, but one didn't need expertise. Her tongue was soft and wet and firm against his length. Her hand pumped upwards from his base.

Max would come down her throat if he wasn't careful.

He opened his eyes. Looked for anything that would slow his thoughts. She still wore that infernal cap. The one that made her appear a prim spinster. He had mistaken that for chastity, fool that he was. Now he grabbed at it, searching for the pins that cleaved it to her scalp.

Miss Preston rocked backwards, one hand on his cock, so that her head was out of reach. "Now, now, Max. If you should like something, ask nicely."

He loved that she called him by his name. Not Berwick. Not Mr. Sims. Just Max. "I want to see your hair. Please."

"That wasn't a question." She twisted her fist, a little tweak to the cock that shot pain and pleasure through Max's core. Then she released him, stood, and started undoing pins.

Even though he knew this was what she wanted, he had to push down his reaction to a genteel lady behaving this way. Wanton. Willful. One would think Miss Preston had no fear. Any farmer could walk into this shed looking for the same shelter they had sought. The maid knew very well they were alone together. A hundred laborers could be gossiping at this very moment that Mr. Sims the carpenter was fucking the baron's daughter.

Yet Miss Preston didn't care.

Max admired her. And feared for her. Which was a strange, new sensation.

Then she removed the cap. Her hair did not fall free as Max had imagined but rather remained where it was, coiled in a braid and pinned in a roll to her head. It did gleam in the candlelight. And it was clearly not brown at all but red, the kind of coppery fire that would turn heads if she wore it for all to see.

The color that Max could never resist.

He grabbed her again, left hand wrapping around her rib cage as his right fingers dipped between her legs. She gasped at the touch. She was wet as the rain, and Max swirled that readiness up the length of her slit and across the little hill that told him she needed him. Max watched her face as he teased her with his fingers. Her eyes fluttered shut. Her lips opened in slack, primal need. Her whole visage had a new countenance now that was framed by color, and Max enjoyed it as her cheeks grew flush in response to his thumb.

"More pressure," Miss Preston demanded as her hips began to buck. Max complied, cradling her body in his left arm so that she could abandon herself when the time came. And it arrived quickly enough. Her body convulsed in great, delicious spasms. Her head rolled backwards against his elbow. And she cried out – as if in surprise – "Max!"

When she had returned to her body, he slid his right hand beneath her thigh and repositioned her so that she was wrapped around his waist again. He growled into her neck, "Would you like to fuck me now?"

She shivered the way he had hoped she would. "Yes, oh please."

Max didn't wait for any further niceties. Gripping each of her buttocks in a palm, he heaved her onto his cock.

Their position wasn't ideal except for protecting them both from splinters, and it took a moment to find a rhythm. She tilted her hips forward and back as he bounced them both up and down. He would have preferred to lay her to the ground and pump into oblivion.

And yet. Miss Preston felt like heaven. Soft, wet, tight, hot, needy, desperate heaven. The pads of her fingers dug in as ten pinpoints across his back. She claimed his mouth as she worked her hips. Max had never liked kissing during actual coitus before, but now the taste of her drove his pleasure deeper under his skin, almost to the bone. He heard himself moan. He nearly lost his balance, almost tumbled them both against the twelve-tined rake behind him, because she drove everything except carnal oblivion from his mind.

But then – just before his peak – her whisper hot against his ear. "You mustn't spend inside me."

Of course not. He wouldn't have. The reminder was good, though, and Max set her on the ground in a fast second before his cock lost all control. His seed dripped in disappointed spurts into the air between them.

Disappointed, because he had almost forgotten.

Disappointed, because he could not claim her in full.

Max turned away, catching up the tails of his shirt to wipe off his cock. It had been a good fuck. It was not as if he actually wanted to spend inside her, with the possibilities of children and the promise of matrimony that entailed. He did not need to let his head rewrite it into some great tragedy. This sometimes happened to him in the aftermath. A dark swirl of emotions, as if his pleasure had been so strong that his body's only response was to plunge into the exact opposite. To offer up a price for such an exquisite experience.

When he looked back, he discovered Miss Preston had sunk to the ground against the door. Her legs spread open, her eyes closed, her fingers working at her slit. Her braid had started to uncoil from its pins.

She must have felt his gaze, for she blushed – pink enough that he could see in the candlelight – and looked up at him. "Do you think me very bold? Only, I was so close to another peak before you had yours."

Her eyes were clear and glassy with desire. It was the first embarrassment she had expressed since demanding he kiss her, and something in the way she said it filled Max with tenderness.

Or perhaps that was only the cesspit of emotions currently warring in his chest.

He put on a grin for her, dropped to his knees, and crawled between her legs. "Let me."

Max traced his tongue where her fingers had just been. He waited for the gasp to which he had so quickly become accustomed, but Miss Preston made no sound, only threaded her fingers through his hair encouragingly. She truly was close – he could tell from the desire drenching his mouth. She tasted like all women and yet like no woman who had come before her. He focused on her swollen flesh, adding pressure as she had requested before, and in only a few breaths, she orgasmed.

This one was different than the first. Her body did not convulse like a witch possessed. Her legs trembled, and her fingers seized in his hair. But mostly, she expressed it, great loud sounds that might be heard across the fields if not for the pounding rain. At the crescendo, she claimed his name again. "Max!"

He rocked back onto his heels. "Are you quite satisfied, Miss Preston?"

Miss Preston smiled. It was lazy and sated and wide. "Quite, thank you, Lord Berwick." She stretched her arms and legs.

Usually, after an interlude such as this, Max's mind was a pleasant blank slate. He didn't know why it was not so with Miss Preston. Only his thoughts raced with a thousand questions. Who had taken her virtue? Had she given it willingly? Why had no one called the rogue out? What would she tell a prospective husband? How many men had she spirited into dark sheds?

A relationship such as theirs could only handle so much honesty. Max curled his arm around her so that she nestled against his chest and pushed out all questions but one. "Why do you always hide your hair?"

She sighed into his skin. "Everyone loves to comment on my hair. Oh, it's so bright. Oh, it's the sign of the Devil. Oh, I am only excitable because my hair is red. I hate it. I don't want anyone to stare at me or assume anything about me simply because of the way I look."

"There is something about women with red hair, though. You must all have the same spirit," Max mused. "I can never resist them. Even though I didn't know what color your hair was, I couldn't resist you."

He meant it in the way they had been speaking all day. A small confession so that she might know him better.

Miss Preston reached for her clothes. "How quickly I grow cold."

There was a stiffness to her movements that cued to Max he had said something wrong. Perhaps it was the mention of other women.

He pushed away the urge to beg her forgiveness. They meant nothing to each other. He did not owe her any care for her feelings.

He retrieved his own apparel from the ground. "Perhaps I should fetch a conveyance for you."

She paused before answering. "Yes, I suppose so. The rain still hasn't let up."

Max dressed, then assisted her with the corset. He even drew the cap back over her head, allowing himself only one indulgent stroke of the braid. Her hair was surprisingly coarse in its pins.

When she was fully dressed, Miss Preston peeked out the shed door. "I hope you won't catch a cold."

The fields were a wet, muddy mess. "Let's hope Mr. Maulvi has the horses ready, then," Max said. He tried to add his Norwich accent back in, and his words came out brusquer than he intended. Almost like an accusation of laziness against Mr. Maulvi.

Miss Preston's face narrowed with annoyance. "Once you've sent the grooms, you may go to the kitchen and ask Cook for mulled wine to warm up."

As if he were a servant, and she extending her good will as mistress of the house.

Yes, it was best they both remember what they were to each other. Nothing.

Max stalked off into the rain.

CHAPTER NINE

T HE HOT BATH FELT good. Not quite as good as having Max inside her, but a close second. Ordinarily, Ellen hurried through her washing, guilty about how much effort it took for the servants to boil and haul the water. That afternoon, she languished in it. She refused to feel remorse for anything that day. Sending Layla away, Ellen glided the lavender-scented soap across her skin, washing off the rain and mud. As a girl, she and Sophia had spent hours charting their bodies, but Ellen hadn't considered hers in what felt like eons. Now she fondled the roll of fat at her hips and traced the birthmark twisting inside her elbow. She counted freckles. She forgave her second toes for being longer than the first. She searched, too, for evidence of Max on her: bruises or scratches or love bites.

She didn't find any. His only mark was the way her whole body felt like liquid gold, even an hour after the encounter.

When guilt threatened to return, she pushed it away. She had not allowed herself to feel shame after Percy Thistleman, and she would not allow herself to now. No matter that Max was Lord Berwick. No matter that in a month or two, he may ruin her family's reputation once and for all.

Max had drunk her in as thirstily as she him; she felt rather like a beast who had consumed his whole being. They were fond of each other, not for the spaces they occupied in the world but for who they were as people.

And therefore, she would allow herself no guilt.

She kept her hair braided tightly against her scalp the whole bath. Ellen was feeling rather angry with it. As if it were another woman entirely who had captured Max's attention away from her. Ellen had never liked her hair, in truth. It was too bright. Invited too many comments. Percy had written a whole sonnet to it, which he recited to her after she tried to ask him whether there was room in Heaven for people who practiced religions other than the Church of England.

If she sheared it all off as if fleecing a sheep, would Max still smirk at her?

When the water cooled, Ellen pulled herself out of the tub, toweled off into her dressing robe, and called out for Layla. If she could have her way, she would slip into her work dress and run off to the carpentry to work on the shutters. Rain still spattered against the windows, however, so she supposed she would stay in the Hall the rest of the day. Perhaps return to the pillowcase needlework.

Perhaps find a block of wood to whittle. She could make Max another sheep to keep Elinor company.

It was not Layla but Mrs. Chow who answered her call. "We haven't chatted in too long," she said, folding Ellen's muddied gown into the hamper.

"No, you're quite right. I have been so busy trying to finish the shutters for the cottages."

Mrs. Chow had begun as Mama's lady's maid, then had been nurse to all the children except Caroline, and by now had been the housekeeper for nearly a decade. She pulled out fresh undergarments and started dressing Ellen with familiar, efficient tugs. "You have been spending time with Mr. Sims, too."

Ellen heard the note of censure in her tone. Guilt pricked – and Ellen pushed it down. "I believe I can discover his true purpose, since we know he wasn't truthful about his experience with carpentry."

"He is very handsome."

That wasn't something Ellen could lie about. "Yes."

Mrs. Chow lifted the dress over Ellen's head and fitted it into place. "Those are two things that you know about him, then. He is handsome, and he is a liar."

"It is not as if I am trying to marry him." The words were an echo of what Max had said on their walk. Somehow, they were less comforting alone in her dressing room.

Turning away, Mrs. Chow started cleaning up the bath. "Your mother had many good ideas. I don't think she was right about men and women, though."

Ellen grabbed a towel to mop up the puddle that had dripped beneath her when she stepped out of the bath. She tried not to let anger leech into her response. "What is not right is that men are given license to copulate whenever, wherever, and with whomever they please while women are expected to remain chaste for their husbands."

"The idea is fine. It feels good to say, too." Mrs. Chow took the towel from her, then wrapped a cool palm around Ellen's wrist. "Your mother forgot that you have to live in reality. You may think what you like about the rights of woman. No one else will care. If they think you are too free with your attentions, they will talk. If you get with child, will Mr. Sims marry you? Do you even want to be married to a man like that?"

"If one measured all of one's ideals based on how other people would react, we would all be conservatives. I prefer to do what is *right* and let others worry about their own opinions."

Breaking free, Ellen settled on the bench beneath the window to tie on her stockings and boots. She didn't care if it was raining; she would go to the workshop and let loose her frustration on the wood.

Mrs. Chow bundled the laundry into her arms. "Campaigning against blood sugar is a good thing. It has a good goal. What else matters than liberating a hundred thousand people from slavery? I don't know what the goal is of chasing Mr. Sims. Other than physical pleasure. Seems like it will do more harm than good, to me."

"I am setting an example of a woman who is property of herself, not any man!"

Mrs. Chow shrugged. "Until you have a baby, and then you had better hope some man takes responsibility for you." From her pocket, she withdrew a letter. "This came for you from Miss Sophia."

Sweeping out of the room, Mrs. Chow left the envelope on the washstand. Ellen was trembling too hard to think of reading it. Mrs. Chow was wrong; she was letting fear warp her ideals, something Mama had always warned against. Ellen had every right to kiss or fuck or marry whichever man she chose, assuming he would have her, just the same as a man could woo as many women as he liked. There was nothing wrong with the principle.

Yet Mrs. Chow was right, too. There was fault in how Ellen applied it. Max was openly plotting to humiliate her family! And somehow, Ellen had allowed lust to consume her. To agree to *help* him. She was fooling herself if she thought she had kept his secret as some sort of strategy to protect Papa.

Ellen had wanted more time with Max. Plain and simple. Even now, she yearned to rush off into the rain to find him. To let him kiss her worries into oblivion.

She jerked from her seat, revolted with herself. She had been weak; fine, everyone gave into temptation now and then. Now Ellen would simply have to do better.

Seizing the letter, she read:

Dear Ellen, Nate, Caro, etc.

London is quite miserable this week. It is overly warm, which means the coal sticks all the worse in my lungs and the air stinks with sewage. Worst of all, the flowers decided to bloom late here, so the allergies I already suffered at Northfield Hall in April are plaguing me now in June. There is no more faithful a friend than my handkerchief.

Caroline, in answer to your question, Aunt Charlotte provided me my own box of candles upon arrival so that I might burn them as needed at night for reading, correspondence, or any other nighttime activities that require light!

Nathaniel, I will not answer any questions about the Navy for I absolutely refuse to allow you to run off to the high seas. You promised me ten years ago that you and I would rove the countryside as traveling actors until we were too old to walk, and I intend to hold you to that.

Ellen, you asked me if I have any suitors, which is a question I find insulting. I am a beautiful young woman who is not actually interested in a husband; of course I have suitors! The question is whether there are any whom I find interesting enough to take pleasure in riding through Hyde Park with, and that answer is no. They all prove far too pompous about their horses.

Speaking of suitors, I believe our Benny has fallen quite in love with a Miss Amanda Fairchurch of Bath. She is very beautiful and charming, as one would expect, but alas for Benny, she also counts a duke and an earl as suitors, so I'm not sure his time is well spent there. In any case, I see very little of him unless Miss Fairchurch happens to be attending the same event as I.

Papa has been much more around, for the bill is not faring well. His friends have advised him to let it be this year and wait for the next elections to see if he can gain more support. He alternates between despair, during which he hardly leaves his chambers and sends all his food back uneaten, and rage, which is when I see him most and am subject to his ranting about how no peer in England has the proper amount of courage.

I say this facetiously but also truthfully. I'm sure you would be of more comfort to him, Ellen, but Northfield Hall needs you more than he does.

I hope to send more cheerful news soon.

All my love,

Sophia

Ellen read it the once, and then twice more. Her fingertips drifted to her throat, which she only noticed when she felt the nails pressing too painfully against her skin.

Papa was in rare form, indeed. He needed consolation, or at least commiseration, two emotions that neither Sophia nor Benny were well-suited to provide.

He needed Ellen. And she needed to leave Northfield Hall, before she did something even more stupid than fuck her family's sworn enemy.

By her fourth reading, there was no question remaining in her mind.

She would go to London for Papa, as soon as the arrangements could be made.

M ISS PRESTON DIDN'T RETURN to the carpentry workshop on Saturday, nor did she send word to Max privately. Max resolved not to notice, and each time she popped into his head – suggested by the toolchest sitting unused in the corner, the oatcakes at dinner, the scent of lilacs along the path – he pushed her away. On Sunday, sweeping his writing materials into his pack and adding Elinor for good luck, Max decided to avoid her altogether by searching out Mr. Griswick. He waited until after church, in case the man attended services, and then followed the innkeeper's directions all the way to the opposite side of town, through a cow field, and along the stream.

He smelled the dyeworks before he saw them. There was no work being done on Sunday, of course, so the stench was left over from years of dye labor. Which, Max knew from having toured other dyeworks, included adding urine to elicit a permanent color from pigments.

He couldn't imagine making one's living from such filthy labor, any more than he could imagine Lord Preston building a dyeworks to stink up Northfield.

Max discovered Mr. Griswick in a small garden behind the dyer's cottage wrestling slugs from his lettuce heads. At this first vantage point, Mr. Griswick was a short, old man with fierce white hair that went off in all directions.

"Would you like some help?" An unfortunate side effect of living at Northfield Hall, apparently: there he went, offering his services left and right when really, he had no interest in kneeling in dirt or touching slugs.

Mr. Griswick moved with the aches of an old man as he first rested his hands on his knee, then cranked around his spine, and finally lifted his chin to spy Max. "Who are you, then?"

"Mr. Maxwell Sims. Carpenter at Northfield Hall." Max swept off his hat and bowed his chin to show respect.

"The one that is shite at his job?"

Max decided not to take offense. "Ah, so you have heard of me."

Mr. Griswick took another series of movements to stand. He brushed the dirt off his hands with two claps. "I can't think what Miss Preston wants us to meet about, Sims. I don't say no to a lady such as herself, but seeing as it is just you and me, I'd rather not make a pot of tea just to toss you on your ear."

Max could respect a plain-spoken man. "Perhaps I may trust you with a confidence, sir. I am not actually a carpenter, but a reporter for the London newspaper *The Perceptive*. I am writing a report on Northfield Hall." He paused to withdraw a card from his pack – printed *Maximilian Hainsworth, writer for The Perceptive* in small, plain letters – and presented it to Mr. Griswick. "I am particularly interested in speaking with you, sir, because you provide such a crucial service for Northfield Hall and yet resist the allure of its...peculiar...lifestyle."

Griswick examined the card. "They pay me in full every month."

"I plan to speak to the dyers' guild, as well. I see no need to name which dyer said what." Max waited a moment, watching the old man's protruding eyebrows catch the afternoon breeze, then prodded, "At the very least, could you show me around your dyeworks?"

So they went on a tour of the place. Max made sure to exclaim over the size and cleanliness of the rooms, as well as to ask follow-up questions, as if he would ever include details on mordants or water temperature in his report. The whole time, too, he managed not to reach for his handkerchief, though he very much wished it were pressed up to his nose to relieve the terrible smell.

"Your vats," he said when Mr. Griswick paused, "shine so beautifully."

They were copper and, in fact, looked a little green and beaten-up. Mr. Griswick beamed with pride nevertheless. "Lord Preston bought those for me, he did, as a present at the start of the new century."

"Did he now?" Max tried not to sound too eager. "I am very curious about where Lord Preston finds the money for Northfield Hall. Have you any sense of his income?"

The old man looked as if it were the stupidest question he had heard in his whole life. "He is a lord, isn't he? Well, lords have money."

Max decided it would be impolitic to explain that in fact, most lords earned their money from the rent and crop sales of tenant farms, which Lord Preston had abolished from Northfield Hall. That, or investments in the colonies.

Even Max didn't believe Lord Preston was hypocritical enough to ban imports from his home and then invest in shipping.

"Do you know, Mr. Griswick, in the past few years, a new kind of linen has become the most fashionable cloth for summer clothing in London? It is known as Berkshire linen. I cannot help but wonder if it originates at Northfield Hall."

The man turned as red as if a vat of cochineal dye had been splashed upon his skin. "You would have to ask Lord Preston about that."

Excitement shivered down Max's spine. That was a far cry from a denial – rather, it practically confirmed Max's suspicion altogether. He resisted the urge to grin and waited, in hopes that Mr. Griswick would speak more into the silence.

The dyer, however, stalked into the yard. Max followed, noting the fabric currently hung up to dry. Most of it was the dull colors of locally-sourced yellow, pink, and blue dyes. On the back line, though, flapped bright reds, purples, and a deep indigo.

"Those are for my other customers," Mr. Griswick said defensively, following Max's gaze. "The ones that aren't afraid of dyes from the New World."

"Lord Preston doesn't mind that you use imported ingredients?"

"He doesn't own me, does he? He has no say in what kind of business I take, no more than he can force me to talk to that man of business of his either."

Something in the way Mr. Griswick spat out "man of business" stuck out unpleasantly. "Mr. Maulvi, you mean?"

Mr. Griswick set rheumy blue eyes on him. "Don't you think it unnatural that Lord Preston allows a man like him to run the place? It never sat well with me, not all these four decades that it has been so."

The man was looking for someone to agree with him. A month ago, Max could have done so without hesitation. Now, knowing Northfield as he did, he felt the desperate need to pivot. "How do you feel about Lord Preston's experiment, Mr. Griswick? Do you feel the lives at Northfield Hall are improved with the abolition of rents and whatnot?"

"I don't mind doing away with the rents. My own cousins were turned out not ten years ago by their landlord, and all for not being able to switch to wheat as fast as he liked. No, that part I don't mind. The problem is that Lord Preston takes in the worst sort of characters. He should stick to good Englishmen, that's what I think."

"Has there been trouble in town from the people living at Northfield Hall?"

"No fisticuffs, if that's what you mean." Mr. Griswick sounded a little disappointed about this. "I wager they happen all the time at the Hall, though. How could they not, with all those Irishmen and Hindustanis and the like? Not to mention the women, parading around unmarried."

That was the moment that Max understood: Mr. Griswick had no concrete objections to anything about Northfield Hall. The only comments he could give Max for the report were the same hot air readers already spewed.

Max withdrew his handkerchief for relief at last. "You have been very generous with me, Mr. Griswick."

The man's eyes gleamed. "How much are you being paid for your report, then?"

Max pulled five shillings from the purse in his pack. "I appreciate your time."

Grinning, Mr. Griswick slapped his back. "If you do ever need to learn the dye trade, I'd be happy to teach you."

Max walked back to town with an uneasy spirit. He should have stayed to ask more questions about the Berkshire linen. Only, once Mr. Griswick started sputtering about the people at Northfield Hall...It shouldn't have bothered Max. He had speculated the same before arriving, that the whole property would be overrun with uncommon licentiousness because of the type of people Lord Preston hired.

Max would have thought Mr. Griswick would know better by now. Everyone at Northfield Hall was earnest. It drove Max mad, but it was also admirable. They were there to make an honest living, and they didn't deserve to be jeered at simply because they didn't fit Mr. Griswick's definition of an Englishman.

Mr. Maulvi himself had been born at Northfield Hall and raised as a retainer to the family. There was nothing more English for the serving class than that.

It being only midafternoon, Max decided to head to the inn for a pint or two. He needed to decide his next action. At last, he had something tangible to investigate about Northfield Hall: how involved was it in Berkshire linen, why did it not claim its involvement publicly, and what other secrets did it pin in place?

He could return to the textiles in hopes of asking Mr. and Mrs. Shayler more pointed questions. But Max doubted they knew much about the business beyond the confines of Northfield Hall itself. What Max needed for his report was a more thorough investigation that tracked exactly how much Lord Preston profited from the linens – and why he was hiding it.

Miss Preston could help him. Max indulged a short fantasy of that: searching her out in the Hall and convincing her to sneak him into her father's study to examine his records. Her gray eyes sparking first with outrage, then with desire. Her hair tumbling down around her shoulders...

But Max couldn't ask that of her, no more than she would actually give him access to her own father's papers. Even Miss Preston wasn't *that* trusting.

She was right to ignore him. No doubt she was treating it like their first kiss: a carnal lust that had been satiated and need not be revisited. Lust was the sum total of it, of course. Max found her charming and beautiful, but not a woman he would make a long-term paramour, much less his wife.

They were simply too different.

Somehow, this line of thinking was no better than turning over the question of Mr. Griswick and Berkshire linen. As the road curved towards the inn, Max found himself completely blue-deviled, and he hoped desperately there would be no one in the taproom who wanted to speak with him. Such was his attitude as he noticed the stagecoach sitting in front of the inn.

It was a bulky black box led by four horses, who were currently being minded by a boy who looked as dusty from the road as the coach did. The driver stood by the side of the coach, strapping a trunk to its top.

Only as Max drew closer did he notice the passengers waiting to board. Two women, both in gray wool travelling suits. One was middle-aged and squat with tight silver curls springing from beneath her bonnet.

The other was Miss Preston.

Max's whole body ran cold. Why, he couldn't say. He had spent the last two days trying desperately *not* to think of Miss Preston, and now here she was.

Leaving on a common stagecoach.

The coachman turned to hand Miss Preston to her seat.

Max launched himself between the two of them. "Where are you going?"

Miss Preston jolted in surprise, her hands raising in two fists as if to defend herself. She let them fall as she responded, "To London."

"On a stagecoach?" He didn't know why it mattered to him. "You must take your family carriage."

"My family carriage is in London."

Damn Lord Preston and his frugality. As far as Max could see, he spent his money everywhere except on the things that would make his family most comfortable. "You cannot travel alone."

Miss Preston's expression sharpened into reproach. "The way you speak to me, Mr. Sims! One would think you were a viscount."

Max hadn't even been thinking about his accent, much less the authority with which he snapped at her.

The older woman stepped forward, her hand landing on Miss Preston's shoulder. "I am Mrs. Croft, Miss Preston's chaperone. You must be the carpenter's assistant about whom I have heard so much."

The Widow Croft. Max had heard of her at the supper table. Mr. Maulvi's common-law wife.

He didn't have the energy for curiosity at the moment, however. His body still thumped with panic at the idea of Miss Preston travelling on a stagecoach.

"Miss Preston is better suited to private travel," he said to Mrs. Croft.

The widow smiled in amusement – at his expense, no doubt. "I will see she comes to no harm, Mr. Sims."

He wanted to growl in frustration. Anything could happen on a stagecoach. Highwaymen, brawls in the posting inns, thieves in fellow passengers.

An elderly widow could not protect herself against such occurrences, much less a pretty young woman such as Miss Preston.

The coachman had grown impatient behind him. "Excuse me, Miss, but you must take your seat if we are to keep our schedule."

"Certainly. I am ready." Miss Preston glanced at Max expectantly. He was still in her way. A hundred questions flooded his mind again, pinned under her gray gaze. Why was she fleeing to London? Had she known she would do so even as she spirited him away to that shed on Friday?

Had she even tried to say goodbye to him?

"Sir." The coachman added a threat to the word this time. "You must move."

In the span of a second, Max did the calculations. Berkshire linen – sold in London. Lord Preston – currently in London. And Miss Preston.

He reached into his purse, found a whole pound, and handed it to the coachman. "For a seat to London."

It was wildly more money than such a seat would cost, and certainly more money than a carpenter's assistant should be throwing around. Well, it was about time he gave up the ghost on Mr. Maxwell Sims, anyhow. Max swung himself into the coach with a buzz of satisfaction.

He was ready for his next adventure.

Chapter Ten

How Ellen wanted to tell Max off.

The gall of him, to vault himself into the carriage after her like some kind of squire. And then to grin – as if she should be glad to have him squeezing onto the bench beside her! She nearly told the coachman to eject Max, but the man shone from the pound in his hand and cheerfully shut the door.

Ellen had no choice but to swallow her protests and pretend, for the sake of the other passengers, that absolutely nothing was wrong.

There were six of them in the coach. Ellen, in between Aunt Croft and Max, occupied the bench facing the direction of travel, while opposite sat two governesses and a young man on his way to Magdalen College at Oxford. It was a friendly group, yet crowded enough that Ellen had no choice except to sit with her arms and hips lined up against Max. Her head only came up to just above his shoulder. If she wanted to, she could have used the swell of muscle between his shoulder and collarbone as a pillow.

The two governesses kept stealing appreciative glances of him.

At the very least, he did not spend the whole afternoon oozing aristocratic condescension at the rest of the coach. Second to Aunt Croft, in fact, Max was the chattiest person in the carriage. He asked the governesses about their positions, listening attentively even as they trilled on and on about various children in their charges. With young Mr. Ogilvie, Max swapped theories about the best cricket bat to buy in London. As conversation flew about the coach, Ellen need only sit back and try to keep up.

They had made it past Reading when Aunt Croft asked Max, "And you, Mr. Sims? What are your plans for once we arrive to London?"

Ellen should have known Aunt would spring something like it upon Max. There was none better than Aunt Croft for keeping a secret – but she also loved to stir up trouble whenever possible.

"Visit my mother, of course." Max's fake accent seemed especially thick in his answer. "Then, I suppose I'll make my way up to Norwich."

"Ah, yes, to marry your sweetheart."

"If she'll still have me." Max smoothed on a charming grin.

Ellen looked away. She knew the Norwich sweetheart was false, but he likely did have someone waiting for him in London. An actress or courtesan or whoever it was that aristocratic rogues like Max dallied with.

It wasn't her, that much Ellen knew. Whatever his plans were in London, they would not include publicly courting a member of the

Preston family. Even if he considered it – which he would not – Ellen would not allow it.

"I was just reading about a by-election in Norwich," Mr. Ogilvie said. "Great Yarmouth, I think it was. The sitting MP died, and they haven't yet stood up anyone for his place."

That was the seat the Earl of Meretta controlled, the one that was supposed to go to Max if he wrote his report. *When* he wrote the report.

Max leaned forward a little, his arm brushing past hers. "A rotten borough, if I remember right. I wonder if they'll have a candidate by the time I get back."

He threw out the term as if it *rotten* meant nothing. As if it was perfectly natural to take advantage of the situation – a district with only a dozen voters whose votes could be coerced or bought, leaving great swaths of the country without proper representation at all – rather than try to fix it. She couldn't help herself but to say, "It is too bad you are not able to vote."

The sunlight gave Max's hazel eyes a glow as he glanced back at her, lips twitching in amusement. Poor Mr. Ogilvie coughed, embarrassed by her manners, and rummaged in his sack to procure a crumpled newspaper. "Here, if you want to read about it."

As Max took it – grabbing it rather eagerly, Ellen noted – she spotted the block-printed masthead: *The Perceptive.*

This was the great publication that would write about her family, then. A single broadside with tiny lettering printed along every inch of space. Popular enough that even a young man about to sequester himself in clerical studies might have a copy.

She tried to keep her interest sounding innocent as she asked, "Is that a London paper? I have never heard of it."

Mr. Ogilvie replied, "It is. It only started last year. Split off from the *Times* in protest of their coverage of the Irish anti-unionists."

"On account of the *Times* being too conservative?" Ellen knew a little of the issue. Last year had been a decade since the Act of Union joined Ireland into the United Kingdom of Great Britain. More than a few Irishmen had used the anniversary to lodge complaints against the union, on account of the unfulfilled promises of economic improvements and Roman Catholic emancipation. From what she remembered of the *Times*'s coverage, they had not been very sympathetic to the Irish arguments.

Mr. Ogilvie chuckled. "Oh no, Miss, on account of it being so Whiggish as to print an opinion article in support of the Irish. *The Perceptive* bleeds for the Tories, through and through. I myself like to read papers of both parties, which is why I subscribe, but it does take a rather harsh view of anything that even smells like a Whig policy."

"Ah. How interesting." She should have known. God forbid Max's politics include an ounce of compassion. The Tories only wanted to protect the traditions of the Crown so that no power ever slipped from their grabby fingers.

"Much the same as the Prestons take a harsh view of anything that reeks of Tories, I wager," Max said with a smirk.

Ellen hated the way his smirks lit desire all the way to her core.

"It is the substance of the thing that we object to, not its stench," she retorted. "Otherwise, I'm sure I would have tossed you from the coach in Thatcham, sir."

He did not actually smell. Well, more precisely, he did smell: of himself. Skin, sawdust, sweat. A cologne that made desire turn to molten liquid between her legs.

Vain man that he was, Max actually looked horrified. He lifted his coat to his nose for inspection. "I do apologize. I visited Mr. Griswick at the dyeworks this morning."

"My nose does not work very well," the elder governess volunteered, "so if it bothers you, Miss Preston, Mr. Sims could always come sit beside me."

Devil take him, Max returned a flirtatious smile as she fluttered her eyelashes. Aunt Croft said, "I see why you have not made it back to your sweetheart in Norwich, Mr. Sims."

"Indeed," Mr. Ogilvie chuckled, "I wish I did not have to take my leave, otherwise I would apply myself to learn from you." He had been watching the road more closely than Ellen; they were in Great Marlow now, approaching the posting inn to switch horses. Mr. Ogilvie would change routes to continue on to Oxford, while the rest of them might take supper, if there was enough time.

The head porter handing them out of the coach frowned when Max intoned, "A private room, if you please," for all the world forgetting he was still pretending to be a carpenter's assistant.

"That is quite unnecessary," Ellen said in her best *ton* accent. "My aunt and I are happy to eat in the common dining room."

Max turned his aristocrat's glare on her. "It is not fit for a young lady, Miss Preston."

That was too much. First, for Max to attach himself to her like some kind of attendant. Then, for him to be such an annoying flirt. And now for him to order her about, as if she were his responsibility.

To the porter and Aunt Croft, Ellen said as politely as possible, "Will you excuse us for a moment?" Then she grabbed Max by the arm and marched him away from the crowd, to the side of the stables where they might speak without being overheard by everyone. "You cannot simply invite yourself onto a trip and start ordering people about. You are a carpenter's assistant, though I think you must have forgotten, since you have been speaking like a dandy from Mayfair all day!"

Max blinked at her through the shadows of the eaves. His hat sat crookedly on his head, and his hair had come loose, as it always seemed to do. "I am not ordering anyone about. I am trying to keep you safe, as any sensible person would do."

"It is not your place to do so. You may stop concerning yourself with anything to do with me."

"May I?" He edged closer. They stood between the inn and the stable, a narrow space to begin with. Max's one forward step felt as significant as another man striding across an assembly room. "You and I are linked. Didn't we decide that? We have an affinity towards each other. That cannot be dismissed like some inconvenient servant."

Ellen's mouth felt desperately dry. "Neither does it mean you may involve yourself in my affairs. I am not your wife. I am a friend, nothing more."

"This is how I treat my friends."

Ellen couldn't tell if that was a lie or not. Max might have friends like her across the English countryside. He might follow them all to London on a whim, depending on what other plans he had that day.

She didn't know if she wanted to be special to him or not.

With a glance back to the yard, Max angled her deeper into the shadows between the buildings. "How long have you known you were going to London?"

The change in subject caught Ellen by surprise. "Only since – it – I received a letter from my sister. My father needs me."

"Oh." Something that Ellen thought might be relief raced across his face.

"I thought you might use church as an excuse to speak with me."

"I don't attend services." His eyes were dark in the shadows, but she could feel them raking over her. "I went to see Mr. Griswick."

"So you said." Where Ellen had yearned to see him again, Max had thoughts only for his report.

"Was there something you wanted to speak about?"

Us. Naked. You inside me again. She hadn't wanted any of that, of course. They had to say goodbye. "Only to tell you that I was leaving for London."

"Ah."

The air filled between them. Ellen wished she could speak the thoughts that hammered against her heart. The ones that made her want to tuck against him and let the world melt away.

But she had resolved to be better. To put her family and her principles ahead of the greedy lust racing through her blood.

She squared her shoulders. "As much as I appreciate your willingness to keep Aunt Croft and me safe, you must not involve yourself. I am superior to Mr. Sims, after all."

Max didn't meet her eyes. "I will say goodbye to Mr. Sims when we reach London."

"You are ready to write your report, then." Ellen wondered what Mr. Griswick had said.

"Close. I hope it will..." Max broke off, and she waited for him to find the right words. "I hope the report will not disappoint you, Miss Preston."

An impossible hope. Ellen swallowed against it. "I wanted to delay you by a few weeks."

He didn't ask why. She almost wished he did, because that would mean he didn't realize the report was designed to interfere with Papa's parliamentary agenda. "I have more research to do in London. And then I still have to write it. Perhaps that will be long enough."

"Perhaps." She was glad she could not see much of his face. If there were better lighting, she would be avoiding his gaze now, looking at his nose or his lips or his ears so as not to see any kindness softening his eyes.

"So long as I am still Mr. Sims..." Max stepped closer, his hands landing at her waist. There was so much heat to him. Ellen's body tilted closer of its own accord. Even though she knew she should resist, she nearly purred to smell the sawdust on him.

The kiss he gave her was new for them. It was not the hurried, desperate desire that had spurred Ellen onwards for the last few weeks. His breath touched her first, and then his lips. They were soft – she had never realized that before. One hand rose from her body to cup the back of her head. His thumb teased across the nape of her neck. Ellen kissed back, pressing herself against him, relishing in the heat and the muscles and the feel of wool beneath her fingers.

They could have kissed all night, she thought, never removing an inch of clothing, if Aunt Croft hadn't called, "Miss Preston?"

"Coming!" Ellen pushed Max away. He stepped backwards into the shadows, a hand brushing across his lips. His eyes were glazed with the same happy desire fuzzing up Ellen's thoughts.

She wished he were anyone but the Viscount Berwick.

"We might not get a chance to say goodbye in London," Max said. "I hope you know I appreciate your friendship."

"Thank you."

"If you ever need me, I am only a letter away."

"Thank you." Ellen could think of nothing else to say. When they parted, he would write some story about her family. And she would...

She supposed she would continue with life, just the way she wanted. Caring for her family, worrying about her father, escaping to the carpentry.

The thought should have cheered her more.

"We will take that private dining room," she said. "If it will make you more comfortable."

Max ducked his head. As if he had been hoping for something else. "I will wait here so as not to cause any talk."

Ellen nodded. She paused, willing better words to fill her mouth. But there was nothing to say except goodbye. So she left.

Chapter Eleven

LONDON WAS OVERWHELMING. FROM the moment Ellen descended from the stagecoach, she felt the pressure of too many people crushing around her. Her lungs seized from the soot in the air, and she had to hold a handkerchief pressed to her nose and mouth like some kind of snob. There were so many noises, too, more than she could ever have imagined before. Men yelling instructions across the yard, peddlers hawking wares on the street, laughter from the alehouses, and the urchins begging...

Ellen couldn't think about the urchins.

Max hovered behind her. His pack on his shoulder, he carried her valise in one hand and Aunt Croft's in the other and ushered them into the posting inn.

"We are hiring a hackney coach to the Partridge House," Aunt Croft informed him. Even though she tried to sound as merry as usual, Ellen heard how carefully she pronounced it, imitating exactly the cadence Uncle Maulvi had used in his instructions. "The Countess of Pemberly will receive us."

Ellen turned, watching Max's reaction. For some reason, she wanted him to stutter at the connection. Perhaps it was that Aunt Charlotte's title counted for so much more than Papa's. Ellen wanted Max to be cowed by the person patronizing her trip to London, the way Ellen herself was cowed by Max's title.

He didn't blink. Grabbing a nearby porter, he pressed a coin into the man's hand and directed him to hire the hack.

"You have taken good care of us," Aunt Croft said. "You are a kind man to go out of your way to see to our safety."

Max corrected her quickly: "I am not kind."

A strange thing to say. Ellen couldn't think why anyone shouldn't want to be described as kind. Though she supposed it was true. Max was intelligent, and she believed he followed his own sense of honor. But he was selfish and single-minded. So consumed by his perspective that he couldn't consider anyone else.

She was glad for the reminder. That was the type of thing best remembered, especially upon parting.

As they waited, Ellen tried to fight back her unease with the city by listing reasons she was glad to come to London. She would see Papa, Sophia, and Benny again. She would get to know Aunt Charlotte better. Perhaps she could even seek out Martin Chow at the dockyards, if that was where he was living, and catch up with him at last. All connections that should outweigh the panic rising unreasonably in her breast.

The porter returned to guide them to the hack. Max still followed, only a handsbreadth away from Ellen. He meant to escort them all the way to Aunt Charlotte's, she supposed. Ellen felt she should object. Or she should want to object, considering that he was unkind and plotting against her family.

But the truth was, fear roiled beneath her skin. There was nothing familiar about London. She felt as if a hundred eyes were crawling across her at any moment. And the hack wouldn't be driven by old Ned or one-armed Gregory but by some stranger, who could as easily take them to their deaths at the docks as to Aunt Charlotte's.

Max may not have been a kind man, but he was kind to Ellen. For the moment, it was enough.

Except when he handed her into the hack, he released her gloved palm and shut the door. Ellen slid in a panic across the bench, her neck sticking out the little window frame as the coach started clopping down the street. "You aren't coming?"

He stared at her. At first, she was close enough to see the hazel of his eyes. The flicker of uncertainty across his brow. But the hack kept rolling, and Max didn't move. She could barely hear him when he finally responded, "You wanted me to?"

The hackney coach turned onto the main road. Ellen closed her eyes, pressing that last image of Max into her memory. Tall, proud, his carpenter's clothes a little too large and his pack a little too light slung across his shoulder. Despite the people and animals and carts streaming about the road, Max stood as if alone. A man who needed no one else to determine his worth.

They had never had a future together, and yet tears stung her eyes at saying goodbye. Only moments ago, she could feel the heat of his body behind hers – and it made her feel safe. Now, she would likely never see him again.

Her heart thumped painfully.

It was a long journey to Mayfair, punctuated by a wait for a dead horse to be cleared from the street, a dozen urchins surrounding the hack beseeching money, and the pervasive underlying stench of stale urine. Aunt Croft filled the time with chatter. She had been to London as a newlywed with Mr. Croft – three decades or so ago – and she compared everything they saw to how she remembered it. She found the press of people exhilarating. There were so many smells, she cried with delight. And she particularly enjoyed pointing out every brown-skinned man they passed, wondering, "Perhaps he is Bengali like my dear Mr. Maulvi!"

Ellen focused on mustering the energy to cheer Papa.

The coach came to a stop in front of a great big building overlooking a green square. The building itself was half the size of Northfield Hall. Painted a bright white with Grecian columns marching down its façade and marble stairs spilling to the street, it stood as if declaring to the world that no greater structure had ever been built. When the driver opened the carriage door to help them out, Ellen asked, "This is Partridge House?"

"Right it is, miss, though you'll want to go around to the side for the service entrance." He handed her to the street and placed the valise in her grip before driving away.

Max must have paid him in advance, Ellen realized. Another kindness.

They knocked at the front door and were greeted by a fresh-faced footman who looked down his nose at them. He wore a bright red livery jacket that included gold braids, white gloves, black pantaloons, and white stockings. Ellen had never seen fabric so bright, nor so supple as it folded around his body.

Imported cotton, she supposed, made from the labor of slaves.

"Miss Ellen Preston to see her ladyship," Aunt Croft informed the man.

He hesitated, his eyes running dismissively across both their grimy travel costumes, and then he disappeared into the house with an overly polite, "If you will please wait here."

Ellen supposed Max would be insulted to be kept waiting. He would expect the servant to fall flat on the ground in gratitude that a personage such as Max's graced the household.

She should find the thought unpleasant, but at the moment, it comforted her. She almost wished Max were there to kick up a fuss on her behalf.

When the footman returned, he was a changed man. "Do come in, Miss Preston. Her ladyship is eager to greet you in the Orchid Room."

As if Ellen or Aunt Croft knew the difference between any of the rooms in the house. They followed the man at a bit of a clip across the entranceway, up a set of stairs, and down a long corridor until finally he stopped before a set of white double doors. These he opened to reveal a room done up with glittering wallpaper patterned with orchids.

Another import, designed to show off the fact that it was imported.

A small, plump woman rose from a settee to greet them. For a moment, Ellen lost her breath: the woman looked just like Mama. Then she smiled, and the illusion disappeared. Aunt Charlotte had Mama's eyes, perhaps, but her nose was too long, her smile too broad, and her whole body otherwise proved her not to be anyone but herself.

"What a surprise, my dear Ellen! Come here and let me look at you."

Complying, Ellen curtsied and allowed herself to be turned about. "I apologize for arriving unannounced, only my sister intimated that Papa is out of sorts, and I am anxious to set him to rights."

"Oh, you have such the look of your mother about you." Aunt Charlotte led her to the settee. "Let me feed you, child. You too, Mrs. Croft. What shall you have? Tea? Chocolate? Coffee?"

"Mint tea, please," Ellen said quickly.

"You keep your father's diet, then." Aunt Charlotte gestured to a servant in the hall. "He is currently at his club, otherwise, I would retrieve him immediately to greet you. What is this about him being out of sorts?"

Ellen hesitated. It was one thing to feel overprotective of Papa and another to explain it to a woman she hardly knew. But Aunt Charlotte was family, no matter that they had only met once before.

"Sophia told me he is discouraged about the abolition bill and has been keeping to his rooms."

Aunt Charlotte frowned. Though her hair was mostly silver, her eyebrows were still dark and her face mostly uncreased. "I would not say discouraged. Just last night at supper, he was crowing over some of the recent conversations he had with the more conservative of the Whigs. He certainly hasn't been keeping to his rooms."

Ellen didn't know what to make of that. Perhaps Sophia had exaggerated for dramatic effect – but, no, Ellen was sure Sophia knew how that would make her worry.

"In any case," Aunt Charlotte continued, "I am beyond myself that you have joined us. Tonight you must rest, of course, but to-morrow, we are going to a lovely little salon at Mrs. Spurrier's. I'll write to let her know you will join us."

"Only if Papa is happy for me to attend."

Aunt Charlotte peered at Ellen. She looked to Aunt Croft, and something about the concept tickled them both, for they chuckled together like old friends. "Why, of course he shall be happy for you to attend. Why else would you be in London?"

Why indeed. Ellen's fingers itched for a chisel and a block of pine. If only she had stayed at Northfield Hall, she wouldn't be surrounded by silk and marble and Chinese wallpaper. Her body wouldn't still be rattling from the terrible city.

Max would still be in the sawpit, and Ellen's greatest concern would be how to ignore the ripple in his muscles as he worked the whipsaw.

It was at that moment that Sophia swanned into the room. In a fashionable green dress that rather resembled one of the columns outside, her hair swept in great poofs above her head, she was hardly recognizable.

"Do mine eyes deceive me? Why, Ellen, it truly is you!"

They embraced. Sophia's arms were as soft and welcoming as ever. But she smelled of a new perfume.

"You of all people should not be surprised," Ellen rebuked, releasing herself from her sister's grip. "You are the one who wrote me, after all."

"I didn't expect you to arrive so speedily." Sophia turned and kissed Aunt Croft's cheek. "I am so excited you are here. Papa will be glad. Perhaps Benny will even appear for supper one of these nights."

There was something about the way Sophia said it that pricked Ellen's suspicion. Her sister almost always spoke with a layer of irony, but now, she acted as if she meant every word she said. Ellen tested, "How is Papa? Aunt Charlotte says he has been in good spirits of late."

"Oh, but you know how Papa is." Sophia did not quite meet her eye. "Have you had any of Cook's pippin tarts yet? I vow, I have never tasted anything so good."

That must have been what the London set said. *I vow.* While swathed in cotton, wearing jewels stolen from conquered kingdoms, eating foods seasoned with West Indian sugar.

Sophia, apparently, hadn't even tried to resist temptation.

"No, I am not interested in food made from imports, and neither should you be."

"Oh, don't be such a bore. Here, Hannah is bringing them in now."

A maid set a silver tray of miniature crusted pies on the table before them. She also brought out porcelain teapots and cups for each person.

Ellen lifted the top off hers to ensure there really were only mint leaves brewing.

Sophia's tea poured out a rich brown color. Real tea, then. Papa had shown them paintings of tea plantations and the poor Indians and Chinese bent over picking the leaves. Condemned to do so for the rest of their lives, since the East India Company bullied them into selling the tea for too low prices.

"Really, Sophia, what would Mama say?"

Anger tightened Sophia's lips into a pinch. "Mama would encourage you to think for yourself, just as I have done."

It was suddenly too much. Ellen had travelled the full day, gotten her head further muddled over Max, and subjected herself to the wretched city all because her sister had said Papa needed her.

As if Sophia knew a thing about Papa. If he avoided her, it must only be because Sophia flouted everything he believed directly before his face.

Aunt Charlotte tittered nervously. "Ah, to be with sisters again, isn't that right, Mrs. Croft?"

Ellen launched from her seat. The porcelain teapot teetered on the table from her movement, but she didn't care whether it crashed and ruined the imported Arabian rug, anyhow.

"I find I am overtired. Please excuse me."

A servant showed her the way to her room. Sophia didn't chase after her. Alone, Ellen peeked out the window to the square below.

Max hadn't chased after her, either.

A BATH, HOT SHAVE, and proper set of clothes – administered by his valet, Downes, whom Max would never again undervalue – went a long way to restoring him to the Viscount Berwick. So, too, did the supper his mother hosted that night, which included eleven courses and eighteen guests. In a space of hours, Max shed the dusty persona of Mr. Sims to become the charming, witty, flirtatious Lord Berwick once again.

Although Max had to admit the dinner jacket fit a little too tightly around his arms after so many days in the sawpit. As well, his mind kept drifting away from the conversation, returning instead to Miss Preston hanging pale and vulnerable from the window of her hackney coach.

They would have said farewell eventually. He didn't know why it haunted him so that she had wanted him to take her all the way to Partridge House.

In any case, it was heaven to be in London again. French wine, properly-seasoned meats, sugared desserts, cigars in the smoking room. A mattress stuffed with goose feathers, and a coal fire in the hearth. Max slept clear until noon the next morning and didn't feel an ounce of guilt about it, even with Elinor the sheep judging him from her new perch on his bedside table.

He wondered how Miss Preston fared with her aunt. He tried to imagine her drinking coffee for the first time, but somehow, Max could only picture her puckering her nose. She would refuse it with some kind of judgment, like "I would rather not drink the blood of the West Indian slave," and leave everyone else in the room feeling like a perfect barbarian.

Max couldn't bring himself to turn down coffee, even knowing that it came from exploited labor.

Then his father summoned him to the conservatory. The Earl of Meretta famously kept country hours even in town, which meant he had been awake with the sun. He was rather in need of luncheon, Max thought, when he snapped in greeting, "You are supposed to be in Berkshire."

"A fine day to you, too, sir."

As always, Max felt awkwardly large in the presence of his father. The Earl of Meretta rose to no more than five feet five inches, and his features were as petite as his stature. Yet he did not move about the world as a small man. Rather, he made one feel like one was occupying too much space, particularly when he glared at Max's shoulder for catching the fronds of a palm tree.

"Have you abandoned your purpose so soon?" the earl asked, his attention on the small cactus he was currently repotting. Persuading tropical plants to grow in the English climate was one of his many interests.

As was finding reasons to complain about Max's comportment. "No, sir. I needed to return to London to confirm a theory."

He outlined what he knew about Berkshire linen, what he had observed at Northfield Hall, and Mr. Griswick's reaction to his questions. "If I am right, then Lord Preston funds his whole enterprise by selling linen outside his region."

"The bastard. After all that talk about only selling to the common man and keeping things local. I knew he was a hypocrite. Now, if only you could prove something criminal…"

Max wondered if, when excited about the report, he wore the same expression as the gleam in his father's eye now. It shone rather dark and maniacal in the strange light of the conservatory.

He shouldn't like Miss Preston to see him like that.

"I still need to check my theory," Max cautioned. "Talk to the shopkeepers, find out where they order it, not to mention discover whether it is included in any international exports." Though he doubted it. If Lord Preston was anything like his daughter, he wouldn't go *that* far beyond his principles.

"When will it be published? Preston is trying to force a vote on the abolition bill."

"A month." It was longer than Max needed. Long enough, perhaps, to satisfy Miss Preston.

Not that he owed her any satisfaction. She concerned herself with her father's needs, and he with the earl's.

"A fortnight would be better. The more air he wastes discussing abolition, the less I am able to advocate for actual governance. Getting Prinny in order and garnering a war budget. Each day you delay, our soldiers go without boots on their feet."

"Understood."

His father's attention returned to the cactus.

Max hesitated. Then cleared his throat. "I have been reading more about Great Yarmouth, so that I may be prepared."

The earl upended a planter so that its soil spilled to the ground. The sandy silt stank, though Max couldn't quite place what was off about it.

"The election is coming up fast. Perhaps you would announce my candidacy now, so that there is no needless speculation."

His father pointed an iron trowel at him. "Don't get distracted. Finish the report. Then we will discuss your future."

This time, the dismissal was clear.

CHAPTER TWELVE

THE NEXT MORNING, ELLEN agreed to take a walk with Sophia in the green that tied Aunt Charlotte's house with its neighbors, all similar temples to aristocratic largesse. Last evening, Papa had been overjoyed to discover Ellen, but too busy to sup with her because of his activities preparing for the vote next week. They had breakfasted together, and it was clear as day that he was in good spirits – had always been.

On their walk, Ellen decided to try to be pleasant and forgiving and remember that Sophia only had the best intentions at heart.

Except, Sophia never stopped talking. Ellen remembered that now. Somehow, in the month they had been separated, she had forgotten how her sister loved to run her mouth. How many opinions Sophia had, too, and how little she expected Ellen to participate in the conversation.

"Anyhow, you'll like Mrs. Spurrier," Sophia assured Ellen, wrapping up a trail of thoughts to which Ellen had long ago stopped paying attention. "I heard she discovered Mr. Spurrier's affair with a mistress and retaliated by carrying on with his valet!"

"And that's why I shall like her?"

Sophia pouted. "No, *you'll* like her because she is sympathetic to Papa's cause."

The underlying accusation – that Ellen was stuffy – was an old one among the siblings. As eldest, Ellen had always seen it as her duty to quash the younger ones' more ridiculous schemes, which in turn earned her a reputation as uninterested in anything fun.

Sophia usually only wielded it as a joke, though.

"It isn't Papa's cause," Ellen replied, weary of the topic. "It is a cause about which Papa is passionate, as am I. As should anyone who has a logical head on their shoulders and a compassionate heart in their breast."

"Must you sound so much like one of those Methodist preachers when you say so?" With a sigh, Sophia turned the corner of the path sharply. "Never mind, it's neither here nor there. I do not want to pick a quarrel with you."

"Then what *do* you want?" Frustration rushed forth at this first opportunity. "I left Northfield Hall in haste because of your letter. Traveled on the first stagecoach I could get rather than wait for a more sensible option. Not to mention, I left behind the shutters only half-finished. All to find that Papa is in no more need of me than the Prince Regent is!"

"How was I to know you would be so imprudent? It's not as though I wrote that he was dying. I thought you would think on it for a few days and then send for the carriage."

As if this were Ellen's fault.

"You wouldn't have come to London for any other reason, that you can admit, can't you?" Sophia didn't wait for Ellen to agree. "You only do things if you think they are in service to others. So, I invented a service. All is well that ends well. There is no need to be so surly to everyone about it."

Ellen *had* been surly, and she was impatient with herself about it – especially the way she had snapped at a footman earlier – but she certainly didn't appreciate Sophia pointing it out. "I did not come to London before because I did not *want* to come. It was not some kind of martyrdom. The sacrifice is that I am here instead of at home, where I would much prefer to be, finishing the shutters for the cottages."

It was unfair that she had to explain this to her sister, who was supposed to know Ellen better than anyone else living.

"Well, perhaps this will cheer you up." Sophia glanced over her shoulder to make sure the maid trailing them could not overhear. "Percy Thistleman will be at Mrs. Spurrier's salon tonight."

The name speared through the storm that had been clouding Ellen with anger and loneliness the past day. Percy, the rector's son. The square-jawed, serious-minded boy who had eagerly enjoyed her body in the private glades of Northfield Hall. A man who had once promised her marriage.

It was she who owed him a letter, Ellen suddenly remembered. Aunt Croft had been their intermediary, and sometime the summer following Percy's departure, Ellen had received a letter and never written a reply.

She had been unable to find anything interesting to say.

Sophia watched her carefully, an excited gleam in her dark eyes. Ellen frowned. "Never say you are being a romantic, Sophia Preston."

"Not a romantic." Though her lips curved into a mischievous smile. "Only I know you were fond of him once, and I thought you might be fond of him again. Especially when you hear his new position."

"Oh?" Ellen couldn't think what would be interesting, unless perhaps Percy had thrown off the clergyman's cloak and apprenticed himself to some trade.

"He leaves next month for Saint Kitts to lead a mission."

There was that gleam again. Sophia expected Ellen to be impressed by this news.

Did her sister know her so poorly?

The nicest thing Ellen could find to say was, "That sounds like Percy."

Sophia actually didn't speak for a moment. Uncertainty – rare for her – flickered across her face. It was a few steps before she said, "I rather thought it sounds like you, too."

"Me?" The weight pressing against Ellen's breast was familiar. Did everyone see only Ellen's outline, and not who she truly was? "I am hardly devout enough to be a missionary. Besides, you've heard Mr. Hamlyn's stories. The missionaries don't actually do abolition work. They only force the slaves to give up their religions while excusing the unholy behavior of the masters."

"I don't think of it as a matter of devotion. Being a missionary's wife is rather like what Mama did at Northfield Hall. Setting up a school, administering to the sick, offering solace and kindness to people who have been spurned elsewhere. You won't single-handedly abolish slavery, but you would make a difference to people in need." Sophia paused, then asked, "Isn't that what you want?"

Ellen remembered Mama as a joyous woman who delighted in every corner and soul of Northfield Hall. Laid out as a series of tasks, Sophia made it sound so sanctimonious. And dreadful.

Ellen wasn't at all sure she could stomach seeing the realities of slavery firsthand. She bore witness to it by listening to Mr. Hamlyn's recollections and by reading other accounts; if she were to see it day after day, she thought she might go mad. Or grow immune to it.

Neither option sounded very appealing.

Sophia took her silent ruminations as a cue to keep talking. "It sounded to me like the perfect kind of life for you. Better than marrying a peer of the realm, anyway."

"When did you go marriage mad?" Ellen objected. "I thought you were determined to remain a spinster to your deathbed."

A merry spinster with endless lovers, was Sophia's exact turn of phrase, but they were in public, after all.

"And so I am. You want to marry, though. I know you do. You were made to be a wife and mother, besides. What would you do without someone to care for?"

"Care for people at Northfield Hall," Ellen responded automatically.

They turned to begin the square path for a third time as Sophia exhaled in frustration. "I don't mean care for, like a nursemaid. I mean *care for*. As in, love. You always said you wanted a dozen children and a husband who would never leave your side. Surely you still want a family of your own?"

The image that popped into Ellen's mind was not very familial at all. It was Max, silhouetted by the posting inn's lamps, smiling down at her. A false memory: they had been arguing, so he would have been glaring.

Ellen shook it off. "What I want is to stay at Northfield Hall." Where she needn't worry about whose blood was spilled to secure the food passing into her mouth, and where she felt part of a community that depended upon each other to survive, and where she could carve her own path without minding how deeply she curtsied to anyone.

"Yes," Sophia said, as if speaking to Caroline, "but you can't stay there forever."

"What is your plan, then?"

"I am going to have an independent income as a governess," Sophia supplied. "Once Benny marries, Northfield Hall will change, you know. He and his wife will need the rooms, and they may redesign, and who knows what else they will do when Benny inherits. You don't want to be an old woman cared for by your nieces and nephews when they need a handy chaperone, do you?"

That didn't seem much worse than a governess, but neither fate appealed.

Ellen supposed it would be too much to expect she could simply work in the carpentry workshop until she dropped dead. And she did want to marry and have children.

Just not as a missionary.

"So, to be clear, you called me to London because you want to marry me off to Percy Thistleman?"

Sophia huffed defensively. "I don't *want* to marry you off. However, this is your last chance to marry Mr. Thistleman before he leaves indefinitely for Saint Kitts. I thought you should have the opportunity to consider it, at least. He is still very handsome."

Ellen didn't quite remember his face. And – compared to the way Max had set her on fire with mere kisses – she didn't think Percy's touch was quite as exciting as she had initially experienced it.

Still, pushing through her surliness at being tricked to London, Ellen could admit her sister made some salient points. She could, at the very least, think on it.

"I'll see how I feel after meeting him again," Ellen decided.

Sophia grinned that gleaming, mischievous smile. "It wouldn't hurt to kiss him once or twice, to be sure."

But Ellen's imagination had already leapt from meeting Mr. Thistleman to encountering someone else at Mrs. Spurrier's party. A viscount with a smirk and particularly strong shoulders.

Max wouldn't be there. If he was, he wouldn't acknowledge her. Neither should she acknowledge him.

Those facts didn't stop her from daydreaming.

IN THE EVENING, MAX accepted his mother's invitation to escort her to a salon hosted by their cousin, Mrs. Spurrier. The woman had never held a title, married further beneath the family bloodline, and had Whiggish tendencies, but she was a favorite relation on account of her good sense of humor. "We'll only stay long enough to be polite," Lady Berwick promised in the carriage. "Then on to Lady Randal's crush. Or we could stop in at Almack's, if you so desire."

"I would rather eat glass." There was only one reason to attend the Almack's assembly, and that was to present oneself as a future husband.

He hoped Miss Preston did not find herself at Almack's. Though he supposed one day, she would marry. Some undeserving Whig, no doubt.

The thought made Max rather ill.

Mrs. Spurrier's three parlor rooms were practically bursting with people when they arrived to the salon. Seeing his mother to a seat with their hostess, Max began to make his rounds. The crowd invigorated him; it had been too long – over a month! – since his last party, and despite the crush, he had missed the conviviality, the challenge of a witty conversation, the easy ridicule of people making cakes of themselves.

"Have you seen the poor creatures in that corner over there?" his friend, George Hisk, asked from the champagne table, a little nod indicating behind Max.

"Be more specific." Max helped himself to a flute of champagne and a roll of cold boiled ham.

"Drab clothes. They don't fit properly, do they, Lady Sylvester?" – this an aside to their other companion, who was always up for a good insult – "and they are terrible colors. The man is in black. Oh, perhaps he is clergy. The poor woman's gown is faded to the color of dust. They have been talking to each other and no one else for at least a quarter of an hour, which must be because they are so dour that no one else can stomach their conversation. Although you might like a go at the female, Hainsworth, given her hair."

A premonition sunk Max's stomach even before Lady Sylvester leaned in to say, "Oh, but didn't you know, Hisk? That is the eldest Miss Preston, recently arrived from the country."

He managed to stop himself from whirling around. Taking a deep sip of his drink, Max casually rearranged himself so he could survey the room. It didn't take him long to spot her. She was exactly as George described –

Only so much more.

Max recognized her gown as the pink one she had worn that Sunday she discovered his scheme. She had added white ribbons to it as a nod to style. Her hair shone in the candlelight, pinned up and free of any covering. Of most interest to him was her face, tilted upwards toward her companion and suspended with animation as she spoke.

Hot jealousy surged his stomach. He wanted her to be speaking to *him*.

"Have you been introduced?" Max asked Lady Sylvester. He couldn't admit to knowing Miss Preston, after all. He had to request a formal introduction, or else spark a hundred rumors.

Lady Sylvester laughed. "I can't imagine why I would have been."

Max excused himself to find Mrs. Spurrier, who was more than happy to oblige. "That is so kind of you, Lord Berwick, but of course I would expect nothing less. Miss Preston has only just arrived to town and hardly knows a soul. Ah, now, here she is."

He couldn't explain why his heart sped up as they approached her, but it did. His hands grew clammy, too. He waited for her to notice them approaching, but Miss Preston's attention was entirely on her companion. Then Mrs. Spurrier interrupted.

Miss Preston's eyes widened, seeing Max. Her face paled. In fact, for a moment, he was afraid she would faint.

He bowed. "Miss Preston. A pleasure to meet you."

She curtsied. The graceful little bob a dozen women had already executed that afternoon upon meeting him. It felt strange – as disorienting as if Mrs. Spurrier started calling him Maximilian instead of Berwick. Up until now, Max had been the inferior to Miss Preston.

As she rose, he flashed back to the moment in that shed when she had breathed out his name.

Her companion spoke before she could. "An honor to meet you, Lord Berwick. Of course, I knew our hostess Mrs. Spurrier is acquainted with your family but I never imagined an introduction myself. How do you find the salon?"

Mrs. Spurrier, who used the man's soliloquy to extricate herself from their group, had mentioned this man's name. Max did not remember it at all. Moreover, he resented being forced to tear his eyes away from Miss Preston. "Delightful, as Mrs. Spurrier's gatherings always are. Don't you agree, Miss Preston?"

She had regained some of her color. Max wished he could tell how she felt about encountering him. "It is my first of such events, my lord, but I am sure I cannot disagree with you. I am certainly delighted to discover I know some people here, Mr. Thistleman included."

This, with a nod to their companion, informed Max of his name. Jealousy heated him again: he hated not only that she knew Mr. Thistleman but also that she could declare it publicly. Max surveyed the man more closely, noting his thick hair, handsome jaw, and well-pressed – if ill-fitting – clothes.

Mr. Thistleman was the kind of man Miss Preston might admire.

The thought soured Max's stomach.

Without prompting, the clergyman explained, "Miss Preston was quite dear to me when I stayed with my father at Thatcham a few years ago. That was when I awaited a curacy, of course. When I met her sister Miss Sophia a week ago at Vauxhall's, I said, Miss Sophia, you simply *must* convince Miss Preston to come to London before I go. And here she is!"

Max watched her lips draw into a flat line. Annoyance, he thought. At this man's endless speech or her sister, Max couldn't quite guess.

"I sail in July for Saint Kitts," Mr. Thistleman continued. "I am leading a mission to baptize those poor slaves. If we cannot free their flesh, we must at least free their souls, as I was just saying to Miss Preston. Do you not agree, Lord Berwick?"

Having never much thought about the state of an enslaved man's soul, Max didn't have a ready opinion. Except, Mr. Thistleman grated on his nerves. So he said, "Why should a man whose master worships God almighty on Sunday morning and whips him senseless that afternoon find solace in believing in Jesus Christ?"

While Thistleman sputtered, Max slid a glance over to Miss Preston, who made a point of not looking at him.

"The one has nothing to do with the other," Thistleman said. "Miss Preston was just agreeing with me that the missionaries are doing the most important work towards abolition of the great sin of slavery. Why—"

"Pardon me, Mr. Thistleman," Miss Preston interrupted. "I was agreeing with you that we must abolish slavery. However, I am not sure my opinion is the same as yours on the role of the missionary. Should not your guidance be directed towards showing the plantation owner the error of his ways?"

This seemed to startle the clergyman. "I have not explained myself well, Miss Preston, if you cannot understand my point." He started gearing up towards a lecture, almost pawing at the ground like a racehorse.

Max had humored the man long enough. "Mr. Thistleman, I cannot help but notice Miss Preston has run out of punch."

The man took the cue like an actor on stage. With a deep bow, he said, "Allow me to fetch you a fresh glass," and rushed off into the crowd.

Miss Preston appraised Max with a cool, unreadable look. "You know I will not drink the punch."

"Too much blood in it." What a rush it was to have her alone. They had only been parted for a day, yet Max felt as if he had agonized through years without her company. "Have you seen Mrs. Spurrier's collection of Chinese scrolls? You shall find them utterly abominable and may lecture me on the evils of importation."

Her lips twitched in a hint of a smile. Max felt almost giddy, having earned that. Or perhaps he was giddy merely from being in the same building as her. Leading her through the crowd, Max could admit to himself that there had been barely a moment this past day when Miss Preston had not been in his thoughts.

Ensconced in her presence, he didn't feel the need to interrogate that fact.

The scrolls were featured in an upper story corridor, away from the main rooms. Only a few other bunches of people milled about. Up there, the air was cool as the evening sky, and it was quiet enough that Max could hear Miss Preston's exhales.

"How do you find your father?" he asked as they paused before the first silk scroll, a sprawling ink painting of mountains and waterfalls and rocks.

Miss Preston looked at Max. It felt like the first time her eyes had landed on him all evening.

He would have been happy if she never looked away.

"He is well," she said at last. "In good spirits and in good health. My sister, it seems, exaggerated in hopes that I would join her in the Season."

That fit with everything Max had heard about Miss Sophia at Northfield Hall. A mischief maker. "Her scheme succeeded."

"Yes." Miss Preston walked on to the next painting – which was another landscape featuring mountain and waterfall and rock.

Max would ordinarily admire Miss Sophia's scheme. Except he had been seated next to Miss Preston that entire journey to London. It was not kind to make a person worry so, only for one's own amusement.

He didn't know how to say as much to Miss Preston. He wasn't sure she would want to hear it. Besides, there were still three other couples admiring the Chinese paintings. "How do you find London? Do you understand now why so many of us consider it the center of the world?"

"It is—" She took a deep breath. Her pointed chin raised, which Max knew meant she was trying to find strength in kindness. He waited for some diplomatic response.

Then her shoulders sagged. "There are too many people here. Not enough space. I can barely see the sun for all the buildings and the smoke. Everything – everything – is made from imports. And no one cares. Not even my sister. Only Papa and me and I don't know about Benny. The people here tonight have been staring at me like I am some strange curiosity. They talk to me as if I am an idiot. All because I have some principles."

Impossible principles. Max didn't voice the thought. "I'm sure that's not true."

Miss Preston's fingers tangled furiously with a ribbon on her dress. "And why are you speaking to me? I thought you and your father loathe my family. Surely you should be asking Mrs. Spurrier to eject me from her house. Or do your friends think you have brought me up here as some kind of humiliation, to rub my nose in our hostess's Oriental collection?"

Was that how she saw him? Did she believe him to be nothing more than a petty schemer? Max swung his gaze back to the scrolls. "I am delighted to see you here. That's the sum total of my motivations." Although he didn't quite feel he had made his point. It was one thing for the earl to cast him as a frivolous fop; that was the moral right of fathers. Miss Preston knew him better than that. Or at least, Max had tried to make her know him better than that.

Perhaps this whole time, Miss Preston had dismissed his honesty as drivel.

She remained silent, although a flush had crept up her neck, pink skin clashing with her magnificent red hair. Max pressed, "Are you not delighted to see me, too?"

Miss Preston dropped her ribbons. Looked down at her hands. And, as if sentencing herself to death, admitted, "Of course I am."

IT WAS INSUFFERABLE, THE way Max beamed at her. Ellen was supposed to keep away from him, and yet he looked at her like *that*.

She should have lied. All she had to do was tell him she wished she had never set eyes on him. Then Max would leave her alone, and she wouldn't have to do any work of ignoring the way her heart began racing the instant he approached.

It would have been more convenient if Ellen's body had responded this way to Percy. He was perfectly handsome in a bland kind of way, though his cheeks hung with jowls rather more than Ellen remembered. He had been hanging onto her for the entire party, alternating between rhapsodizing about her beauty and lecturing her on his plans for Saint Kitts. Ellen had tried – really, she had – to be excited to see him. To imagine herself inside the life he plotted.

She would keep trying. Until she no longer felt Max's gaze as if it were fingerprints across her skin, and until she could decide clear-headed whether Percy's life was the one for her.

Max moved along to the next painting. "Ah, just what I needed. Another stream falling from a mountain."

"Didn't your tutors teach you anything? Even my ten-year-old sister could look at this and see more than a stream falling from the mountain."

"Could she?" Max pretended to pull spectacles from his pocket and placed them on his nose. "Ah, yes, through my ten-year-old glasses, I can see this is a masterpiece. The technique! The composition! The miniscule people he included in that distant path!"

He mocked her. But he softened it at the end by stepping close and placing the invisible spectacles on her face. His gloved fingertips brushed like ghosts against her cheek.

"There, now you tell me what you see."

She willed herself to still be cross with Max. "I see the context. This is a scroll from the Yuan dynasty. That's when the Mongols conquered China, and the scholars were censored or expelled from the ruling class. The mountain is China. It is always there, will always exist. The stream is the imperial rulers. Present but not constant, impactful on China without erasing China. And the people are the Chinese, who must simply trust the path is taking them in the right direction." Ellen's words were not her own but Mr. Chow's – or at least, what she remembered of them. Vivid in her memory was the afternoon when he had climbed up to their schoolroom to unroll his tattered print and explain its significance. His voice had gone rough with homesickness.

If he had stayed in China, he would have applied to become a scholar. He might have begun painting himself. Instead, he had eloped with Mrs. Chow, gotten work with Viscount Folkestone, and fated himself to life on the opposite side of the world.

Behind her, someone clapped. "Oh, brava! I had no idea this art had so much to say!"

Ellen caught the annoyance on Max's face as they turned to discover their observer. She was glad she was not alone in wishing the newcomer away.

In fact, it was a couple, middle-aged and dressed head-to-toe in imported goods. Their eyes swept over her with unabashed curiosity as the woman continued, "Why, you must be an artist yourself!"

This, Ellen supposed, was a commentary on her day dress, which Sophia insisted looked very poor. Ellen hadn't cared when she entered the party, and she reminded herself that she still didn't care, no matter that Max stood right there, observing the exchange.

He had likely already condemned her outfit along with all her other beliefs.

Except, he was delighted to see her.

"No, ma'am," she responded, "only a connoisseur."

"Lord and Lady Bowden, may I present Miss Preston, daughter of the second Baron Ashforth?" There was an edge to Max's introduction. Ellen liked to think it was a warning to the others not to slight her. But it could also have been a warning to her not to embarrass him.

She curtsied.

"You are recently come to London, are you not?" Lord Bowden asked. "I've heard of what it is like at Northfield Hall. Come to see how people live in the real world, eh?"

His phrasing made it plain what answer he wanted. Like every other peer in this godforsaken town, Lord Bowden wanted to gloat that even Papa's daughters couldn't stand being banished to a medieval lifestyle such as the one at Northfield Hall.

Ellen wished she could shut her eyes and transport herself back to Mr. Chow's workshop.

Max saved her from answering. "What is your opinion on importing artwork, Bowden? We all know that blood sugar is an evil we should do without, but what about prints like these? Is it inherently sinful for a British man to bring artwork back with him from a trip to Foochow?"

What a chameleon Max was. Insisting to her one day that he didn't care about the labor behind sugar, then throwing out *blood sugar* as a banner of virtue the next. Ellen didn't know which version of him to believe.

"I cannot see the harm in it," Lord Bowden said before shifting his gaze to Ellen expectantly.

He thought he was baiting her. That she would launch into some lecture like Percy that later he and his wife could pick apart and laugh at.

"If one can make assumptions such as that the artist is not compelled to produce the artwork for low wages and that the artwork's owner is paid fairly for parting with it, then I agree," she said as placidly as possible. "The issue is never with the physical item itself but instead the context in which it is procured."

"There is that word again," Max murmured. Almost as if the comment were only for the two of them. "Context."

"Isn't that what all debates are truly about? We do not argue that the poor riot over bread prices. We argue over the context: is it because they are lazy and ungrateful, or because the government spends too much on the war and parties? My family does not argue that linen gowns are prettier than muslin, only that the context of procuring muslin is unacceptable. You ask for my opinion of London because you think I will have changed my mind after seeing the context of all these worldly goods."

Max clasped his hands behind his back. "What about when the context changes? If Scotland's crops all fail, will your family send its surplus north to feed our poor countrymen, or even under that context, would you restrict your estate to selling at local markets?"

Heat spread across her cheeks. Ellen was used to debates in her family's drawing room, where there were no observers who might turn around and whisper afterwards. "We do not limit our sales to Berkshire out of some blind malice. It is only that we have limited surplus, and why not offer it to our neighbors first? In an instance such as the one you propose, I am sure we would do all we could to assist the hungry."

"But you do not currently sell any products outside of Berkshire," Max persisted. There was an intensity to his gaze that felt new and significant.

Ellen didn't know what to make of it. "No, we don't."

For a moment longer, Max looked at her – and only her. Then he turned to Lord and Lady Bowden. "I promised I would return Miss Preston to her aunt within the quarter hour. Will you excuse us?"

Ellen curtsied, as expected, and followed Max out the way they had come. Instead of taking the stairs back down to the party, however, Max looked to his left and right, then – out of view of anyone – waved her into a side room. It was some kind of morning room with delicate armchairs and the smell of wood polish in its air. Shutting the door, Max dragged a low cabinet to lean against it.

No one would enter the room by surprise.

Her body heated with immediate, stupid desire.

"Max, we shouldn't."

He cocked his eyebrow. "Shouldn't *what*?"

"You know very well what I mean." Her fingers caught her skirt in bunches.

Max stalked towards her. His legs were so long, he was breathing on her within just a few steps. "Why not? Did you not enjoy it last time?"

Somehow, Ellen summoned the strength *not* to kiss him, even though he was so delectably close. "Are you still writing your report?"

"Yes." At least he didn't lie. His eyes dipped away from hers.

"Then we cannot do this. You have your principles, and I have mine." Oh, but his breath was so hot on her cheek. Ellen swallowed. "You are going to take your seat in the House of Commons."

Max remained where he was, not quite touching her. Yet Ellen's nerves were on fire, as if his very gaze caressed her skin. "While you will...what? Marry a Whig and rally your friends against me in every Parliamentary battle? Start an orphanage for the urchins of London? Build cottages across the countryside for landless peasants?"

Once upon a time, Max might have said this to tease her. He was serious now. Honest. She shut her eyes and focused on the linen in her palms. "Whatever my future holds, it will be in service of others. That much, I know."

"That did not stop us before." He trailed one finger, soft in kidskin, down the line of her cheekbone. "You are fond of me, aren't you, Miss Preston? I can't quite recall if you ever said."

She was still Miss Preston to him, then. Even in the honesty of this moment.

Ellen wondered if he only liked her for the thrill of fucking Lord Preston's daughter. Or perhaps it was the hair: she did seem to be the only ginger-haired woman at the salon.

"It does not matter whether I am fond of you, if you still plan on publishing an account of Northfield Hall in your paper."

"By that logic, only like-minded individuals can be fond of each other." He spoke in a murmur that whispered across her cheek like a breeze. "Can we not respect each other from opposing viewpoints? Or are you condemning yourself to the exclusive company of people like that missionary, who are so full of their own importance they cannot tell when to stop speaking?"

"*You* are full of your own importance, too." She liked it in Max, though. He knew his own arrogance, and he didn't mind laughing at it – as he did now, a little intimate chuckle.

Percy, on the other hand, had tired her with his opinions within the first five minutes of renewing acquaintance. Or rather, he had spent those first five minutes regaling her with opinions without asking her a single question.

The life of a missionary's wife might be precisely the calling for Ellen. But she couldn't imagine surviving with Percy as her husband.

Max stepped back. "I don't mean to push you. I am simply intoxicated at finding myself in your presence again, when I had thought we wouldn't mingle in the same company. Let me return you to your aunt now."

It was the parting that was her undoing. The sudden absence of his heat. The prospect of returning to that party, with everyone sneering at her.

Latching onto his arm, Ellen pulled Max back and threw herself upwards into a kiss.

He moved his mouth to her ear before it could elaborate into anything deeper than a peck. "The trick to illicit trysts at a party like this is to touch only where clothing will hide any marks." Hands roving to cup her arse, Max navigated them as one to an armchair by the empty fireplace. He landed in the seat and positioned her to straddle him. "We can't use our mouths at all."

That barely felt like a constraint with Max pulling her skirts slowly upwards, letting the hems trail on her bare thigh. Just that was enough to make her quim quiver.

She was wicked to want him so much when he was so very wrong for her.

"What about hands?" she asked. She could feel the hard ridge of his member teasing her arse through his trousers. She wanted to free it. To hold it in her palms and watch him grow helpless in her grasp.

"Only if you take off your gloves." Even as he said it, Max discarded his gloves and started unbuttoning hers at the elbow.

Ellen ground down against his lap, too impatient to wait for bare hands. Max let out a little groan.

Pulling off her gloves, Max captured her right fingers and brought them down with his own hand to touch her quim. She felt her wetness alongside his carpenter's calluses. "You're wet enough to leave a stain on my trousers," Max breathed.

"So take them off." Not waiting for his response, Ellen opened his fall front, so handily designed to free his cock from the stricture of clothing. It stood at an angle, throbbing angrily to match her quim's impatience.

She coated her palm with her own juices, then slid it around Max's member. "Is this one of your principles?" she teased, watching his head tip backwards in delight. "Always find a pretty girl to fuck at a salon?"

"Not a principle, just luck." Grinning, Max dipped his finger against her again, tracing her folds. Her rhythm around his cock grew irregular as he teased her. "My principle is to always make the pretty girl peak so hard she'll fantasize about me for the rest of her life."

"You have already achieved that principle for me, but I invite you to try again." Ellen braced her spare hand against his shoulder. She wished it were bare, that they were in the workshop surrounded by the smell of wood. She could add that to a fantasy later, in Max's honor. For now, she focused on how his lips fell slack as she increased her pace, and how he tried to match it with his own fingers against her quim.

It wasn't enough to hold him in her hand any longer.

"I want you inside me."

Max groaned again. His hands moved to frame her hips beneath her petticoats. It took only a little maneuvering to position herself, and then his cock slid in.

It was immediate pleasure. The kind that evaporated all thought from her mind. And that was good. Ellen wrapped her arms about his neck, her forehead against his ear. He didn't smell like sawdust anymore. Only skin and a little sweat and some fruited hair pomade.

He drove the rhythm from beneath, thrusting deeper and deeper inside her with fast jerks. Ellen pushed downwards in response, grinding her hips into his. Max's hands squeezed her arse beneath her shift. She felt mounted, overwhelmed, overjoyed.

And then he changed his angle. Filled her long and hard in a new way that was like unlocking a secret. Before she could understand it, she exploded. Pleasure spilled into every corner of her body.

Max lifted her away, draped her in the chair, and stumbled towards the fireplace before catching his own orgasm in a handkerchief.

He settled at her feet, her ankles dangling from her perch as they both basked in the afterglow. Ellen didn't care for the cut of the London suit. She wanted him naked, or at least in his loose work shirt.

She reached out to trail a finger across his jaw. "You have lived up to your principle again, Lord Berwick."

"Then I will sleep well tonight." Catching her hand, Max started fitting her glove to her fingers. Taking them off had been seductive. Putting them back on felt intimate in a new, different way.

Ellen's thoughts returned to the debate earlier. The way Max had thrust that question upon her, as if she alone could make the moral choice. "I am not the arbiter of right and wrong, you know. I try to live my life in the best manner possible, but that does not mean I always know what that manner is."

"I know." Their eyes tangled as he worked the buttons at her elbows. "You have spent more time thinking about right and wrong than I have, though. For example, I have been wondering..."

For a moment, it seemed he wouldn't complete the thought. The bliss had disappeared from his face, replaced by something more thoughtful and inscrutable. Finishing with her gloves, Max kissed her covered fingertips.

At last, he asked, "Should I offer to marry you?"

"No." She said it before she could even feel the way his phrasing battered her. "We do not suit." If he *wanted* to marry her, Max would have asked it differently.

He would have changed his mind about Northfield Hall.

"Quite." Max fixed his fall front, tucked his shirt back in, and stood. "I'll leave the room first and ask your aunt to find you, on account of your having come down with a megrim."

Max glanced backwards at her. Guilt in his hazel eyes. Or was it pity?

Either way, he shoved the cupboard back in place and left the room.

Chapter Thirteen

*Northfield Hall operates by its own set of rules,
which, to the outsider, appear dangerously stupid.
For example, instead of references, I simply spun a
sob story about being a reformed convict recently returned from Van Diemen's Land. Not only did they
give me a position, but they paid me thrice: in wages,
in food and board, and in free access to materials
such as homespun fabric. What, your correspondent
asks, keeps a murderer from claiming a position,
eating himself fat, and slaying every one of his filthy
thirsts at the first new moon?*

MAX SHOOK OUT HIS hand. He barely knew what he had just
written. His mind kept wandering – or rather, sprinting –
back to the previous evening. Marriage. What a fucking fool. Max

had enjoyed plenty of women of all classes and never once had he been seized with such idiocy as he had with Miss Preston.

Should I offer to marry you?

Like some kind of simpleton.

From the windowsill, Elinor the sheep condemned him for having asked the question at all.

It was only that Max was accustomed to trysts with married ladies or fallen women. At Northfield, he had easily forgotten that Miss Preston must one day catch herself a respectable husband.

He should have remembered better yesterday. Miss Preston might have to marry one of those very fops sneering over their champagne glasses at her. Max should be protecting her reputation, not fucking it to shreds in the spare morning room.

He forced his attention back to his draft. He was trying to arrange all the details of living at Northfield Hall in such a way that would keep the reader's interest while still making his key points. Homicide, however, seemed to be taking it too far, even though it might sell the most newspapers.

MURDERERS AT NORTHFIELD HALL!

Miss Preston would never speak to him again.

He had been at this futile draft all morning. Every time he wrote a paragraph, he struck it out for being too macabre or melodramatic or dry. The problem was that Max didn't yet have a point to make, beyond what everyone already knew: Northfield Hall was different, which made it an uncomfortable place to be.

Although Max couldn't help wishing himself there, if it meant he could kiss Miss Preston under the lilacs.

Pushing away from his desk, he called for his hat. He would do better to find his evidence rather than dither on with this draft.

Max visited three different stores, whose addresses he had found in advertisements in *The Times*, that claimed to sell Berkshire linen. Located at various points along the fashionable New Bond Street, the shops all catered to the richest in England: their storefronts were freshly painted; they boasted various fashion supplies such as silk ribbons and ivory buttons; and they also offered coffee or tea from delicate silver dishes for the waiting customer. At two of them, their stores of Berkshire linen were completely out, but all three were happy to provide him the name of the mercer who supplied the fabric. A Mr. Martin at 100 Salmon Lane, Limehouse.

Unfortunately, that direction was near the dockyards, meaning the linen could have been shipped from anywhere in the world before being branded as a Berkshire creation.

From the last shop, Max purchased a small sample square of the linen. The shopkeeper leaned close to point out the fine weaving, including the little idiosyncrasies that proved it to be from a handloom. "I am down to my last two bolts of it," the man said apologetically, "and Lady Pemberly asked me to save those for her. Later in the summer, I should have more, my lord."

Max waved the man away, biting down a smile. How lucky for him that of all the ladies of the realm, it was the Countess of Pemberly – Miss Preston's aunt – who had ordered the last of the Berkshire linen.

Why, even the Earl of Meretta would surely agree that required Max to pay a visit to Partridge House.

In another stroke of luck, it was the countess's afternoon at home, which meant she had dressed to match her wallpaper, set out silver trays of food and drink, and received sycophants for hours on end.

Max spotted Miss Preston as soon as he entered, sitting with embroidery beside the countess. In her white linen and lace cap, she looked every bit the part of demure virgin waiting for a man to whisk her into marriage.

Yearning twisted in Max's gut. She was right, of course: Max could never marry her, not when she hated so very much about the way he lived his life.

That didn't stop him from wanting her anyway.

On her other side sat a brunette, both taller and wider than Miss Preston, in a muslin afternoon gown that dipped low across generous breasts. They didn't resemble each other, yet from the way the brown-haired girl moved, Max could tell this was Miss Sophia. The sister who had tricked Miss Preston – and him – away from Northfield Hall.

Also in the room were a dark-haired man, a young debutante and her chaperone, and Mr. Thistleman. The latter hovered behind Miss Preston and, upon Max's entrance, was laughing too loudly at something Miss Sophia had said.

The ensemble welcomed him with an array of expressions: delight from the countess, confusion from Mr. Thistleman, narrowed interest from Miss Sophia. As for Miss Preston, she smiled – a blossoming of relief across her face.

She was glad to see him.

Max caught himself just before echoing back a stupidly big grin.

"Lord Berwick, what a surprise!" the countess exclaimed. "Do have a seat. I was sorry we had to leave last night before I had a chance to catch up with you. Where have you been hiding this whole Season?"

"My lady, you would not believe me if I told you." Max bent over the lady's hand and received introductions to the debutante – a Miss Fairchurch – her mother, and the dark-haired man, who turned out to be Miss Preston's brother Benjamin.

"Tea or coffee?" the countess offered as she ushered Max into the armchair beside her.

In his periphery, Max saw Miss Preston's lips twitch. No wonder she had snapped with impatience yesterday. She may as well have been staying in the East India warehouses themselves with the amount of imports in her aunt's house. He replied, "I would prefer to follow the Preston family's lead and have whatever drink they have deemed least offensive."

Miss Preston raised a wry eyebrow. "That would be a rose tisane, my lord."

"How wise of you to broaden your taste, Lord Berwick," Benjamin Preston interjected, his tone tilting towards sarcasm. "Our late mother swore by rose tisane at least once a week to fortify one's constitution."

As Max accepted the tisane from the countess, he considered his possible replies. Miss Preston had reacted immediately upon learning Max's identity; no doubt young Preston was similarly threatened by his presence. Even as Miss Preston shot a communicative glance at her brother, he only watched Max with a steady gaze.

It was Mr. Thistleman that saved Max from a reply. "I myself developed a fondness for tisanes of all sorts during my time at Thatcham. Lord Preston has many useful ideas by which we should all live. He is, if I may say so, my most significant mentor outside the clergy."

"Oh? I did not know you corresponded regularly with my father." This came cool as ice from Miss Preston.

"A mentor when we meet in person, I meant to say," Mr. Thistleman corrected. "I have not had the opportunity to correspond regularly with anyone save my own family these last years."

The undercurrent of their conversation was palpable. Miss Preston was unhappy with Mr. Thistleman's comments, but Max could not quite figure out why. Perhaps she was protective of who laid claim to her father's attention.

Perhaps she simply found Mr. Thistleman as annoying as Max did.

From the other settee, Miss Fairchurch asked, "Have you been making many visits today already, Lord Berwick?"

The debutante was willowy, blonde, and wont to flutter her eyelashes, as if that would so captivate Max that he would spontaneously offer marriage.

Benjamin leaned forward to obstruct Miss Fairchurch's view of Max. Of more interest to Max, Miss Preston tightened her lips into a firm, annoyed line.

In lieu of whisking Miss Preston away to a private room, Max responded as if the debutante had stolen his heart. "None. This is the first and only salon I am visiting this afternoon, and perhaps even this whole week." Having earned another flutter of eyelashes, Max turned to the countess. "Actually, I have just come from New Bond Street, where I am informed the Countess of Pemberly has claim to all the remaining bolts of Berkshire linen that are to be found in London. I wonder how you came to be so lucky."

Miss Preston's eyes darted upwards in alarm as the countess responded, "Now, Lord Berwick, I can hardly give you my secrets, otherwise it will be the Countess of Meretta who is the best-dressed matron of London, not me." Then, holding out a length of her generous skirt, she added, "If you will indulge some impropriety, you may examine the linen here. It is the perfect weight for summertime, especially for an old woman like me who cannot wear a delicate muslin without looking like a stuffed doll."

Max leaned forward to see the same confident weaving as on the sample provided by the shopkeeper.

"Why are you so interested in Berkshire linen?" Miss Preston asked. As if hearing the sharpness in her own tone, she added – with an imitative flutter of eyelashes – "If you don't mind my inquiring, my lord."

"Or is it the Earl of Meretta who is interested?" her brother pressed.

Max bristled. That he would jump at his father's orders like a puppet, with no brain of his own, insulted him.

Even if there were a tiny bit of truth to the accusation.

Max smoothed on a smile. "Why, I am merely trying to follow your family's example to understand how my favorite products are manufactured." Unfolding the sample fabric from his jacket pocket, Max offered it to Miss Preston. "I know Northfield Hall has its own textiles. Can you tell me whether this linen is similar to what you produce?"

Her gray eyes met his. As she ran her fingers across its weave, Max remembered those same fingers running across him yesterday. He shifted in his seat, commanding his thoughts back to his mission.

"It was woven by a handloom, that much I can say."

"Then you may rest easy, Lord Berwick, knowing no children were employed in the steam manufactories to make your linen." Benjamin clapped his hands together, as if to finish the subject. "Thistleman, how go your preparations for Saint Kitts?"

"It is a headache, sir, but one I welcome with eager arms." As Thistleman launched into a lengthy explanation of choosing the correct trunk for the sea voyage, Miss Preston returned the sample fabric to Max. She was careful to keep her face blank, but that was enough for Max to read. He wasn't surprised when, announcing his own departure after another ten minutes of interminable conversation, Miss Preston made an excuse to follow him out of the room.

"What is your interest in Berkshire linens?" she asked when they were alone in the corridor, save the footmen posted along the way.

The sun filtered through Partridge House's endless windows to bathe Miss Preston in white light. Her hair shone red as fire even beneath the lace cap. Every fiber of Max's being called out to spirit her into a spare room and lock the door.

"Does it have to do with your report?"

"Yes."

He opened his mouth to explain, but she rushed to say, "Northfield Hall barely has enough surplus to supply Thatcham with linen, much less London. You must be mistaken."

So she had said multiple times now. Max eyed her as he asked, "Would you still like me to be honest with you?"

She glanced up and down the corridor. For a moment, Max thought she might really pull him into privacy, and his whole body responded. In the end, however, she simply whispered: "Yes."

"Mr. Griswick all but confirmed to me that Northfield Hall linen ends up in London. I am gathering evidence to prove that your father has been selling it."

It felt foul as he said it. Max didn't mind the report, didn't mind holding Lord Preston accountable to the ideas that he espoused; but he *did* mind that it hurt Miss Preston as he did so.

She lifted her chin. "You won't prove it because it is not true. It can't be."

"I am going tomorrow morning to the mercer who supplies the shops with linen. He should be able to tell me once and for all where the fabric comes from."

"And if it is Northfield Hall?" Miss Preston still whispered, which delivered her words hot and intense into the air. "How could that be worth writing about?"

He did not actually need to explain this to her. She was the one whose very backbone was made of Northfield Hall principles. "It wouldn't be, except your father has spent years arguing that prices of goods should be based on what the common man can afford, not driven by the richest person willing to pay for them. Meanwhile, a yard of Berkshire linen costs more than my own monthly allowance. Not to mention that your father preaches about shopping with merchants who restrict their goods to free labor products, yet Berkshire linen is sold in shops that also stock cotton and silk."

With each of these points, Miss Preston grew paler. Even the freckles framing her cheeks seemed to fade.

Guilt washed over him again, and he took her hand, no matter that the servants could see. "I could be wrong."

"You are." But she didn't sound sure at all. Her fingers squeezed around his, and Max cursed that he wore gloves. "I will come with you tomorrow," she murmured, stepping close enough that they could have kissed. "To hear it from the merchant myself."

An unwise idea. She had a reputation to maintain, and traipsing to the dockyards with the Earl of Meretta's heir would spark the worst controversy, if anyone found out.

But there was a steel to Miss Preston's eyes that said she would brook no argument. Max didn't have it in him to refuse.

Especially since it meant he would steal a few hours in her company.

"You would have to be in disguise."

"Fine." Her lips twitched into a smile. "I shall be your maid, Miss Sims."

"Mrs. Sims. My housekeeper." The role added respectability. The fantasy of a marriage – even between two fictional identities – drove a fever of desire deep inside Max.

Miss Preston's eyes had darkened into pools, too. Realizing he still clung to her hand, Max forced himself to release it. They couldn't afford the footmen talking, not now that they were starting a proper scheme.

"I'll fetch you in the morning from the service entrance."

She smiled once more. "Tomorrow morning." Then, peeling away to complete her excuse of fetching scissors, Miss Preston left him.

Max found his way out of the townhouse, a whistle on his lips. He knew the plan was reckless. Perhaps even counterproductive to getting an honest answer from the merchant.

He didn't care. Max didn't need to weigh the plan against morals or wisdom. It felt right to share this discovery with Miss Preston.

That was enough for him.

I T WAS SIMPLE TO steal away the next morning. Ellen enlisted Sophia's help – telling her only that she wanted to sneak off to meet *someone* – so that in Ellen's absence, Sophia would direct the maids away from her room, claiming Ellen had a migraine and was to be disturbed under no circumstances. Then, outfitted in her serviceable gray dress and friendly starched cap, Ellen snuck through the shadows of ill-used corridors, hid in a closet, and timed her exit through the kitchen for when Chef closed his eyes after the staff breakfast.

The only hiccup arose just as a black hackney coach pulled up to the lane. In the same moment, an urchin boy darted up to her. "Is this where I can find Miss Preston?"

Ellen's heart lurched. Was the boy a spy, and put upon her by whom? He was short, grubby, and possessing luminous blue eyes that made her want to take him in for a good scrub and hot meal.

"I'm her maid," Ellen lied, resisting the urge to help him.

He stuck a letter in her hand. "A gentleman hired me to deliver this to Miss Preston. Will you see that it gets to her?"

Ellen had barely even replied before the boy took off, racing into the square as if the Devil himself chased him. Expecting the letter to be from Max, she tore it open without even looking at the handwriting on its front.

My dearest Ellen –

A sharp whistle pulled her attention back to the street. The hackney coach still stood at the end of the lane, and Max hung out its window, gesturing her in. His golden hair glinted, despite the clouds depriving the morning of sun.

Letter in one hand, skirts in the other, Ellen walked as nonchalantly as she could to the cab and climbed in. Her heart, however, was thumping. Why had he sent her a letter when they were about to meet, and why did he use such sweet language?

She shouldn't want to be his dearest.

Max pulled shut the hack door behind her, drew the curtains across the windows, and knocked on the ceiling for the driver to go. "Did you have any trouble getting away?"

"No." Ellen smoothed the letter in her lap. "I haven't had a chance to read your note yet, though."

From the bench opposite, Max adjusted his cuffs. He smelled again of soap and hair pomade. "I didn't write you a note."

"The boy said this came from a gentleman," Ellen said stupidly – as if Max might be mistaken about his own actions.

"Three days in London and you already have competing admirers." In the dim lighting, his smirk looked strained. "Go on, then. What does it say?"

Her mind whirling – why had she thought Max would call her his dearest, anyhow? – Ellen took it as a cue to read the letter aloud. "*My dearest Ellen, Please excuse this breach of propriety, but I know you do not set store in conventions and I must bare my heart to you...*"

She stopped. The words would have been embarrassing enough read in silence; aloud, with Max as witness, they mortified her. And the poor author. Whose handwriting Ellen now recognized.

"No, this is definitely not from you," she joked.

Max had turned his head down so that she had only a view of his broad hat and the tips of his ears sprouting from beneath its brim. "I haven't the talent for such a confession," he agreed. "Dare I ask whom it is from?"

She really shouldn't say. It was a private matter and not at all Max's concern. The kind act would be to fold up the letter, change the subject, and muster up a reply in the privacy of her own room.

Just that opening line – *My dearest Ellen* – had made her heart jump with hope when she thought the letter was from Max. And now, knowing it wasn't from him...watching him no more than twitch at some other man confessing love for her...Ellen supposed she was trying to punish Max when she disclosed, "Mr. Thistleman, of course."

"'Of course'? It hardly seems obvious to me." Max snapped upright. Some fierce emotion glittered from his eyes – which looked black in the darkened carriage – but Ellen didn't dare interpret it.

"I suppose that is heartening to hear. I was afraid I was blushing every time Percy entered a room." This was wicked. Her blushes were entirely reserved for Max these days. "He and I were very close when he stayed at the Thatcham rectory."

Max braced his elbows on his knees, which effectively thrust his face into hers. "As close as you and I?"

Wetting her lips, Ellen tried to remain nonchalant. "Physically. Emotionally, I suppose he and I were closer. We had several months to get to know each other. We would get into great intellectual debates on the walk home from church." That was how Ellen had perceived it back then, anyway. Now she could see they hadn't been debates but lectures, with no room for her own questions or thoughts.

Max was the one who debated with her.

"Then why didn't you marry him?" Max growled. There really was no other description for it: he was ferociously angry, his eyebrows and lips drawn in a scowl.

At least she knew she had this modicum of power over him.

"He couldn't yet afford a wife. We decided to wait a few years." Ellen looked back down at the letter, reality erasing the giddiness of making Max so jealous. "Sophia thinks he wants to marry me now, before going to Saint Kitts. I suppose, if I keep reading, this letter is a declaration of some kind."

"Don't keep reading." This was almost a whisper. Max's scowl had disappeared, replaced by that boyish earnestness she so loved.

"Sophia thinks I would be happy as a missionary's wife."

The coach swerved, jostling them to the side and back. Max's hands landed on her thighs, not salaciously but as bolsters to keep her in place. "A missionary's wife? You would be bored to tears in a month. How could you keep up with carpentry when you must care for the invalid and poor?"

Ellen's thoughts exactly. She replied with the counterargument she had already levied to herself a hundred times. "My conscience would not be in good health if I choose to turn my back on the needy in order to indulge my own interest in woodwork."

"Your carpentry helps plenty of needy people at Northfield Hall," Max snapped, even though they both knew she was inconsequential to the completion of the cottages. After all, she was here, and the cottages were still being constructed. "There is not only one way to help the needy. Spouting Bible verses at them will hardly be effective, especially if you yourself are not...well, I've begun to suspect you have as little interest in religion as I do."

"I would leave the preaching to Mr. Thistleman and dedicate myself to creating a safe haven for those less fortunate than I."

In a sudden, heady movement, Max pressed forward. His hands reached around her waist. His knees landed on either side of her thighs. His mouth traced against her neck. "And what of Mr. Thistleman? Does he fuck you better than I do?"

Ellen locked him in a kiss in response. Max was so large, his arms and legs and torso so muscled, that his embrace almost felt like a blanket wrapping her into a cocoon. Except the heat between them was not that of cuddling on a cold winter's night. It sizzled like iron set into a fire. Their kiss was ferocious enough that their teeth collided. Max's hands blazed across her torso. He pulled down her bodice with fierce, efficient tugs and palmed her breasts, one and then the other, until they were free from her corset. It was rough – it should have felt like manhandling – but it set Ellen alive, made her instantly wet, and she wrapped her legs around his waist, trying desperately to get close to him. The coach took another sharp turn, cries of outrage rising from pedestrians on the street. Max rolled with the movement, his hat falling to the side, so that he sat on the bench now and Ellen rested on his lap.

The very position that had been so pleasing just two evenings ago.

Max ducked his head to suckle her breasts. His fingers slid to her quim. His touch there was delicate compared to the rest of the interaction, yet thorough. Exactly what she wanted. Ellen tried to remember if she had ever breathed instructions to him, or if Max knew intuitively that she needed his index finger just *there* and that she wanted the rhythm that slow and that she would peak if only he bit her nipple at the same time as –

The carriage shuddered with her movements, or she shuddered with its. Ellen didn't know. Didn't care. Didn't listen to whether her cry of ecstasy was loud enough to carry to the driver. Max held her steady, still worshipping her chest, until she had settled enough to smell the manure and sweat and stale straw of the carriage again.

The hack, incidentally, was slowing down.

"We are almost there," Max groaned. His head leaned back against the wall, his expression a daze of lust and frustration.

Ellen reached for his hard length. "I could..."

"No." He batted her away, then smirked. "At least, not now. I may accept your offer on the ride home."

It took a few minutes to tuck her breasts into the corset and pull the bodice back into its place. Ellen's body still craved more, and even the whisper of cloth across her flesh made her squirm to take Max inside her. He looked steadily away, drawing the curtain from the window an inch to peer out at the street, until even Ellen couldn't tell that he had so recently been aroused.

Just before the coach stopped, she retrieved Percy's letter from where it had landed among the straw and stored it in her pocket.

The reason for this journey came rushing back as Max paid the driver and handed her down into the street. They were close enough to the river that the air stank almost exclusively of seawater and sewage; gulls squawked in the air above; the lane was narrow, covered with muddied boards of wood, and packed with people.

"Stay close to me," Max ordered Ellen with a frown.

She didn't argue. This many people so close together already had her breath coming short. She followed Max like a shadow, trying to focus her thoughts on the task at hand. The linen Max had shown her was as fine as any Northfield Hall had ever produced. She needed to know if Max was right.

She feared what it meant, if the linen had indeed come from Northfield.

Max checked a piece of paper from his pocket, then stopped and frowned at a narrow wooden building. A painted sign hung above the door: *East India Lodging House*. "This is the address the shopkeeper gave me."

The name alone curled distastefully in Ellen's stomach. She looked up and down the lane. There were no other signs that would indicate a merchant. "This must be where Mr. Martin boards."

Max pounded out three knocks. They waited for what seemed an interminable amount of time. Ellen almost hoped no one would answer, or that whoever did would never have heard Mr. Martin. Anything to put this matter to rest.

But then the door swung open, and she could only gasp. It was no stranger answering to the name of Mr. Martin.

It was Martin Chow, the eldest son of Mr. and Mrs. Chow, lately of Northfield Hall.

Chapter Fourteen

F OR A MOMENT, ALL Ellen could do was stare. Her mind knew it was Martin, and yet her heart refused to believe it. There were his square jaw and the same broad shoulders as his father. Except he wore a cotton suit, and he was answering the door at an East India Company lodging house.

Beside her, in his perfect viscount's accent, Max said, "Let me guess: you are Mr. Martin, otherwise known as Mr. Chow. I am Lord Berwick, sometimes known as Mr. Sims. I lately worked in the sawpit with your brother Oliver."

A hundred memories rushed Ellen as Martin evaluated Max. A year older than her, Martin had always been in the periphery of her life. Playing in the nursery with her and Sophia. Snacking on pork buns with Mrs. Chow in the garden. Footraces through the garden, birthday celebrations, learning to read and write together. Even when she had first ventured into the carpentry, it had been to follow Martin as he started working with his father.

He had been in London for over a decade. First as an apprentice for a ship carpenter, and then in private employment.

For two years, he hadn't been back to Northfield Hall, yet now here he was.

A linen merchant using a false name.

Ellen wanted to say something about how she missed him. When she opened her mouth, however, all she could sputter was, "I have a letter for you from your mother. She didn't have your direction. I didn't bring it with me today. I didn't know."

"I've been meaning to write her." Martin did not quite smile. He looked at her and then Max. "I suppose I should invite you in."

Inside was a shabby sitting room with wallpaper stained brown from tobacco smoke. A painting of an East Indiaman ship hung above the ragged settee. Awkwardly, Ellen perched there. She didn't know the protocol for visiting a boarding house. She didn't know if she was supposed to sit at all.

Martin glanced back to the front door. "Did you come here alone?"

"I thought people would assume me a maid." She couldn't help sliding a look at Max. Martin was acting as if they were all family, not as if he were in the presence of a viscount, and she worried that Max might take offense. He loomed near the sitting room door, hands loose at his sides. The effect suggested he wasn't paying attention, but Ellen could feel him tracking Martin's every movement.

She smiled at Martin. "It is good to see you. You haven't visited for ages."

He looked older, in fact, a few permanent lines sneaking across his forehead. He had gained weight, too, so that he looked more like his father than ever.

Except for when he smiled, as he did now. That expression was Mrs. Chow's, through and through.

"Long enough to finally get you to London, apparently." Martin turned to Max, his eyes cast obsequiously past Max's shoulder. "How may I help you, my lord?"

Of a sudden, Ellen remembered she had not arrived at this sitting room in order to catch up with Martin. She saw Max begin to answer and jumped in to explain, "Lord Berwick is curious about Berkshire linen. Since it is so rare and expensive. He thinks it comes from Northfield Hall."

Her cheeks grew hot. Even she could hear the request beneath her words: *Tell him it's not true.*

Max clasped his hands behind his back in that lordly way of his. "Perhaps you could begin by telling me your involvement with Berkshire linen. I expected to find a warehouse here."

Martin, of course, was no fool. He knew as well as Ellen did that, as the Earl of Meretta's heir, Max couldn't be trusted. His brow furrowing, he looked between her and Max again. "May I ask what your interest is, my lord?"

Shifting his weight from one foot to another, Max hesitated before answering, "I am investigating it for a report in my newspaper, *The Perceptive.* I ask for honesty, nothing more."

Martin looked amused, yet his words hung darkly: "Do you believe me to be a dishonest man?"

Ellen could see their words hurtling towards collision. She leaned forward to clarify, "What Lord Berwick means is that he has promised to write the truth and not spin it into some ridiculous story that will get Papa arrested."

She couldn't help but glance at Max as she said this. He looked so much more a viscount than when she had first met him, his golden hair clean enough to match the filigree brocaded at the hems of his coat. And yet, Ellen didn't find him threatening at all.

Why, he even smirked a little as he met her glance.

Then he addressed himself to Martin. "Quite. If there is anyone dishonest in the room, it is me, and I have promised Miss Preston to be on my best behavior."

For a long moment, Martin still frowned. Then, he shrugged. "There is not much of a story for you to do anything with, my lord. I act as intermediary. The shops order linen through me, I send the orders to Mr. Maulvi, and then I coordinate the shipments, collect the payments, and deposit the money in Lord Preston's account at the bank. In return, I earn ten percent of each order."

Again, Ellen's brain worked against her senses. She heard his words. And yet, they made no sense.

The shops Max had found the linen in were high-end mercers. They stocked the finest muslins spun from slave-grown cotton, silks imported by the East India Company from China. They invited clientele whose wealth came from those economies, too, like Aunt

Charlotte. She had heard they even served tea and sugared cakes as the ladies evaluated fabrics.

Her father wouldn't sell to that kind of shop. Uncle Maulvi wouldn't place those orders. Martin had to be wrong.

She shook her head. "Lord Berwick refers to the linen sold on New Bond Street, Martin. Northfield Hall does not sell in shops that stock slave-produced cotton, and we don't price so high that the common man cannot afford it. You must be mistaken."

"Did you really not know?" Martin frowned at her. He sounded puzzled – and a little bored. "They increased production last year so we could keep up with the shop orders. Didn't you wonder why your father bought a new loom?"

"For our own needs." That had been last summer, just before the flax harvest. Caroline, with the Shayler children and Edward Chow, had dressed as sheep for a chorale, and Mr. Hamlyn had broken out his fiddle for dancing.

Ellen hadn't thought twice about why they needed a loom. Only that Papa had decided they did, and now they had it.

What kind of fool didn't wonder about the why? What kind of simpleton merely jumped at the chance to jig?

This whole time, Ellen had thought the laborers at Northfield Hall had drawn away because of who she was. But was it simply this: that she was too self-absorbed to question even the basics of how Northfield Hall operated?

Max sat beside her. The settee was small enough that this brought their bodies in contact, knees and thighs and sides aligned. Strange, how that faintest touch restored her to reality.

He asked, "What does Lord Preston use the money for?"

Martin shrugged. "Taxes and wages, I assume."

He was so apathetic to it all. Here was Max – a man Ellen *knew* Martin recognized as a political enemy to Papa – asking about their business, and Martin laid it out as if he were explaining the difference between oak and elm.

Ellen reviewed the information again. Papa sold Northfield Hall linen to the London shops using Martin as his intermediary. Martin, who earned ten percent of each order, and who answered the door at an East India Company lodging house.

No wonder he didn't come home to visit. Ellen realized – with a surge of anger – that he was a completely different man than she had ever imagined. "And what do you use the money for?" She circled her hands to encompass the room. "Are you an East India shareholder now? Do you drink their tea and eat their sugar and reap their profits?"

She didn't care that her words flew so violently from her mouth that spittle accompanied them. She wanted an explanation. She wanted to shake him, as if Martin were only under a spell and if he blinked, he would see what he had become.

He scowled at her. "You know you cannot actually control anyone else's actions, don't you, Ellen?"

"I am not trying to—"

But he didn't let her finish. "Whether you put sugar in your cakes or not, that slaveowner is going to buy another slave. Whether you drink tea or not, the East India Company is going to coerce more leaves from the Foochownese planters."

An old argument, and one Sophia employed often. "If there were no market for sugar or tea, then they would not—"

"Then they would find ways to exploit people in producing whatever product *is* selling." Martin cut one hand angrily through the air, as if it were a blade. "I am not interested in your economics. Nor am I interested in being told that I must live life on your family's terms." He spat *your family* as if it were a poison on his tongue. "Yes, I live here. This is the boarding house for their Chinese sailors, and they trust me with my English to act as their representative. Which means, Ellen, that I have discounted lodging, so that I can save more money earned by selling your precious linen to British fops who think that owning something rare makes their lives more meaningful. Yes, I drink the Company's tea and eat their food. And when I have saved enough money, I will buy myself a ticket on one of their ships and sail with them all the way back to KwongChow. I do it all without guilt or shame, and you may not sit there and judge me."

Ellen was not sure she had ever seen Martin so upset. He spoke physically, rising to the balls of his feet and gesturing with his whole body, until he seemed to take up more space in the room than even Max. And his words –

She didn't want to hear them. Tears pricked her eyes. He acted as if she had done him wrong, when he was the one turning his back on everything their families believed in.

Beside her, Max had grown tense. Martin was not a peer, after all; it was wildly inappropriate in Max's world for him to speak to her this way. Ellen stretched her palm across his wrist – glove against cuff – to restrain whatever impulse he might follow.

She tried to choose the most salient point to pursue from Martin's diatribe. "Why are you going back to KwongChow?"

"It is my family's home."

And yet, his initials were carved alongside all her siblings' on a lilac tree by the pond. "Northfield Hall is your home."

His scowl lifted. What replaced it was more inscrutable. Sadder. The expression of a man about to break someone's heart. "Your father thinks he did us a kindness, when he took my parents in. As if hiring a man and woman to labor is a great act of charity. But Ellen, having shelter is not the same as a home. Being employed is not the same as being part of your family. Being controlled is not the same as being loved."

The sitting room suddenly felt very small. Martin's words crowded it like the tobacco stains on the wallpaper. "My father does not control you."

"He won't, once I return to KwongChow."

Ellen didn't know what to do with the bitterness seeping from Martin. She knew she should try to hear it. Try to absorb it. But all she could think was:

Whatever it was she could offer Martin, he did not want it.

And beside her, Max still sat. Silent. Observing. Wildly, Ellen wondered if he would write up this interview in his report. *NORTHFIELD HALL RESIDENT CHOOSES CHINA.*

Max cleared his throat. With the lightest pressure – so much that she might have been fantasizing his support – he leaned into her and asked, "Why isn't it called Northfield linen, if that is where it is from?"

Calmer now, Martin replied, "Lord Preston didn't want it to be tied to the family name."

"Why not?"

Martin looked away. Frustration added lines to his face, making him look old and weary in the dim light of the sitting room. "You would have to ask him. I have told you everything I know about the matter."

Papa. It came back to him. Papa who had failed Martin. Papa, who was selling the linens.

Ellen rose from the settee. She needed to get out of that sitting room.

She needed to think.

At the door, she and Martin both paused. He watched her shoes rather than face her. Ellen's anger subsided long enough for her to realize this might be the last time she saw him, if he didn't visit Northfield Hall again. She reached out to hug him, as if he were Benny or Nate.

Martin stopped her, catching her hands. "I will write to my mother."

But not to her. Not to anyone in her family.

Ellen tried to find the right thing to say. All she could muster up was, "I'm sorry, Martin."

He latched the door behind her.

MAX COULDN'T SORT OUT what he felt as they stepped back onto the street. The air inside the sitting room had been oppressive, summer heat trapped within the papered walls, yet it didn't feel any fresher outside. His cravat was too tight, his jacket and waistcoat too heavy.

He should be feeling excitement. The heady thrill of triumph. The saltwater buoyancy of hope. This was the evidence he had been looking for. Northfield Hall selling its products right alongside calicoes and muslins spun from slave-grown cotton. At prices too high for the common man to achieve.

A concept so out of line with Northfield's utopic promise that poor Miss Preston had looked positively ill to hear it.

She stumbled as they turned from the alley onto Salmon Lane. Max caught her, stretching an arm across her waist. He thought she was about to faint.

Then he saw the flush in her face. No longer was she pale as bone, as she had been while Martin Chow scraped away her understanding of Northfield Hall. Her cheeks, ears, and neck were pink – and her gray eyes glittered with emotion.

Max suspected it was anger even before she pushed out of his arm. "I don't want to believe it, but I suppose I have to. You were right all along. Oh, how am I supposed to believe it? Oh, the nerve of him!"

"He forgot himself entirely in the way he was speaking to you," Max agreed. If she hadn't put a hand on Max's arm, he might have lunged at Chow as soon as that scowl had descended. The man had spoken as if he were Miss Preston's brother, not her family's servant.

"Not Martin. Papa! How could he do this?"

A cart trundled past, its horse running faster than it had any business going, and in her flurry, Miss Preston nearly stepped directly in its path. Max grabbed her wrist to pull her into safety. "Miss Preston—"

"Is that all I am to you?" She stilled. "After everything we have done, I am only Miss Preston? The Baron Ashforth's daughter? An extension of Northfield Hall and not a woman unto myself?"

Max's tongue might well have been numb – but she carried on before he even had a chance to respond.

"Apparently I am nothing more than that to Martin. I consider him a brother. Someone I have *missed* all these months – sixteen, it must be! – since he last visited. But to him, I am – what? A symbol of a great folly? My father's foolish hope that we might be able to help the Chows in their moment of need?"

Max slid his fingers from her wrist down to her waist. He wasn't sure if it was wise to be honest. But that was the tenet of their friendship, so it was what he would give her. "I rather thought he was saying something more personal than that. Your father's generosity was not enough for him. Worse, even you – who he considered a sister – can't see it. You want him to live life on your terms, rather than his. You missed him, yet here you are in London, and you didn't even *mean* to visit him."

"I meant to..."

"You expect him to fit into the role of Friend, yet there is no room for him to be himself."

That seemed to stop the wildness of her emotion. Her gaze lifted to meet his, eyes wide. "As your father does to you."

Max let go of her wrist. He couldn't hold onto anything at the moment with shock from her words.

He was no victim of his father. His father expected him to be Berwick, and Max consistently failed. It was his father who had to suffer Max, not the other way around.

Yet her words unlocked something inside him.

Something that felt dangerously like sorrow.

She turned away, not noticing. "Come along then."

"Where?" When she didn't answer, only reached out to hail a hackney coach, Max plodded after her. "Miss Prest—Ellen. My dear Ellen. Where are we going?"

Ellen looked back. The gleam in her eyes was different. Perhaps because he called her by her name. Or perhaps because she had made a decision.

She lifted her chin. "It is time to ask my father what exactly he is doing."

Chapter Fifteen

Max followed her into the hackney coach with a thumping heart. After all these weeks, he was finally to meet Lord Preston. Hand-delivered by the man's own daughter.

Ellen. Max had very deliberately resisted the temptation to think of her as anything but Miss Preston. As the latter, she remained aloof and apart. Out of reach.

As Ellen, she was something else. Carpenter. Friend. Woman with hopes and fears and a dangerous swirl of emotions.

The difference between a clay figure and a human of flesh and blood.

On the bench opposite him, she sat stiff, her hand clinging to the door as if without that support she might collapse. Max's own mind was spinning too fast to catch onto any one thought. Except he could tell she was upset. He slipped an arm across her shoulders.

"Perhaps your father has a perfectly reasonable explanation for selling Berkshire linen as he does." Max couldn't think of what it might be, but he had been proven wrong before.

"Or perhaps he is merely like everyone else. A selfish hypocrite."

Her words pelted into the air like bullets. Max considered them for a moment. Admitted to himself that he was guilty of both adjectives. Then, he ventured, "At the salon, you said you are not the arbiter of right and wrong. Your father isn't either. If there even is such a thing as an objective right and an objective wrong."

Ellen glared at the opposite bench. "He raised me to know certain things as right and certain things as wrong. He could at least have the decency to follow his own rules."

"My father raised me to believe in the interests of our family above all else. Yet, for all that I am trying to prove myself to him, my views have recently altered." Almost without thinking, Max dipped his free hand into his pocket, where he had tucked Elinor for good luck. "Perhaps Lord Preston has left room for his opinions to be impacted by new perspectives, too."

She did not question him about his altered views. She did not even respond to his suggestion. She only looked at him, a hundred emotions pooling in those gray eyes, and rested her head against his shoulder.

Max held her close.

They arrived at a modest building two streets away from the Palace of Westminster. An iron placard beside the door proclaimed *The Society for the Propagation of Free Produce.*

A serving man in a plain, fine gray suit showed them up a creaky wooden staircase to the third story. The building was not completely import-free, but Max noted the walls were whitewashed instead of papered, the furniture upholstered in traditional English wool, the cabinets built of oak or elm instead of the more fashionable mahogany.

Lord Preston answered the servant's knock with a distracted, "Enter."

This was the moment, then. Max swallowed against dust on his tongue. Whatever happened in this meeting, whatever Lord Preston disclosed, it would make or sink Max's report. He was surprised to find himself nervous, almost as if it were the Earl of Meretta he faced, not a complete stranger.

Ellen pressed open the door, stepped through, and bobbed a curtsey. "Good morning, Papa."

Here, then, was Max's first glimpse of the Baron Ashforth: a man behind a round oak table jerking his head up in surprise.

Lord Preston's hair was completely white, except for his eyebrows, which were dark enough to match his daughter Sophia's coloring. He rose, revealing he was almost as tall as Max himself, though leaner and listing a little forward from years of bowing across a desk.

Most surprising to Max was how familiar he looked. The tilt of his eyes, the curve of his mouth, the slash of his jaw – they were all Ellen's.

"May I present the Viscount Berwick?" she continued, making room for Max beside her.

Confusion flickered across Preston's face, but he bowed his head politely. "Lord Berwick." Then his gaze returned to Ellen. "Are you here unaccompanied?"

Without even flinching, she lied, "I left my maid in the carriage."

Max pushed away the guilt that twisted his gut. She didn't want him to worry about her reputation; therefore, he wouldn't.

What a different meeting this would be, though, if she had brought him here so that he might beg her father's permission for her hand in marriage.

Max summoned as much of his old bluster as he could. "I have imposed myself upon Miss Preston, I'm afraid. I am fascinated with Northfield Hall and, having called at Countess of Pemberly's yesterday and missed you, begged an introduction."

Lord Preston hesitated for just a moment before gesturing to the chairs around the table. "Of course. Shall I call for refreshments?"

The conversation danced around the weather and mutual acquaintances as they waited for the man to bring up a tray. When he did, Ellen served from an old Wedgewood abolitionist teapot. For herself and her father, she poured the water over chamomile flowers. When she made to pour for Max, too, Lord Preston stopped her. "Perhaps Lord Berwick would prefer tea to tisane."

Max watched annoyance flicker across Ellen's face as she turned to him. "What may I offer you, my lord?"

He himself was surprised. He would have expected Preston to enforce the import ban upon his visitors, or at least not go out of his way to accommodate them. "Tea of chamomile is fine, thank you."

When the flowers had steeped, Lord Preston leaned back in his seat and surveyed Max. "So, Lord Berwick. Are you here on your own curiosity, or your father's?"

Max inhaled. He had pictured this moment a dozen times: what would he say, if and when he found himself before Lord Preston?

Ellen didn't give him a chance to reply. With a raise of her chin, she said, "Mine, actually. We have just come from 100 Salmon Lane."

If this were the Earl of Meretta, he would not so much as look at Ellen in response to her accusatory tone. Max considered it to Lord Preston's credit that he replied, "What is at 100 Salmon Lane?"

"Martin Chow." Ellen almost sounded dispassionate. "Your linen merchant, apparently."

And here, the Earl of Meretta would end the interview. One cutting diagnosis of Max's character and a nod to his private secretary, who would bring Max his coat and escort him out the room.

Sweat drenched Max's palms at the thought of Lord Preston doing the same to Ellen. He inserted himself forward. "I have been investigating the origin of Berkshire linen. Miss Preston did not believe it possible that it came from Northfield Hall until Mr. Martin Chow confirmed that it does."

"Sold in the same shops as cotton." Ellen's fingers, trembling, rose to grip her teacup.

Lord Preston's brows drew together. Gently, he asked, "What is it you are trying to say, Ellen?"

"How could you?" Her voice shook. Max sensed her fury had disappeared, replaced by something deeper. Rawer. "Everyone at

Northfield Hall thinks we are living one kind of way. You told us we were sacrificing for the greater good. That it is worth refusing tea and chocolate and all of that because it will turn the tide against exploiting the colonies. We live this way because you told us it would make a difference."

Lord Preston set his palms evenly on the arms of his chair. "It does."

"How can it, if you turn around and sell our linen to shops that price it so high only the richest may purchase it? To shop owners who profit at the same time by selling other fabrics from the very economies we are trying to change? It is hypocrisy. Worse than hypocrisy."

"It is reality." Even now, Lord Preston's tone was kind.

"Then what is Northfield Hall? A fantasy?"

"Life is not so simple as either this or that." Her father leaned forward. "How we live at Northfield Hall *is* worth it, Ellen. At the very least because you and I can go to sleep at night knowing we have not consumed anything that required barbaric labor conditions to produce it. If others follow our example – or at least think about it and start to consider whether they *should* follow our example – then it is that much more worth it."

"But why sell our linens here? Martin said you invested in the new loom so that you could increase production and sell even more. How can we claim to live one way and turn around and behave like a Manchester manufactory instead?"

"Would you have me stop paying the laborers? Spend all your dowry money? Leave Benjamin no bank with which to run the estate?"

"Mama would never have approved of this."

At last, Lord Preston winced. He looked down, directly at the ground, as if the very reminder of his late wife might send him to pieces. It was a long moment before he looked up again, his eyes settling in great focus on his daughter. "I am doing what is best for Northfield Hall. I have to trust that your mother would understand."

Max sucked in a breath. The strangest thing about the whole exchange was that Max did not feel the need to duck his eyes or creep out of the room. The Prestons both spoke with such bare emotion, and yet it did not make Max cringe.

Envy curdled deep in his gut instead.

Latching onto Ellen's comment about her mother, Max set down his cup of the tasteless chamomile brew and asked, "How long have you been selling Berkshire linen in the London shops?"

Lord Preston looked at Max as if seeing him for the first time. A sheen of tears glimmered across his eyes, though he quickly blinked it away. "Three years or so."

About when Lady Preston had died, then.

"She had a wasting disease," the man continued, as if he could hear Max's thought as a comment. "I brought in all the doctors I could. I paid for the best treatments." Lord Preston looked at his daughter again, his shoulders rising helplessly. "I had already spent our money on the Hall. So I went into debt trying to save her."

Max knew a handful of peerages gone bankrupt. For spending too much on their country seats or investing in the wrong schemes or gambling it all away during a foolish evening at the tables. The usual recourse was to find a rich heiress to marry into the family, hawk the jewels, or flee to the Continent to avoid debtors.

Selling linen in a London shop hardly seemed a scandal compared to that. Except for who Lord Preston was.

This story was enough to embarrass him in *The Perceptive*. It was exactly what Max's father had wanted him to find. Bankruptcy, Berkshire linen, and class divides at Northfield Hall would be enough to ruin the myth of Northfield's progress once and for all.

Ellen looked at Max. Her expression was blank, her gray eyes empty. "I should like to go now."

Lord Preston reached out to her. "Ellen, there is more to say."

She rose to her feet. "Later, Papa. Let me alone to think."

"I will see you home."

She stepped away from him, which landed her directly beside Max. "My maid is waiting for me in Lord Berwick's carriage."

Lord Preston darkened. Max could see the objection on his lips. It did not do at all for her to be escorted home by an unmarried peer.

"Good afternoon," Ellen said, and she swung into the corridor.

Following, Max flagged down a hackney coach and settled in across from her. He tried to focus on the bright white of her cap, the dumpy gray of her dress, the freckles spattered across her nose.

His mind still lagged on what Lord Preston had revealed. The way the man had not even tried to say it in private. How he was not attempting to hide his connection to Berkshire linen.

How he demanded nothing of his daughter. Even as she abandoned good sense to travel through London with Preston's political rival.

He wondered if he could ever ask the same of his own father.

IF SHE LOOKED OUT the window to discover the sky had turned green, Ellen wouldn't be surprised. The day had already upended her understanding of life; for all that she understood about Northfield Hall, she might well not even know the principles of the physical world.

She didn't understand how Papa could excuse the Berkshire linen enterprise. If they needed money, then surely there was a way other than selling their produce to shops that didn't care what kind of labor created it. He was the one who had always cautioned against doing the easy thing.

She wondered whether Martin had lost his faith in Papa before or after he started selling their linen for such huge profits.

Ellen did not want to think anymore. It felt like all she had done these past few months was *think* – and try to defend Northfield Hall against Max, against Martin, and now against Papa. She had had enough of asking questions of the world around her.

She wanted to plunge back into an existence where she did not need to question right or wrong. Where she simply existed and knew that wasn't hurting anyone.

In his corner of the coach, Max leaned his head against the carriage wall, eyes closed and legs strewn sideways to stretch as much as the small space allowed. He really was a specimen of a man. Ellen tried to clear her mind by memorizing the lines of his body: his nose veering aristocratically downwards, his jaw tightening against his breath, his arms crossing his chest, and his thighs creeping with every jostle of the hackney coach a little bit closer to her.

This was the gloried son of Britain, born to power and wealth and beauty. The epitome of everything Ellen deplored about her nation.

Why, then, did her heart feel more complete each time he touched her?

Max's report wouldn't be long in the making. Her father had said it plainly: Northfield Hall would be bankrupt, if it weren't for selling Berkshire linen at shameful prices. It would be a few days, perhaps, until Max had written his draft. A week, then, until the news was splashed all about London.

Ellen didn't fool herself that Max would visit her now that he had finished his investigations. They had said goodbye twice already, but this time it would stick. These were their last moments together. Her last opportunity to bask in the glory that was Max before she vaulted herself into whatever the future held.

Max cleared his throat just as the carriage reached the alley that led behind Partridge House. "Ellen..."

Her name had never felt so right, like an old familiar nightgown wrapping her for bed.

She couldn't let their last moment be here, in this miserable hired carriage that stank of manure.

"They think I'm in bed with the megrim. Sophia forbade anyone from seeing me. If there is no one around...if they don't see you..."

She didn't need to finish her sentence. Max's eyes gleamed at the hint. The air between them grew as hot and electric as a summer storm.

"For old time's sake," she murmured.

He grinned. "The way you think, Miss Ellen Preston, is one of my favorite things about you."

MAX WAS WELL-VERSED IN sneaking through a townhouse undetected. It was one of his favorite past times: choosing exactly where to place one's feet without emitting a creak, ducking into shadows when a servant emerged unexpectedly, always staying one heartbeat ahead of one's thoughts so as not to get caught. He rarely did it in broad daylight, but that only made the game more fun. Especially knowing what would come next.

When he successfully ferried Ellen into her bedchamber.

They were nearly discovered as they turned down the corridor to her apartment. A door ahead of them opened, and Max whirled her into the crevice between a lacquered armoire and the window casing. The footsteps walked away from them, not even drawing near. But Ellen, eyes shining with the same glee surging through Max, giggled.

Whoever it was paused.

And then – after a million years – continued on their path.

"You'll be punished for that," Max breathed, checking over both shoulders before letting Ellen free from the hiding spot.

She whispered back, "Do you promise?"

Hand in his, she darted down to the bedchamber at the end of the corridor. Locking the door behind them, she set the key on a nearby table. The curtains had not yet been thrown open for the day; they were alone in the dark, cool room.

He could still see the flush across her cheeks as she turned to him. "Here we are."

Max had spent more time than he cared to admit imagining what he would do if he were to ever to get Miss Preston – Ellen – alone with a proper bed. He started with her cap. Six pins held it in place: these he removed as gently as possible and set on the dressing table along with the discarded cap. Then came the braid. Another ten pins uncoiled it from her scalp. Max threaded his fingers through her hair, releasing it from its plait, his whole body coming alive under its soft, wiry weight.

Ellen brought her hands to rest on his chest. Her right palm above his heart. A gesture that had no business making his cock throb, and yet it did.

"You only like me for my hair," she accused.

"I didn't even know your hair color before I—" He caught himself. He had almost said *before I fell in love with you.*

"Before you caught my eye," he corrected. Her hair flowed about her shoulders now, igniting her whole countenance with fire.

No, that fire had always been there. It was only that Max had poor eyesight, and he needed the cue of her hair to notice it.

Impatient, Ellen started untying his cravat – which, luckily, Max had instructed Downes to keep simple that morning. He settled his hands on either side of her waist, happy to watch as her bottom lip jutted out in concentration. If he looked down, he had a direct view of the gap between her bodice and her breasts. A nice view, at that.

It would be better when she was naked, though.

"I didn't know your name before you caught my eye." Ellen threw the cravat to the floor, then set to work unbuttoning his waistcoat and the shirt beneath it. Each brush of her fingertips made him harder – and he had already been standing at attention.

"Which was when?" he asked, teasing a finger across the rim of her bodice.

Embarrassment slid into her smile. "When you demanded to know who I was."

At least someone had enjoyed that moment. "I do make a good first impression."

Smirking, Ellen wrestled off his jacket, waistcoat, and shirt, almost all in one. Her body slid against him. Her perfume had changed since coming to London – the result of French soap instead of Northfield's homemade stuff, he supposed – but underneath was the familiar scent of Ellen. Kind, giving, demanding Ellen.

"I'm going to miss this prospect." She danced her fingers across his chest. "I hope your next lover appreciates how many hours in the sawpit went into your physique."

He didn't like that. Not one bit – not even though it was true. Catching her hands in punishment, Max nipped at her fingertips. "There is only you and me in this room."

She met his glare with wide, watchful eyes. After a long moment, she smiled. "Then why haven't you kissed me yet?"

A better question: why was she still fully clothed? Dipping his mouth to hers, Max maneuvered her backwards to the bed. The kiss was a little lazy, in that tantalizing way of knowing one had time to enjoy it. Max laid her across the mattress and climbed on top, still teasing her tongue with his. Her legs had wrapped about his waist; now he stretched them into a vee and – blindly, since he was loathe to break the kiss – removed one at a time each slipper, garter, and stocking. They dropped in a heap somewhere past the bed.

Ellen raised her hips, rubbing bare legs upwards towards his groin. They moaned as one. "You're quite right," Max said, leaning back. "It is time I took off my trousers."

She presented quite the view as he did so. Dress and petticoats bunched up at her hips, legs spread, nothing but wet desire between him and her cunny. When she caught him watching, she brought her fingers to her clitoris, and he nearly spent.

"Take off that terrible dress." He hurried out of his trousers.

Impish, she teased, "You do like to order me around," before rising to her knees and drawing the dress and petticoat over her head. Next, she shimmied out of her corset and shift.

Then she hooked her hands beneath each of his elbows and tugged him onto the mattress. He fell onto his back.

"Here is an order for you," she murmured, throwing her right leg across his hips to straddle him. She took his cock inside her in one slick jerk. Immediate starbursts rushed Max – he almost didn't hear her command, "Don't finish until I give you permission."

And then came the fucking. Mercifully, the bed and mattress were well anchored, so that they needn't waste any energy worrying about someone hearing their frenetic thumping. Max pulsed into Ellen with every muscle he had, and she ground down just as hard. Then she leaned into him, her breasts dipping at just the right angle that he could catch them in his mouth and nibble at her nipples. Her fiery hair draped all over him. It was everything he had ever wanted.

Not nearly enough.

"Please," he heard himself breathe. He didn't know what he begged for. He didn't want to spend. He wanted this to last forever.

"No, you may not finish yet. New position." And they rolled as one so that Ellen was on her back now, Max on top. She spread her legs into the wide vee again. Her breasts jostled with each movement, and he steadied them with his palms. He would spend if this continued. He tried to think of something – anything.

Not Percy Thistleman taking her like this. Max couldn't stand the thought.

"We should have stayed at Northfield Hall," Ellen whispered, wrapping her ankles behind his neck, which only drove him deeper inside her. "We could have done this every afternoon for weeks."

In the shed. In the fields. Under the lilac trees. In the pond. Max nearly went wild with the thought. He tried to picture the workshop with all its sharp blades and unfinished wood and filthy sawdust. But even there – oh, he could have taken her in the pit, with his jacket laid down to protect her from the dirt.

"Not helping," he ground out.

"New position," she responded and pushed herself up by the elbows until she sat in his lap. They were mirror images layered on top of each other, legs stretched behind the other, arms wrapped about each other's shoulders. He could feel almost every inch of her body, from the deep wet folds of her cunny, to her stomach and breasts against his chest, to her mouth kissing his.

They always ended up like this, it seemed. Holding on to each other in sheer desperation.

Ellen broke the kiss to press her forehead against his. Her gray eyes were endless. "Tell me you would fuck me forever if you could."

"I would fuck you forever if I could." And he would spend in the next second if she demanded much more of him.

She was the one to go first, grabbing a pillow and pressing it between her teeth as a wail of delight rose from her mouth. Max drove deeper into her as her cunny seized around him, trying not to do anything except memorize this moment.

When she recovered, her body and hair limp in his arms, she said into his ear, "You may finish when you want."

They were still joined. Max almost let himself go, thought about a glorious orgasm inside her, laying claim to her womb, if only to have a reason to visit her the next few months.

He was stronger than his weakest urges, though. Pulling away from her just in time, Max fell onto his back so that the fluid fell almost entirely onto his own stomach.

Ellen crossed the room to retrieve his shirt and jacket from where they had fallen near the door. She took his handkerchief from its pocket and wiped down his torso with careful strokes. Max almost couldn't bear it; not the touch, but the tenderness with which she did it.

This was supposed to be their farewell.

Catching her at the waist, he pulled her to lie down. Hair spilling down her shoulders and onto his chest, she nuzzled into him as if she had been born to fit beside him. Max had said goodbye to a dozen women, some of them whom he had known months longer than Ellen.

It had never before felt like cutting off a part of his own body.

"Marry me," Max said, meaning it.

Ellen laughed. "Don't be sentimental."

Max told himself she only wanted to make it a challenge. "What makes you think I am being sentimental? I am an eligible member of the peerage in need of a wife. You are an eligible young lady of noble birth. Hence and therefore, marry me."

"Oh, I see. You've never had an affair with a woman actually within the realm of eligibility for you." Now Ellen rolled away from him, her hair tickling his skin as it slid off his chest. "I don't know much about the earlship of Meretta but I imagine you need much more than a young woman of noble birth as your wife. You'll have a handful of properties to manage, tenants, and not to mention political parties so that you can lead our generation to Tory greatness. All of which might be rather lackluster if you marry a woman who refuses to participate in the import-export economy."

"I don't care about any of that."

"Oh, don't you?" Ellen glared at him. "You are drunk from a good time in bed, Lord Berwick. It is understandable, but most annoying."

She emphasized his title, almost the way his father always did. As if nothing else about him existed, except for that.

A damned courtesy title that didn't even *mean* anything.

"I don't have to live that way." The words fell off his tongue, as if he were drunk. As if he didn't know how to speak for himself. "I don't have to be the same kind of earl as my father."

She brought both palms over her eyes. "Max, are you or are you not publishing a report in *The Perceptive* about Northfield Hall?"

"I am—"

"Without delay? While Parliament is still in session?"

"Only to get my seat in The House of Commons."

"And yet, whatever your motivation, it will bring great scrutiny, embarrassment, and pain to my family. Not to mention how it will destroy my father's abolition bill."

He was sick of talking about the report. They had discussed it endlessly. She always threw it at his feet – and it *was* an obstacle, but it was also the reason they even knew each other. If Max could fall in love with a radically idealistic Whig, then why could she not – even for a second – set aside his politics?

"If I weren't Berwick, would you marry me?" Max glared up at the bed canopy rather than risk seeing her face. "I have told you how I feel about you a dozen times. Yet now that I think of it, I'm not sure you have ever responded in kind. Tell me honestly, Ellen. Are you even fond of me at all? Or am I just a passing amusement?"

"Of course, I am fond of you! Must you require me to say it? It is hard enough to be in love with you, much less admit it. You stand for everything I fight against, and you're arrogant about it!" She seized the edge of the quilt in her fists. "It makes no sense for us to feel as we do about each other."

Max couldn't help himself. "Love? Are you quite sure that is how you feel?"

Ellen glared at him. "I yearn to be with you. I hang upon your every word. I adore the way you smirk as much as I do the way you make me feel like I can tell you anything, from a mere look in your eyes. You are a kind man, you know, even though you insist you aren't. And obviously, I worship your body. What else would you call it?"

"Then marry me."

Beneath the blankets, her feet found his. They tangled all the way to their toes. Ellen murmured into his shoulder, "It is not enough for a marriage."

Max understood her reasons. The ideal of Lady Ellen Berwick jarred against the reality of Miss Ellen Preston. But life had always arranged itself the way Max desired. He couldn't believe that there was no way for him to marry Ellen, if it was what they both wanted.

"What will you do, then? Return to Northfield Hall?"

"I don't know if I can go back after everything I have learned today." Her breath rattled against her rib cage. "Perhaps I will throw in my lot with Percy after all. At least in Saint Kitts I could direct the work myself."

He had no words for the pain cracking through his chest. Max rolled off the bed. His bare feet landed cold on the wood floor, and not even his stockings and boots warmed them up.

"I'm not the same man who started writing the report, you know." He shoved himself into the linen shirt and jacket, which he had chosen specifically in honor of her. "I don't think Northfield Hall is an abomination or even all that strange. I admire your father's courage to do what he has done."

"Which part? To gouge the public with high-priced linen, or to lie about it?"

Max hated to hear the bitterness in her voice. "To choose to live by his principles. Even if he can only do so imperfectly."

"And you would have me believe you are beginning to agree with his principles? That you are considering banning sugar from the halls of Montchampion Manor?"

His cravat slipped through his fingers, and he had to start it over again. "At least that I do not wish to humiliate Northfield Hall in my report. And I *will* delay it. I'll take as long to write it as I can."

Still beneath the covers, Ellen turned her head away from him. "I would like to believe that."

"But you don't." Even though she could so readily believe in anyone who Mr. Maulvi hired to work beside her in the carpentry shop.

"It has been a long morning," she said. "I think we are both overwhelmed."

Sentimental. Overwhelmed. How easy it was to dismiss an emotion, even when it thumped with every beat of his heart.

Max had finished dressing. The only thing left to do was to leave.

He leaned into Ellen, taking a final, chaste kiss for his goodbye. "I am in love with you, too." Somehow, he summoned his most regal sneer. "Believe that."

Tears reddened her eyes. Max waited a breath, long enough for her to say something if she wanted to.

It was only when he was at the door that she said, "I love you for you, Max. Whether you are Berwick or Sims or any other name. Anyone who doesn't is a fool."

If only love alone were enough.

Chapter Sixteen

T HE DAY HAD BLACKENED into a rainstorm, which suited Ellen just fine. She did not want to go anywhere, did not want to comment on sunshine, did not want to be in London at all. As soon as Max shut the door behind him, she flopped back into the mattress, buried her face in the smell of him, and willed herself to sob.

The tears didn't come. Perhaps because she didn't know what to cry for. Max. Northfield Hall. Martin. Herself.

After a time – Ellen didn't know how long – she gathered herself. If she wasn't going to cry, she might as well be useful. Straightening the room to eradicate all evidence of Max, she called for the maid and dressed. She let her hair hang loose down her back in a plait, the way she had done as a child.

Max would like it that way, if he saw her.

Ellen pushed out a sigh, as if she could expel the thought. His offer of marriage had been impulsive. Well-intentioned, but poorly thought out. Lovely, but doomed.

The less she remembered it – the less she tried to catch his scent still hanging in the air – the better off she would be.

Ordering a tea service to the drawing room that joined her bedroom with Sophia's, Ellen sent the maid to rouse her siblings. Sophia popped in immediately, a knowing smile upon her lips. "Your migraine is gone, then?"

"Quite." Ellen knew her sister wanted more details. One day, perhaps, she wouldn't feel so raw, and she could confide in Sophia all about Max.

For now, she wanted to focus on the other matters at hand.

Benny arrived at the same time as the tea service. He wore a rumpled set of trousers, a dressing gown, and the heavy shadow of an overnight beard. When he threw himself onto the chair beside Ellen, she caught a whiff of brandy. "Did I wake you?" she asked, bemused.

"I am not sure I ever fell asleep," he sighed. "Miss Fairchurch accepted the Marquess of Thorne last night. At his mother's ball, for everyone to see. Without so much as a word to me!"

Sophia pouted for Benny. "Oh dear. She did seem rather attached to the idea of a man over twenty."

If Ellen weren't heartbroken herself, she might have felt for her brother. As it was, she had room for no more emotion than her own. "I am afraid I will only make things worse with what I have to share with you." As they both turned to her, countenances drawn narrow with concern, Ellen took a deep breath. "The Berkshire linen that Lord Berwick was asking about yesterday is in fact from Northfield

Hall. Papa has been selling it on New Bond Street because otherwise, we would be bankrupt."

Her siblings stared at her. Ellen thought perhaps they didn't understand.

"They aren't free produce shops. The shop owners profit off slave labor as much as they do from us."

Sophia poured herself a cup of tea. "Really, Ellen, I thought you were going to tell us that you were ill, or that you and Percy Thistleman are in the family way."

"Did you already know?" Ellen felt sick at the thought that she might have been the only one in the whole estate thinking Papa abided by his principles.

"No." Sophia took a healthy bite of a cheese scone. "It is annoying, I suppose. He wouldn't allow *me* to purchase anything from those shops, and all the while we had our own linen there!"

Straightening, Benny reached for the tea, too. "I thought you knew, but it must be because I've been learning the estate. I don't understand why you're upset, though. We have always sold our surplus."

"Not in shops like these!"

"It is not as if we are investing in the slave economy. Besides, we need the money." He gulped down the brown liquid, then winced. "That's too hot."

He lives by his principles, even if he can only do it imperfectly. Ellen blinked away the memory of Max, but it was only replaced by the way Papa had looked so hopeless, asking what she would have him do.

Ellen had never stopped to wonder about money. Not once in her life. She had thrown Mama's opinion in Papa's face, but now she faltered. If the estate couldn't operate without income, then what *was* Papa to do? Upend a hundred and fifty people just so he could say he had never engaged in the imperial economy?

And yet. If they started down that line of questioning, how long until they all felt as Martin Chow did, that avoiding commodities such as tea and sugar was a pointless exercise?

On an impulse, Ellen took up the same teapot as her siblings. They watched in shock as she poured a cup to the brim with the dark, amber brew.

She chugged it down without stopping to breathe. It was bitter, like drinking dirt. Ellen's eyes stung from the terrible taste. She wiped her mouth. "That's awful," she said, and then somehow she was crying.

Sophia's hands landed on her shoulders first. Benny just a moment later. Sobbing was so physical, ravaging her face, clotting her nose, convulsing her ribs. She reached for her siblings' hands, holding tight to the hot flesh of their fingers.

Ellen had thought she was angry about Papa, injured by Martin, and bereft about Max. Separate emotions, layered on top but independent of each other. But as her heart broke, she felt them all swirling together. She lost Martin because she had failed him, without even knowing it. By merely following her best intentions.

As Papa failed her now. And how she would fail Max – and he fail her – if they tried to be anything of consequence to each other.

Sophia murmured soft words into Ellen's ears. They were empty, yet not meaningless. The siblings had comforted each other plenty in the aftermath of Mama's death, so every "There, there," and "Time will ease this," was a secret password that meant *I see your pain.* Ellen clung to the whispers. She focused on the weight of Benny's palm drawing circles at her back. The smell of his slept-in clothes and Sophia's flowery perfume. The slowing rhythm of her breath.

When her tears dried, her body opened with the release. Ellen felt light enough that she could float, if needed. Which was good, because she raised her head to discover Papa standing at the threshold.

He hesitated. Ellen held out her hand, as if she were still a little girl, and he came to kneel before her, handkerchief ready as it always was. She mopped up her tears in its familiar linen smell.

"I wish I could live up to your expectations, Ellen. I'm sorry that I can't."

"To be fair," Sophia said as Ellen blew her nose, "no one can."

"Not even me," Ellen admitted, thinking of how Martin hadn't even wanted to hug her goodbye. "It's only that I thought I was living up to *your* principles, Papa, and then it seems they changed."

Benny offered her a sugar bun. "This one goes down better than the tea."

She pushed it away. It wasn't rebellion that Ellen wanted. It all returned to what Papa had always said: *if you cannot be proud of an action, don't do it.*

Returning Papa his handkerchief, Ellen decided it was about time she confessed to her family. "I am afraid I have made a mess of things."

Somehow, she found the words to describe the whole of it, from discovering Max's report to their meeting with Martin that morning – leaving out the physical intimacy but admitting to the emotions that had tangled like brambles through her heart.

Sophia listened with growing intrigue, exclaiming here and there or murmuring her agreement with conclusions Ellen had drawn. Benny ducked his head into his hands. Meanwhile, Papa sat still and stoic through it all.

"I'm sorry," she finished. "I should have burned the report when I first found it and turned him out. Instead, I helped him, and now he is going to print all of it for the whole country to read."

Papa lifted his shoulders. "Well, for *The Perceptive* subscribers to read, which is hardly the whole of England."

"Of all of us, I never thought it would be *you* who would do something stupid for a man," Benny said.

"She does not have exclusive license to that privilege," Sophia sniffed. "I have many more years ahead of me to drag the family's name through the mud."

"As a governess?"

Rather than admit he made a good point, Sophia turned away. "*That* is neither here nor there."

"No, what is here is the mess I have made," Ellen said. "And I didn't do it for Max. I thought I could buy Papa enough time to pass the abolition bill."

Papa rocked back onto his heels, pensive. "It may be a setback. But there have been plenty of scandals about Northfield Hall before. We will recover. As long as you children are on my side, I can weather any storm."

"I had a thought…" An inkling, really, that she hadn't yet puzzled through. "If I marry Mr. Thistleman, we will have a small but steady income. I could send some to you every quarter. Perhaps then, you wouldn't need to sell our linen on New Bond Street."

Papa shook his head. "That is kind, Ellen, but that kind of income would be inconsequential to what Northfield Hall requires to operate, and besides, Thistleman will need all the money he can get for his abolition efforts."

In her usual sarcastic way, Sophia said, "Yes, if you are going to marry for wealth, you would do better to blackmail Viscount Berwick into it."

"He did offer to marry me," Ellen admitted – though she couldn't for the life of her think why she would volunteer this information. "I refused him."

For a moment, the room was silent as all three of them blinked at her in shock. Then, Papa cleared his throat. "If you are going to marry, Ellen, don't do it to save Northfield Hall. Do it because you know he will make your life better. Whatever else, I know your mother would agree with me on *that*."

In a flash, Ellen remembered a moment from her childhood. It was no more than a glimpse, an impression. Papa returning from London, so fresh off the road that he still wore his muddy cloak and boots. They children had surrounded him, demanding kisses, which he gladly dispensed. Then Mama had walked in. And they had fitted together in an embrace – nothing more than a hug – that made Ellen believe their souls had been fated to find each other.

That embrace, she thought, must have felt something like the moment in the carriage when Max had slipped his arm around her, requiring nothing of her and yet offering all the comfort she could need.

Benny flung himself backwards into his chair. "This talk of marriage is making me ill."

Rising to his feet, Papa served himself a cup of mint tisane – the other teapot on the tray – and sat in the remaining chair. He looked at each of them, one by one. "So, at some point in the very near future, our family will be dragged through the scandal sheets and back again. It may well be an unpleasant time. It will not be without its rewards, however. For one thing, we will learn which of our friends are true enough to stand by us. For another, we will learn something of our own characters. The strength of our convictions." Pausing, he sipped his tea. "You are intelligent adults, capable of establishing your own convictions, even if they are different than mine. I should like you each to close your eyes. Clear your mind of everything but the future. And now: what does a good life look like to you?"

Ellen's lashes were still a little wet from her tears, and at first, she could only think of that and the congestion behind her nose.

Sophia announced, "Rooms of my own, paid for by my savings from working as a governess, with no one bothering me about what I'm doing or why."

"Must we speak them aloud?" from Benny.

"You may keep it to yourself," Papa allowed.

Ellen tried again. The world was dark and simple with her eyes closed. A memory of Max popped up, which she banished. He returned almost immediately: that last expression, when he glowered as if to dare her to change her mind, his face perfectly handsome despite all she had put him through.

If she couldn't have him – if she shoved him from her mind – what did Ellen want?

She couldn't think of one thing alone.

What her heart served to her closed eyes were a hundred moments collecting together. The carpentry workshop. Chisel and wood in her palms. Friends at supper discussing their day's work and planning for the future. That feeling of belonging that came with Northfield Hall and the thrill when someone new arrived and, with tears in their eyes, said they finally felt they had come home.

In the past, when she had envisioned this, a veil of guilt dimmed it. Guilt that Ellen wasn't doing more. She should want to fight slavery in Saint Kitts with Percy, or to join the lecture circuit preaching against imports, or somehow upend her world – the way her parents had done – in order to improve the lot of others.

Ellen let this guilt slide away. She need not make great sacrifices in order to live a good life. Especially when she didn't even know which sacrifices would be the right ones. If she only lived her days with joy, lining up her actions so that she could be proud of each one, and if she made room for her companions to do so too – that would be enough.

She fluttered her eyes open and smiled at her family. If she couldn't have Max, then at least she could have this.

CHAPTER SEVENTEEN

July 1811

Three Weeks Later

IN HIS FATHER'S STUDY, Max counted no fewer than a dozen imported goods. The mahogany desk, rattan-caned chairs, and Persian rug were obvious. The silk wallpaper featuring frolicking green nymphs less so. In a glass-encased cabinet were rum, wine, and cognac – the latter two, in fact, Max suspected of being recently smuggled in from France. Then there were all the curiosities decorating his father's shelves: jade figurines from China, a carved ivory tiger from India, a jewel-encrusted snuff box, a nephrite pen case, and the twin marble Egytpian bookends.

Counting imports, Max had discovered, was an interesting way to exercise the mind in idle moments.

His father entered wearing his muslin summer dressing gown and with a delicate cup of coffee balanced in his hand. "It is far too early for calls, Berwick."

Max tilted his head in apology. "You asked for the earliest print of *The Perceptive.*"

The paper, still warm from the presses, waited patiently on his father's desk. Max's article took up the entire front page.

"Ah, the moment has arrived, then. I had begun to fear you would never finish your scribbling." With a gesture, he called in a footman who lit more candles and produced glinting spectacles. The earl smirked at Max as they waited. "I cannot decide if I am most eager to see Lord Preston's face this morning, when all of London has read of his failure, or when you win that Great Yarmouth election and take your place in the House of Commons."

Max had briefed his father on his conversation with Lord Preston before secluding himself to write the report. He supposed that the earl had been crowing about it these last three weeks. Max had declined all society in favor of writing. At the beginning, he had tried to take his time, to delay the report as long as he could without rousing his father's suspicion. Then he hadn't been able to stop.

It felt to Max that he had spent every daylight hour of the past twenty days wringing out words about Northfield Hall's agriculture, laborers, and corruption. And then doing it again for the final draft. Downes despaired over the ink permanently staining Max's fingertips and shirt cuffs. Max far preferred that to the alternative, which would have been drinking himself into the Thames in order to forget Ellen.

He felt only vaguely ill as his father settled down to read the article. This was the moment he had worked towards all spring, when he could prove once and for all that he was serious about a political future.

Max had envisioned it going a bit differently, of course. For one thing, he had always pictured his father toasting him with champagne at the club, not at the break of dawn.

For another, Max had always assumed he would write an article aligned with his father's convictions.

It took about one tick of the clock for the earl to start sputtering. Red splotches appeared at his forehead and neck as he kept reading. At the end of the first paragraph, he lunged from his seat. "Is this some kind of prank?"

Max rose, too, as a sign of respect. "No, sir. That is the truth."

"The truth?" His father fisted the paper and, sneering, read, "*I spent weeks at Northfield Hall searching for its shocking truths for you, Dear Reader, and here it is at last: at Northfield Hall, men and women trust each other to put the good of the community above the good of the individual – and they have made me want to do so, too.*"

Max had rewritten that sentence a dozen times trying not to make it sound sentimental. At one point, he had even juxtaposed a Locke quote to show the stark differences in his attitude towards Northfield Hall from the beginning of his research to the end. This sentence was the best he could do to express it in words.

"Is this a jape to you, Berwick? I cannot think what induced Cabot to read this, let alone print it. Have you taken leave of your senses?"

Max had, in fact, bribed the editor with two hundred pounds – five years' worth of the newspaperman's salary – to print the article as Max had written it.

"I know it is not what you wanted me to write, sir, but it is the sum of what I learned in my time at Northfield Hall. I can do nothing except be honest."

His father wasn't listening. "You did this to embarrass me. I cannot think *why* you should want to do so when I am the one who pays for your clothes and food and those jewels you insist on buying courtesans. Consider yourself cut off, from now until you can worm your way back into my good graces. *If* you can ever do so. I'm sure I don't know how. I can hardly stand to look at you."

A month or two ago, Max would have felt this speech as a failure. He had, after all, spent his whole life trying desperately to earn his father's approval.

Now, Max felt nothing but sadness for the earl. The man was so stuck in his own thinking that he could not even see his son standing before him. Max was nothing but a specter, representing hopes and dreams that would never – could never have – materialize.

Max let the words wash over him. When the earl finished his tirade, he responded only, "As you say, Father." Then, with a short, respectful bow, Max picked up his satchel and exited the earl's townhouse.

For three weeks now, Max had been dreading that interview. Even up through taking that last kiss from Ellen, he had considered writing the report his duty. A commitment that had come long before her and would long outlast her. He had gone so far as to write a draft the way that his father expected.

That had felt rather like flaying himself alive. Because the truth was that Max no longer agreed with his father, or Cabot, or even his previous self. Leading towards an ideal was not dangerous or farfetched or futile. It was hope, and it pushed men to be better versions of themselves, rather than allowing power to settle amongst those who had always held it.

He did not agree with every single aspect of Ellen's principles. But he would far rather live the way she did than follow his father's example. He would rather make her promises and try to keep them than spend his life serving only his own purposes.

Besides, he was beginning to agree that the government needed to curtail the natural greed of man.

And now Max had declared himself to his father. Soon, anyone with access to *The Perceptive* would know it, too: Maximilian Hainsworth, Viscount Berwick considered Northfield Hall a paragon of good leadership.

Max only hoped it was enough.

The sun still hadn't breached the rooftops as Max cut through Mayfair to Partridge House. It was far too early for a social call, but Max suspected Ellen would be up, keeping country hours even after a month in London.

Max knew there was little chance she would change her mind about marrying *him*, but he needed her to read his report, to prove that he had kept his promise to write his honest impressions.

He counted the windows to find her bedchamber. Then, catching up pebbles from the street, he commenced trying to get her attention. The first stone missed the window, hitting the building's façade a few feet away. Max threw the next more carefully and waited.

Not even a flicker of movement from the window.

Rearing his arm back, he tossed up the third pebble.

With a great shattering of glass, it sailed directly through the windowpane.

Well, fuck.

Two footmen rushed from the front door. They nearly accosted Max before realizing he was a peer, not a thief. "I only want to talk to Miss Preston!" he apologized. "I'll pay for the window, of course."

They kept him on the front step, glaring at him, until someone from the family could be roused. Max spotted a simple linen dressing gown flapping on the stairs and his hopes rose – until he realized it was Miss Sophia.

"You do like mischief, don't you?" she greeted him. "I near about had a heart attack thinking the mob had come for us at last."

Max tried to look appropriately contrite. "I would talk to your sister, if I could. Only for a moment."

"I would talk to her if I could, too. She isn't here."

"Where can I find her?"

Sophia shook her head. "She is gone. Quit London forever, if she can be believed. Off to meet her destiny."

Max's heart plummeted. Had she married Thistleman after all and sailed for Saint Kitts?

Lord Preston arrived then. Fully dressed, shaved, and austere as ever. His serious eyes measured Max from top to bottom.

"I was hoping to speak with Miss Preston," Max said, desperate.

Her father nodded, just the once. "You had better come in."

THERE WAS NOTHING BETTER than a holiday at Northfield Hall. Everyone wore their best clothes; Killian and Mr. Hamlyn and Mrs. Shayler made up a musician party with drums, fiddle, and her haunting voice; Cook handed out dozens of baskets with fresh bread, cheese, cured meats, and ale; there wasn't a somber face to be found in miles. Even though it had rained earlier that morning, the day of the theatric was beautiful and balmy, and already, Ellen wished it would never end.

Ellen ducked behind the stage to make sure the children were ready. Mrs. Chow knelt before Caroline, quickly sewing up a tear in her skirt, while Edward held Caro's hand, stoically calming her as she cried over having ruined her costume already. The Shayler girls recited lines to each other, and poor Miss Lockyear tried to herd the Greek chorus into their white robes.

There was no better kind of chaos.

Ellen had built the stage to sit in the clearing beside the pond. Behind the audience stood Northfield Hall. On the horizon beyond the stage was the chalk hill with the great white horse carved into its grassy side. To the left were the flax fields, about ready for harvest to become next year's supply of linen. And to the right was the path to the newly-completed cottages, into which the families would move that very night.

Ellen returned to the audience. All of Northfield Hall had turned out for the performance, so she started skirting around the edge of the crowd to take up a place in the back, where she wouldn't block anyone's view. Layla grabbed her hand. "Sit with us, Miss Preston, won't you?"

The maid gestured to an empty spot of grass beside her group, which included Jacques the footman as well as a couple of kitchen maids. One of them, a redhead, said in a lilting Scottish brogue, "I've been meaning to ask you how you keep the shine in your hair. Do you use a special cream at night?"

Ellen couldn't help laughing. "You would have to ask Layla. If it were up to me, I would chop all this off." Sinking onto the ground beside them, she eased into their chatter, trying not to second-guess her good luck.

When she first returned to Northfield Hall, Ellen sat down with Mrs. Chow to talk about her encounter with Martin. And to apologize for all the things she hadn't seen about what it was like to live at the Hall as a worker, not a family member. "How were you to know?" Mrs. Chow had dismissed, pulling her into a hug. "Martin has his experience. You have yours. I have mine. We love each other, don't we? That's enough."

Ellen didn't want it to be enough. So now, in between finishing the shutters, she stopped to ask her companions what they really thought. Whether they agreed that imports should be avoided. What their goals were. If they wanted something more from Northfield Hall than they had so far gotten.

Not everyone replied honestly. But Ellen found the more she led with her own honesty – breaking the bread, so to speak, by admitting she felt stupid for not knowing about Berkshire linen – the more the other person was willing to open up. And now, here she was, part of the crowd instead of holding herself apart.

If only Max could see her.

Uncle Maulvi and Aunt Croft climbed onto the stage. "Your attention, please," Uncle Maulvi said softly, and then Aunt Croft cried out, "Oi! Stop your chatter!"

The crowd laughed. For anyone familiar with Northfield Hall, this was a feature of their homegrown theater.

"Thank you for joining us today," Uncle Maulvi began. "Lord Preston sends his regrets that he cannot be here, but he remains in London to organize a bill to abolish slavery once and for all." At this, the crowd cheered. "We celebrate this afternoon a great project led by our own Chow Bou Yuen and his sons: the completion of four new cottages. If you have not yet toured them, make friends with their new inhabitants so that they might invite you in." He took the time to name each family and highlight their recent contributions to Northfield Hall. Ellen cheered each one. "And now, without further ado, I invite you to enjoy the world premiere of *The Cottages at Northfield.*"

The children entered the stage all in a jumble. Ellen was just laughing as Caroline stared out at the crowd – at last struck dumb, by stage fright no less! – when Nate tapped on her shoulder. "There is someone to speak with you."

He pointed her attention behind them, to where the path curved backwards towards the Hall and the trade village. Ellen had to lean onto her knees to see anyone. And then she spotted him.

Max. Not quite looking her way. His hair had grown longer again, enough to sway in the breeze even beneath his hat. His travel clothes were simple and homespun. He was neither Lord Berwick nor Mr. Sims. Pure Max.

Handsome enough to stop her breath.

Nate took her spot beside Layla. Ellen barely noticed. She focused on walking as sedately as possible. She wanted to run to Max, like a desert wanderer to an oasis.

He looked nervous. Ellen had never seen him nervous before. The uncertainty as he shifted his weight from one foot to the other endeared him to her.

She couldn't afford to feel this way. He was still Lord Berwick, had still pretended to be Mr. Sims. Ellen should be steeling herself to push him away again.

She nearly laughed with giddiness when she finally got within breath of him. "Max."

He smiled. Earnestly. "Fancy meeting you here."

The nerve of him. Why did she love it so? "You came all the way to Northfield Hall to be smart with me?"

Reaching into his satchel – the old canvas one she recognized from his time as Mr. Sims – Max produced a slightly-creased newspaper and handed it to her. "I came to Northfield Hall to ask you to read this."

She knew before taking it that it was his report published in *The Perceptive*. Ellen didn't want to read it. Not on a beautiful afternoon when everything was right with the world. Perhaps not ever. However, from the corner of her eye, she saw Max's throat bob with a nervous swallow. For his sake, she decided to at least look at the headline.

VISCOUNT BERWICK LAUDS NORTHFIELD HALL

Ellen's eyes sped forward. She was sure she was reading it wrong. Her heart hammered too loudly in her ear; that must be why she thought it said Max found Northfield Hall inspiring. And that he considered her father an example to all of the ruling class. And that he aspired to be more like the Preston family, who designed their life so they could be proud of each action.

Perhaps you are like me, Dear Reader, and were raised
to protect your own interests at all costs. To only spend

*that penny if it will bring you and you alone plea-
sure. To cultivate friendships that will benefit your
future. Even to select your spouse based on what
money or connections she will bring to elevate your
family.*

*This was my framework to view the world until I
met the Preston family. Through their example, I
now see that for what it is: selfish. And what need
have I, one of the richest and most powerful men in
England, to be selfish?*

Ellen couldn't read any further. She searched Max, as if the
way he stared at her would prove this to be true or false. "Is this
truly what you wrote?"

He nodded. "Circulated to all five thousand of *The Perceptive*'s subscribers, and quite a few more, I think, who bought it
on the streets."

"And it is truly what you think?"

Another nod. Max tucked his chin, not quite looking at her. "I
meant it when I said that my views have changed because of you.
I couldn't write the report the way my father wanted me to. Mind
you, I am still a proponent of a strong imperial economy. But I don't
want to imagine the future based on what I think is or isn't possible.

I want to imagine it based on what could be, the way you do, and see how far that can take us."

Behind them, the Greek chorus began a wildly off-beat song.

"Ellen." Max took her hands, and the newspaper floated to the grass. "When I am around you, I feel able to be a different man. One who is not quite so arrogant or self-serving or unkind. In part, because I want to be better for you. More, because I admire you. I aspire to be like you. I love you, with my whole heart, and I've waited these three and a half weeks to say it so that you would know I mean it."

Ellen's heart was swelling and breaking all at the same time. She didn't want to have to refuse him again.

He tightened his grip around her palms. "You think our lives are incompatible. I agree: there will be challenges. But that doesn't mean we shouldn't try. Northfield Hall does not succeed because it is isolated. It succeeds because it brings people who are different from each other in a hundred ways and unites them.

"You and I are different. You are allergic to doing the wrong thing. I am bereft without coffee. You believe the best in people, and I manipulate to get what I want. You are the daughter of a radical Whig; I am the heir to the staunchest of Tories." His hazel eyes glinted in the sun. "Just imagine the example we could set if we joined our lives. If we worked together to forge the best path for Britain."

His words were too pretty. Ellen had to remind herself aloud, "I can't give up the free produce movement. Or carpentry. Or Northfield Hall."

"I am not asking you to. I don't want you to be anything other than exactly who you are. Honest. Kind. Willing to put me in my place. We can live here, if you want, until I inherit, and then we can take the Northfield model to Montchampion Manor."

From the stage, Caroline screeched too high a note.

"Ellen, I have never felt an emotion as intense and as pure as the love – the joy – I feel for you. Whether I am with you or not. If you feel even half that—"

And, oh, she did. Ellen had been trying to deny it, but Max had become part of her soul, without her even noticing.

"—then give me your faith. Believe in me, the way you believe in Northfield. If we love each other every day, we can make a life together. That is my ideal. Please, darling, my dear Ellen, won't you be an idealist with me?"

There were a hundred reasons still why they shouldn't marry. Anyone past the age of sixteen could predict that a marriage based on love alone would not be happy. But Max was right: there were also a hundred reasons why Northfield Hall was doomed, and why the people gathered at the theatric this very moment should be shunned, and why Ellen should feel shame for the way she lived rather than pride. If one listened only to reason, one would remain with the safe status quo for the rest of time.

Ellen loved Max, even though she shouldn't. And here he was, too handsome for words, laying himself bare. Because he loved her, too. Because he knew they were both fuller versions of themselves when they were together.

If one can be proud of an action, do it.

Ellen banished all the fear from her body. It was time to let her heart answer. "I don't know what is right or wrong. I thought it was simple. It's not. You help me see that. I don't know if it is right to marry you. But I know I want to." Oh, she hadn't expected that to feel so freeing, as if wings sprouted from her back and lifted her into his arms. "Yes, Max, I will marry you."

His hands closed around her. He grinned the most earnest grin she had ever see. With the children's chorus wailing terrible notes behind them, they kissed for all the world to witness.

From somewhere in the distance, her brother whooped, and then Sophia and Benny and Papa spilled out from where they had been hiding, and soon all of Northfield Hall was dancing. For her. For Max. For everyone who could steal a spot of joy from life.

It was better than Ellen could ever have imagined.

EPILOGUE

Summer of 1814

Three Years Later

THE TRADE VILLAGE WAS silent except for the stroke of Ellen's stain brush. Well, and the chirp of the birds and rustle of squirrels and chipmunks going about their daily business. Her fellow journeymen and apprentices were gone for the afternoon to join in the Thatcham summer fair, leaving her the quiet heat of the afternoon.

It was one of Ellen's favorite kind of days. In the absence of company, she let herself hum a tune, one that had no beginning and no end and couldn't really be said to carry a melody, either. Her mind fixed on the task at hand, leaving her no room for worries other than whether the stain would set properly. In the spring, she and

Max had disassembled the shed in the southwestern field in order to reclaim the wood for new projects. That had been bittersweet, but now Ellen was rejuvenated to transform the tired planks. All it took was a little carving, sanding, and staining to turn the old into something completely new. Completely hopeful, too: at the moment, she was applying the final stain to a crib for Mrs. Beauchamp's coming infant.

"You make me jealous when you look at wood that way."

Ellen jumped at the interruption. She had been so absorbed in her task that she had not heard Max's footsteps. He leaned against the doorjamb, smirking.

Even after these three years, Ellen's heart leapt when she caught sight of him. Especially when he wore his hair long and it slipped out of its ribbon, as if its sole purpose was to seduce her.

"Back from the fair so soon?"

"Your daughter did not like the crowds, proving once again that she has your good taste. Never fear, though. Nate remained to sell your carvings, and with Aunt Charlotte's party in attendance, I do believe we will clear one hundred pounds from your nativity scenes alone."

This was the part of their new scheme to provide Northfield Hall with income that did not require Berkshire linen to be sold at shops on New Bond Street. Ellen whittled something new every day – sealed and stained by Max, when he was not too busy with work in the House of Commons – and sold it as artwork. They had increased Northfield Hall's honey output, too, so that instead of requiring high profits from linen alone, they could sell multiple goods for reasonable prices – and only at free labor shops – in order to earn the necessary income.

Max liked to tease that he lived at Northfield Hall as a spy, so that he could steal all its successes for Montchampion Manor once he inherited.

At the moment, he continued, "I put Rosalind down for a nap and thought I would remind you of the time."

Ellen wiped her hands across her apron. "It is good you found your way here. I am in desperate need of your help."

He leaned his torso only *that* much further into the shop. "We have Sophia's farewell supper to dress for, and you made me promise that I would remind you not to while away too many hours here because you still need to wrap her present."

Incorrigible man. Parroting her own words back to her instead of ripping her clothes off and ravishing her on the worktable like she wanted. Sophia was off to her new position in the morning, taking up the mantel of governess to Lord and Lady Widlake in Northampton, so they were closing out the summer fair with a feast in Sophia's honor.

Still, that didn't mean there was no time to take advantage of the empty trade village and a handsome husband. "I only need your help for half an hour, at most."

"I have letters to write," Max teased. He did like to make her sing for her supper. Untying her apron, Ellen crossed to the doorway, enjoying the weight of his gaze the whole way there. "How shall I ever pass the bill to increase tariffs on imports if my wife constantly distracts me from my work?"

"Ah, you should have married a simpering miss if you wanted a wife you could ignore."

After their marriage – which had occurred by special license approximately two days after Max's return to Northfield Hall – Papa had helped Max run for a seat in the House of Commons in a nearby Berkshire borough. In the two years since, Max had been particularly focused on building bridges between the Whigs and Tories to create fairer policies for the poor of Britain. Ellen was not always satisfied with the compromises that he struck, but it was certainly preferable to any policies proposed by the Earl of Meretta.

One day, Max would inherit that title and join Papa in the House of Lords. Ellen would be Countess of Meretta, their firstborn son – if they were so blessed – would be Viscount Berwick, and their whole life would shift. Not unlike the crib she was building. Same wood, new purpose.

At the moment, Ellen had little interest in politics, or even the future. She seized Max's necktie in her two hands. "Now, look lively. I need you in the pit."

With a tug, Ellen directed him towards the sawpit – currently nothing but a gaping hole in the workshop, awaiting its next batch of timber to be cut. Max glanced back at her, one eyebrow raised questioningly, before climbing down the ladder.

"I think I know where you are going with this, Miss Preston, and I do believe it is your sauciest idea yet."

"That's Lady Berwick, thank you very much." Hands on his shoulders, she vaulted down to join him in the cool dirt.

"My darling Lady Berwick."

Max pulled her against him in that lovely, cozy way that felt as natural as breathing. "I do love you," she whispered, nuzzling into the scratch of his shaved cheek. She could have stayed like this all afternoon, simply holding him, losing her mind in Max's touch the way she lost herself in the shape of wood.

There was, however, one thing she had been wanting to do for years.

Ellen pushed Max away. "Now, Mr. Sims," she teased, summoning all the haughtiness in the world. "Remove your clothes."

Author's Note

AND SO, DEAR READER, we come to the end of another story. At times, this one was a soaring joy for me to write; at others, I wasn't sure it deserved the light of day. I hope that you are now feeling a glowing reluctance to part with characters who have become dear to you.

If you are one of my newsletter subscribers, you know that I have transitioned most of my historical notes to monthly research deep dives, on account of there being too much to tie directly back to any given story. I do want to highlight a few things here. First, I am even worse than Max when it comes to woodwork. I watched a lot of YouTube videos and consulted a Regency-era joinery book to get the gist of carpentry, but there are definitely inaccuracies for the sake of a good story. One of the most glaring is that England was actually running out of wood, so rather than having fresh timber to cut in a sawpit, they would have been disassembling older buildings for wood (or building with brick). However, the sawpit was too perfect a display of raw muscular power to succumb to such details.

Throughout the story, I used the Whig and Tory labels pretty widely, which may not reflect the nuances of how they were actually wielded at the time. I didn't want to get into specifics of British politics but instead represent the stakes of falling in love with someone from a different ideology, specifically when that ideology is part of your identity. Rotten boroughs existed, where whole seats in the House of Commons represented only a handful of voters, and were used by wealthy people to purchase power, though I admit I did not flesh out the technicalities of how Max would actually have been elected.

If you are interested in the role of textiles in the global economy or the history of dyes, I recommend *A Perfect Red* by Amy Butler Greenfield and *Empire of Cotton* by Sven Beckert.

For those of you who read *The Baron Without Blame*, you may notice a key difference: Mr. and Mrs. Zhou have suddenly become Mr. and Mrs. Chow! I worked with an authenticity reader on this book who pointed out that since the family spoke Cantonese, they would likely spell their name in the Cantonese transliteration (or romanization). Now, I still only have a cursory understanding of the history of English transliteration of Chinese, but it does seem that at the time the family came from China, they would have used the Cantonese transliteration. So, to reflect the true spirit of the family as Cantonese, I have officially changed the spelling in Preston Family Canon.

As always, I have a number of people to thank for their support of this book. My amazing cover designer, Julia Gerbach, who gave me a beautiful image of Max and Ellen to return to every time I needed to reconnect with their spirit. My interior layout designer, Asya Blue, who gives me confidence this ebook will properly load on your ereader device. Crystal Shelley of Rabbit with a Red Pen provided me with a thorough and thoughtful authenticity read to make sure the Chow family's storyline rang true. My amazing beta readers who were honest exactly when I needed them to be: Sarah Flanagan, Jen Trinh, and Danielle Lamoureaux. My parents and aunt, who allowed me to write to deadline even when I was supposed to be on vacation with them. And, of course, my husband, who had to put up with a lot of artistic angst as I wondered if I would ever be satisfied with this plot. Nothing gave me greater joy than when, reading a near-final draft, he declared with some incredulity that this is his favorite book of mine (so far).

Thank *you*, dear reader, for diving into this little corner of my imagination. I hope you visit again soon!

EXCERPT FROM THE GOVERENESS WITHOUT GUILT

One bored governess, one handsome doctor, and unchaperoned nighttime activities. What could possibly go wrong?

1814

The schoolroom at Robin Abbey offered two escape routes: the door to the corridor and the window to the courtyard.

Sophia Preston considered both options as she sat in the front of the room, waiting for her three pupils to finish scratching out French conjugations on their chalkboards. She didn't consider the door much of an option. It might lead her from the room, but she would still be trapped in the drafty old Abbey with no one but the well-meaning Cosgrove family and their household for company.

The window, on the other hand, sat two stories above the courtyard. If she survived the drop, she would surely break an ankle or wrist or perhaps something worse on the gravel beneath. An ominous prospect. One, she knew, a sane person wouldn't consider at all preferable to polite company with conventional people.

In the months since arriving at Robin Abbey, home to the Baron and Baroness Widlake and their six and a half children, Sophia had begun to entertain the idea that she was not completely sane. For this was a good position with kind employers who let her be herself. Perhaps it did not include dances in London and shopping on Bond Street, as she had envisioned when first imagining herself a governess, nor were there gentleman to flirt with, nor were her charges at all keen to heed her attempts to steer them towards independent thinking. Still, Sophia's account grew fat from Lord Widlake's bank draft. She lived free from the confines of her family and their rules at Northfield Hall. And she did it all as a governess, just as she had proclaimed often and loudly that she would.

She must be insane, else she would be happy, not contemplating an escape out the window.

In unison, her three charges—the Misses Danielle, Francesca, and Mary Cosgrove—raised their heads. Sophia heard it, too: the clatter of hoofbeats and carriage wheels coming down the drive.

"Is it him?" Miss Mary asked, spilling her chalk to the ground in her nine-year-old's excitement.

Miss Cosgrove—the thirteen-year-old, eldest sister who considered herself too urbane for excitement—condescended, "Who else would it be, when Father sent the coach to fetch him from the inn this very morning?"

"Oh, please, may we look?" This from Miss Francesca, the eleven-year-old, who clasped her hands together as if to pray as she presented the question to Sophia.

Sophia didn't know if all children were like this or only these three, but she had soon discovered that whatever learning happened in the schoolroom occurred by accident, in between battles over whose personality commanded the most power.

The skirmishes sapped more energy from her than the actual lessons did, and those already stole her enthusiasm for the day.

"Oh, please?" Miss Mary echoed.

The girls might wage their battles, but Sophia was determined to win the war. "Once you have finished your conjugations." She stared them down until they bent over their slates again.

Victory in hand, Sophia permitted herself a sojourn to the window. All morning, she had told herself she would not take too much interest in the new arrival. He was the accoucheur–or man-midwife, to those without French–there to deliver Lady Widlake's coming baby. New blood in Robin Abbey, perhaps, but Sophia knew better than to get her hopes up. He might be dull. Conservative. Unattractive. She could not plan for him to be her antidote any more than she could leap from the window.

That said, it did not hurt to get a glimpse of the man.

The schoolroom boasted an excellent view of Robin Abbey's central courtyard. In one sweeping glance, she could take in the sunlight spiking off the Abbey's white stone, the mud spattering the carriage though it had been repainted just two weeks ago, the shadow of movement as servants hustled through the cloisters to greet the new arrival.

Yet, in the schoolroom a good ten feet above the courtyard, Sophia's view of the man himself was limited. When the coach-and-four came to a stop before the Abbey's entrance, she could see Mr. Anderson's hat extend from the interior of the carriage: a modest stovepipe fashion with expensive beaver felt that glinted in the afternoon sun. From there, she observed the cloak billowing out from his shoulders.

She could not see what interested her most. The length of his legs as he stepped onto the drive. The bulk of the body wrapped beneath that gray wool cloak. The sparkle–or lack thereof–in his eyes.

She watched for these signs, anyway. Impatient to a fault, as her family liked to tease. Sophia leaned forward, her breath fogging the window, as if a few extra inches would reveal to her the intimate details of the doctor's physique.

He was not strictly a doctor, nor did she strictly have no idea what to expect of his appearance. The household had been preparing for his arrival for weeks, almost more than anticipating Lady Widlake's Great Event itself. Sophia knew already that he had studied in Edinburgh, that his glittering reputation stemmed from a successful delivery for the Countess of Gresham, and that he was an Anglo-Indian with skin as brown as his mother's.

None of this told Sophia what she most wanted to know. Did he stride with confidence, or match his shuffle to an obsequious hunch? Was he austere and solemn, as if always a breath away from delivering bad news, or did he cheer the room with learned wit?

When he looked at a woman, did he see merely her role in the world, or did he notice the flesh and blood beneath her gown, waiting to be stirred to ecstasy?

"Is it him after all?" asked Miss Mary. "Did he bring chocolate?"

Miss Cosgrove heaved out a deep sigh. "Don't be a child, Mary. What will our visitors think if you always demand chocolate of them?"

"Mr. Brewer brought chocolate last year for Jacob. And before that for the twins. Francesca told me. Didn't he?"

"Mr. Anderson isn't Mr. Brewer, is he? He has never met you, nor does he concern himself with your sweet tooth. You are being gauche."

"I am not!"

"Miss Preston?" Miss Francesca cried out, just as her two sisters' voices reached the high-pitched peal that guaranteed Sophia a headache for the rest of the day.

When envisioning herself a governess, Sophia had imagined she would be like Mama, who had loved teaching the children of North-field Hall. She would have chuckled at this squabble and settled it with some humorous wisdom.

Now, Sophia didn't have the patience to emulate her mother. She found only the energy to intone, "If you have not finished your conjugations, then you should not be speaking."

The scrape of chalk against its board replaced the bickering. For now. But Sophia had been governess to the Misses Cosgrove for four months already. She knew better than to trust the peace.

Below, Mr. Anderson paused on the drive, head tilted up and away from her, as if to take in the whole of the Abbey in one glance. He wouldn't be able to do that, not from where he stood. It rose two stories–three, if one counted the bell tower punctuating its southwestern arm–and squared its stone wings around him, almost enclosing the courtyard on all four sides, save the drive from which he had entered. Even if he turned in a circle, he wouldn't be able to see where the new wing ended, jutting backwards as it did to accommodate the staterooms.

He looked upwards, all the same. Then the footmen—Frank and Jasper Gibson—joined the scene, claiming Mr. Anderson's bags from the coach with fluid efficiency. The accoucheur's attention returned to mortal beings. Sophia could see his head bob with the movement of speech, though she was too far away to glimpse the specifics of his face. He was shorter than Jasper, who sprouted up past six feet tall, but looked about the same height as Frank. A good height. Sophia liked a man whose eyes she could meet without craning her neck backwards.

"I have a question."

Sophia jumped: the whisper came from right beside her, yet she hadn't heard Miss Francesca cross the room. The girl held her chalkboard like some kind of innocent. She even held it up and pointed to the verb *convoiter* to carry on the charade of scholarship. But she gave herself away when she rose onto her tiptoes and darted her gaze at the window.

"Oh, very well." Sophia stepped aside. "Come see what Mr. Anderson looks like."

Miss Mary rushed to join them. For her part, Miss Cosgrove murmured about how unseemly it all was even as she sashayed up to press her palm against the window glass.

In the courtyard, Mr. Anderson held out a hand to Frank. At first, Sophia thought he was trying to take a valise. Then the footman accepted the hand, bowed, and slipped his palm into a pocket, and she understood the accoucheur had paid a tip.

Mr. Anderson offered a tip to the coachman, too. The coins caught the sunlight as they spilled from Mr. Anderson's black glove into the coachman's. Sophia wondered, if she were closer, whether she would see that the gloves were new, on display like his generosity for the benefit of his new employers. And his boots—did they gleam from a fresh shining, or did they carry the dust of travel?

"He doesn't look anything like Mr. Brewer," Miss Francesca breathed.

"Why should he?" Miss Cosgrove responded. "They share a profession, not a bloodline."

"I still hope he has chocolate for us," said Miss Mary.

Sophia wondered what Mr. Anderson would think, should he look up to discover the spies in the schoolroom window. Would he be flattered to be the center of attention? Grin and give a flirtatious smile to the young girls desperate for his distraction? Or would he be shy and turn away and stutter over his words when they all finally met?

She hoped for something in between. A man who was not unaware of his effect on others, who enjoyed giving a little pleasure here and there when all it cost him was a smile, but who did not abuse the power of his charm.

A man should always be more kind than he is proud, Mama used to say.

Sophia pushed the echo away. Mama's advice had suited Sophia when she was an audacious fifteen-year-old. She didn't like to guess at what her mother would say to her now, if she discovered Sophia as a diffident governess.

"May we go meet him?" Miss Mary asked. "I pressed a dandelion in my Bible to give him as a welcome gift."

"A dandelion? But that's a weed!" protested Miss Francesca.

Sophia placed a hand on both girls' shoulders to quiet them. "We must remain at our studies. You will meet him soon enough. I imagine we will all dine together tonight."

"Besides," Miss Cosgrove sneered, "it is not done for a young lady to present anyone but her family or her betrothed with a gift."

Sophia felt the weight of their eyes on her. Their previous governess had been more concerned with teaching them the minutiae of etiquette than with scholarship. Though Sophia took the opposite approach, Miss Cosgrove in the mighty wisdom of a thirteen-year-old considered anything not related to finding a husband a complete waste of time. She therefore found every lesson of Sophia's both suspect and wanting.

At first, Sophia had found it inspiring. A goal by which to measure her success at Robin Abbey. But now that four months had passed without so much as a begrudging concession from Miss Cosgrove, she found it exhausting.

Everything about governessing, in fact, was exhausting. Which was why she ignored the girls looking at her. Let them condemn her as incompetent or inappropriate or bookish. Sophia had only eight months left on her contract with the family, and then she would free herself for another adventure.

In the meantime, Mr. Anderson was here.

"You may present him with your flower, after the proper introductions have been made."

The valises were sorted, and the coachman was nudging the horses around the well to head out the courtyard to the stables. Shoulders forward, Mr. Anderson followed Frank and Jasper up the stone steps to the Abbey's entrance. Desperation propelled Sophia: she pressed her fingertips into the window glass as if that could freeze him in place. She needed him in sight so she could drink him in, measure him beyond his hat and height and coins, keep tasting an elixir of hope that he might be the distraction she yearned for.

As if he heard her silent plea, Mr. Anderson hesitated on the steps, just within view. He swept off his hat and tilted his face upwards, as if to catch the sun.

He was not the one who froze: Sophia did. Heart, soul, and quim.

Handsome. Even from a distance. She could see the line of his jaw, the slope of his nose, the expression in his brow. The glow of his brown skin.

She got only that glimpse. It lasted less than a second before he resumed his march into the Abbey.

It was enough. For the first time in weeks, Sophia's spirits lifted. With Mr. Anderson around, escape from Robin Abbey might no longer be necessary.

Keep reading The Governess Without Guilt from your favorite bookstore or library!

ABOUT THE AUTHOR

KATHERINE GRANT WRITES AWARD-WINNING Regency Romance novels for the modern reader. Her writing has been recognized by Foreword INDIES Book of the Year Awards, the Next Generation Indie Book Awards, the National Indie Excellence Awards, the Romance Slam Jam Emma Awards, and the Shelf Unbound Indie Book Awards. If you love ballgowns, secret kisses, and social commentary, a book hangover is coming your way.

Her ideal day includes a cup of tea, a good book, and a board game with her husband. Find out more at www.katherinegrantromance.com

Connect with Katherine on your favorite social media platforms:

instagram.com/katherine_grant_romance/

tiktok.com/@katherinegrantromance

facebook.com/groups/katherinegrant

bookbub.com/authors/katherine-grant

goodreads.com/author/show/19872840.Katherine_Grant